PRETCO

U0132908

高等学校
英语应用能力考试
全真模拟试题集

A级

 5套全真模拟

 2套专家预测

 2套最新真题

 1张MP3光盘

 附MP3光盘

北京航空航天大学出版社

图书在版编目（CIP）数据

高等学校英语应用能力考试全真模拟试题集. A 级 /
PRETCO 研究小组编. -- 北京：北京航空航天大学出版社，
2010.1

ISBN 978-7-5124-0018-4

Ⅰ. ①高…　Ⅱ. ①P…　Ⅲ. ①英语—高等学校—水平
考试—习题　Ⅳ. ①H319.6

中国版本图书馆 CIP 数据核字（2010）第 016796 号

高等学校英语应用能力考试全真模拟试题集 A 级
PRETCO 研究小组　编写
责任编辑　姜伟娜

*
北京航空航天大学出版社出版发行
北京市海淀区学院路 37 号　（100191）　发行部电话：010-82317024　传真：010-82328026
http:// www.buaapress.com.cn　　Email: bhpress@263.net
涿州市新华印刷有限公司印装　各地书店经销
*
开本：787×1092　1/16　印张：10　字数：255 千字
2010 年 1 月第 1 版　2010 年 1 月第 1 次印刷
ISBN 978-7-5124-0018-4　定价：19.80 元（含光盘）

编委会

前　言

高等学校英语应用能力考试(PRETCO)是为反映和评价高等学校专科层次(高等专科教育、高等职业技术教育、成人高等专科教育)修完英语课程的在校生英语应用能力而设立的标准化英语水平考试。高等学校英语应用能力考试分 A、B 两级,A 级考试为高职高专学生应该达到的标准要求,B 级考试略低于 A 级考试,是过渡性的要求。

为了帮助考生进一步熟悉所考题型、内容及难度,使考生顺利通过考试,我们特邀专家编写了这套《高等学校英语应用能力考试全真模拟试题集 A 级》供广大应试者复习使用。本套试卷严格遵循国家教育部高等教育司颁布的《高等学校英语应用能力考试大纲》和《高职高专教育英语课程教学基本要求》编写而成。本套书由试题评析与应试技巧、模拟试题、专家预测试题、历年真题、参考答案与解析五个部分组成。本书编写的特点如下:

一、试题评析与应试技巧:大纲解读,直击考点

阐明考试题型的命题特点和试题分析、答题思路及解题方法,均为针对性的知识点讲解,技巧点拨贯穿其中。

二、全真模拟:紧扣考纲,真实训练

试题命制过程中充分体现了"重点、常考知识点反复练习,精确定位;次重点知识全面覆盖,不留丝毫死角"的原则;试题从选材到难度,完全与真题相仿,利于考生了解考试程序,对考试做到心中有数。

三、专家预测:权威预测,逼真演练

汇总历年考查重点,对考前重点进行预测,提高试题命中率;考生通过此套试题不仅可以全面掌握历年考点,还可以洞悉真题的命题特点及难度。

四、最新真题:分析到位,精讲精练

答案解析点出试题考点,并对相关知识点适当拓展,让考生知其然,并知其所以然。并且通过真题演练,让考生在第一时间领略真题的魅力,增加胜利的筹码。

五、随书光盘:地道美音,考场再现

当然,真正的英语学习没有什么秘诀,只有努力。建议学习者每天坚持阅读英语文章,每周坚持至少做一套试题,帮助自己寻找考试的感觉。接近考试前一个月,每周坚持做两份以上试题。每次做完试题之后要及时总结,将自己的错误记录下来。我坚信,只要大家能够坚持不懈,什么考试都难不倒自己。

本书如有疏漏、错误和不足之处,敬请广大同仁和读者批评指正,以便我们再版时进一步改进。最后,祝广大考生考试顺利!

编　者

2010 年于北京

目 录

第1章
试题评析与应试技巧

考试大纲与内容解读

一、考试概述

高等学校英语应用能力考试是为反映和评价高等学校专科层次(高等专科教育、高等职业技术教育、成人高等专科教育)修完英语课程的在校生英语应用能力而设立的标准化英语水平考试。相当于1998年以前举办的"高校专科英语二级考试"或"高校专科英语三级考试"。

高等学校英语应用能力考试分A、B两级,A级考试为高职高专学生应该达到的标准要求,B级考试略低于A级考试,是过渡性的要求。原"大学英语三级考试"相当于"高等学校英语应用能力A级考试",原"大学英语二级考试"相当于"高等学校英语应用能力B级考试"。

参加"高等学校英语应用能力考试"取得60分以上(含60分)为考试成绩合格,颁发有"高等学校英语应用能力考试委员会"印章的国家级合格证书。

凡已设置了"高等学校英语应用能力考试"考点的学校,均可组织本校具有报名资格的学生报名参加高等学校英语应用能力考试。未设置高等学校英语应用能力考试考点的高等学校,须向省教育厅高等教育处和省高等学校英语应用能力考试中心申请设置"高等学校英语应用能力考试"考点,经审核批准后,方可按规定组织本校具有报名资格的学生参加高等学校英语应用能力考试。

高等学校英语应用能力考试每年举行两次,上半年一般在6月下旬举行,下半年一般在12月下旬或下一年度的元月上旬举行。

二、考试报名资格

(一) 专科层次(即普通高等专科教育、高等职业技术教育、成人高等专科教育)修完英语课程的在校生可以报名参加高等学校英语应用能力考试。

(二) 体育、艺术类修完英语课程的在校本科生可报名参加高等学校英语应用能力考试。

(三) 参加过高等学校英语应用能力考试,但考试未合格者,亦可以再次报名参加考试。

三、考试大纲(总述)

我国高等职业教育、普通高等专科教育和成人高等教育的教学目标是培养高级应用型人才,其英语教学应贯彻"实用为主,够用为度"的方针;既要培养学生具备必要的英语语言基础知识,也应强调培养学生运用英语进行有关涉外业务工作的能力。高等学校英语应用能力考试就是为了检验高职高专学生是否达到所规定的教学要求而设置的考试。本考试以《高职高专教育英语课程教学基本要求(试行)》(简称《基本要求》)为依据,既测试语言知识也测试语言技能,既测试一般性语言内容也测试与涉外业务有关的应用性内容。

考虑到目前我国高职高专学生英语入学水平的现状,《基本要求》将教学要求分为 A 级要求和 B 级要求,本考试也相对应的分为 A 级考试和 B 级考试。修完《基本要求》规定的全部内容的学生可参加 A 级考试;修完《基本要求》B 级规定的全部内容的学生可参加B 级考试。

考试方式为笔试,测试语言知识和读、听、译、写四种技能。口试正在规划之中,待时机成熟时实施。客观性试题有信度较高、覆盖面广的优点,而主观性试题有利于提高测试的效度,能更好的检测考生运用语言的能力,为此本考试采用主客观题混合题型,以保证良好的信度和效度。

本考试按百分制计分,满分为 100 分。60 分及 60 分以上为及格;85 分及 85 分以上为优秀。考试成绩合格者发给"高等学校英语应用能力考试"相应级别的合格证书。

高等学校英语应用能力考试大纲(A 级)

(一) 考试对象

本大纲适用于修完《基本要求》A 级所规定的全部内容的高等职业教育、普通高等专科教育、成人高等教育和本科办二级技术学院各非英语专业的学生。

(二) 考试性质

本考试的目的是考核考生的语言知识、语言技能和使用英语处理有关一般业务和涉外交际的基本能力,其性质是教学水平考试。

(三) 考试方式与内容

考试方式为笔试,包括五个部分:听力理解、语法结构、阅读理解、翻译(英译汉)和写作(或汉译英)。考试范围为《基本要求》对 A 级所规定的全部内容。

第一部分:听力理解(Listening Comprehension)

测试考生理解所听对话、会话和简单短文的能力。听力材料的语速为每分钟 120 词。对话、会话和短文以日常生活和实用的交际性内容为主。词汇限于《基本要求》的"词汇表"中 3,400 词的范围,交际内容涉及《基本要求》中的"交际范围表"所列的全部听说范围。

本部分的得分占总分的 15%。测试时间为 15 分钟。

第二部分：语法结构（Structure）

测试考生运用语法知识的能力。测试范围包括《基本要求》中的"语法结构表"所规定的全部内容。

本部分的得分占总分的15%。测试时间为15分钟。

第三部分：阅读理解（Reading Comprehension）

测试考生从书面文字材料获取信息的能力。总阅读量约1,000词。

本部分测试的文字材料包括一般性阅读材料（文化、社会、常识、科普、经贸、人物等）和应用性文字，不包括诗歌、小说、散文等文学性材料，其内容能为各专业学生所理解。其中，实用性文字材料约占60%。

阅读材料涉及的语言技能和词汇限于《基本要求》中的"阅读技能表"所列的全部技能范围和"词汇表"中3,400词的范围；除一般性文章外，阅读的应用文限于《基本要求》中"交际范围表"所规定的读译范围，如：函电、广告、说明书、业务单证、合同书、摘要、序言等。

主要测试以下阅读技能：

1. 了解语篇和段落的主旨和大意；2. 掌握语篇中的事实和主要情节；3. 理解语篇上下文的逻辑关系；4. 对句子和段落进行推理；5. 了解作者的目的、态度和观点；6. 根据上下文正确理解生词的意思；7. 了解语篇的结论；8. 进行信息转换。

本部分的得分占总分的35%。测试时间为40分钟。

第四部分：翻译——英译汉（Translation — English to Chinese）

测试考生将英语正确译成汉语的能力。所译材料为句子和段落，包括一般性内容和实用性内容（各约占50%）；所涉及的词汇限于《基本要求》的"词汇表"中3,400词的范围。

本部分的得分占总分的20%。测试时间为25分钟。

第五部分：写作/汉译英（Writing / Translation — Chinese to English）

测试考生套写应用性短文、信函，填写英文表格或翻译简短的实用性文字的能力。

本部分的得分占总分的15%。测试时间为25分钟。

测试项目、内容、题型及时间分配表如下：

序号	测试项目	题号	测试内容	题型	百分比	时间分配
I	听力理解	1—15	对话、会话、短文	多项选择、填空、简答	15%	15分钟
II	语法结构	16—35	句法结构、语法、词形变化	多项选择、填空、改错	15%	15分钟
III	阅读理解	36—60	语篇，包括一般性及应用性文字	多项选择、填空、简答、匹配	35%	40分钟

续表

序号	测试项目	题号	测试内容	题型	百分比	时间分配
IV	英译汉	61—65	句子和段落	多项选择、段落翻译	20%	25分钟
V	写作/汉译英		应用性文字(摘要、通告、信函、简历表、申请书、协议书)	套写、书写、填写或翻译	15%	25分钟
合计			65+1		100%	120分钟

试题透视与技巧点拨

一、听力理解

(一) 试题分析

听力理解是高等学校英语应用能力测试的第一部分,其目的是测试考生获取口头信息的能力。该部分共 15 题,考试时间为 15 分钟。此部分包括三小部分:Section A 是对话部分,共 5 小题,每小题为一组对话,共两句,对话后有一个问题;Section B 有两个会话,共 5 小题,每组会话后有 2 至 3 个问题;Section C 有 1 篇短文,每篇短文约 200 词,随后有 5 个问题,要求考生在所给的 5 个不完整的答题里填入单词或词语,录音朗读两遍。

英语听力不仅考查学生的听、理解、逻辑判断的能力,还要考查学生的心理素质。就高等学校英语应用能力考试 A 级听力的三种题型来看,主要有三大类型。

1. 具体信息题

主要包括通过对时间、地点、人物职业、颜色、天气、价钱、数量、原因、目的等方面的信息处理,从而得知说话者的意图。其中关键词包括 what, where, how much, who, why, when 等。这类题主要集中在听力部分的 Section A,Section B 两大部分。

2. 主旨大意题

任何一个对话或短文都是围绕一个中心展开的, 常见的问题有:What are they talking about? / Where does the dialogue happen? / Which of the following is right? 这类题的选择项一般由句子构成,难度有所增加。可通过充分预读题目,针对选项进行逆向推测,做到带着问题去理解录音材料中的信息,以提高准确率。

3. 推断题

常见的设题方式有:What does the woman(man) mean? / What do we know about the woman (man)? / What can you know from the conversation? / What can you infer from the dialogue? 此类题对语言运用能力要求更高,也是最容易丢分的部分。大家要根据具体事实、关键细节进行推断,从而找到对话的背景、时间、地点、说话人之间的关系。平时做

题时,注意通过语音语调、固定搭配等提示进行理解。

(二) 解题技巧

在掌握了常见题型之后,答题的时候还应该注意一些解题技巧的应用,这样才能提高解题命中率,达到事半功倍的效果。

1. 把握住问题的类型

把握住问题的类型是从听力内容中获得有用信息的关键。听力的技巧在于分清问什么,知道问什么,才能在听内容时有的放矢,才比较容易听到关键词,抓住有用信息。

2. 做好听力题要注意解题方法和技巧

多数情况下,往往不能从听到的内容中找到与选择项完全相同的部分,即一般不易从对话中直接找到答案。因此,要根据对话内容采用归纳、推论或判断的方法答题。

3. 做好听力题要善于理解言下之意

在对话中,由于语境的作用,同样一句话在不同的情况下可以表达不同的意思。

4. 确认讲话人的目的是听懂内容的关键

确认讲话人的会话目的,是英语对话听力理解的一个重要技巧。通过对讲话人会话目的的确认,能加深我们对会话内容的理解。如果我们不仅能听清对话人在讲些什么,而且能明白他们讲这些的目的是什么,那么,我们就能更好地理解对话内容。

二、语法结构

(一) 试题分析

语法结构部分包括两节(Section A, Section B)。本部分测试考生运用英语句法结构、语法和词性(词形变化)的能力。测试范围限于《基本要求》中的"词汇表"(A 级学生应该认知 3,400 个英语单词,以及由这些词构成的常用词组)和"语法结构表"所规定的全部内容。本部分得分占总分的 15%,测试时间为 15 分钟。

Section A 的题型为多项选择题, 试卷中给出一个不完整的句子,下面有 4 个选择项,要求考生从 4 个选择项中选出最佳答案。本节共 10 题,每题 0.5 分,共 5 分。测试要点为测试学生对英语基本语法知识掌握和运用的能力。测试的范围含有"语法结构表"的全部内容,但主要涉及以下基本语法知识和内容:谓语动词、非谓语动词、词类用法、句法结构、常用句型等。

Section B 的题型为填空题,共 10 题,每题 1 分,共 10 分。本节的测试要点为词性转换和语法结构。词性转换主要指动词、名词、形容词和副词四大类实词之间的转化。题干中给出词的原形或词根,要求考生根据句子的含义以及构词方法填入正确的词形。语法知识的范围主要有:动词的时态、语态、语气及主谓语一致,非谓语动词,形容词和副词的比较级和最高级等。

(二) 解题技巧

Section A　多项选择题

本节主要包括五种题型:常用句型题、谓语动词题、非谓语动词题、语法搭配题、句法结构题。如果考生熟悉并掌握了这些测试题型(考点),明确题目测试的要点和关键就能做到有目的,有重点,有条理地分析句子,并能在较短的时间内选择出正确答案。在做本节的选择题时,考生应注意以下解题技巧:

1. 分析句子,理解题意

在做本节选择题时,考生要先分析句子成分,该句的结构以及主要成分(主语、谓语、宾语等)了解该题的大致意思。因为如果题意没有看懂,就谈不上选择出正确答案。

2. 辨认题型,确定考点

考生在读懂题意之后,要大致推断出该句的测试题型,即考点。按照上述的五大考点,结合该题和选项进行分析,认准该题的考点,然后运用掌握的英语知识进行分析、判断和选择。

3. 注重惯用搭配

在做此类选择题的时候,考生所选答案不能只考虑语法结构方面的要求。而且还要考虑到英语中有不少的惯用词语搭配、习惯表达法和特殊用法等。

4. 利用已给信息,拓宽做题思路

考生在做此类选择题时如果遇上生单词,不用慌张,因为考生可以利用题目中以及答案中所给出的信息开阔自己的思路和分析方法,不要用一成不变的思路和方法去选择答案,可以从不同角度去思考和分析每道试题。

Section B 填空题

本节的测试要点为词性转换和语法结构,该试题主要考查考生正确、熟练地使用词汇的能力,一些考生在做这一节试题失分,究其原因不外四个方面:对英语词性的准确判断不够;对英语构词法的掌握程度不够;对英语语法结构的理解和运用不够;对英语词汇拼写和规范注意不够。

根据考生存在的具体问题特提出以下建议:

1. 判断成分

首要认真细心地读懂每道题的大意,判断句子的结构以及空格处应填什么句子成分,从而认准考题的考点是词性变化还是语法结构。

2. 熟记四大实词的转化规律和语法功能

考生应认识到英语四大实词(动词、名词、形容词、副词)在句子中的重要作用,他们是句子的主干、中心和关键。本节试题的重点就是动词、名词、形容词和副词,考生不但要熟练掌握这四大实词之间的转化规律和方法,而且要明确并掌握这四大实词的语法功能。一般说来,动词在句中一般作谓语;名词在句中作主语、宾语或表语;形容词在句中作定语来修饰名词,作表语时置于联系动词之后,或作宾语补足语;副词在句中作状语,修饰动词或形容词等。

3. 了解英语构词法

若考生推断并确定试题的考点为词性变化题,则根据对句子的理解和句子结构的分析推断出应填入空格处的词的词性,再根据括号中所给出的词,运用构词法中的派生法,进行相应的变化——加前缀(prefix)或后缀(suffix),将其正确的形式填入空格处。

4. 认准语法点

若考生推断并确定试题的考点为语法结构题,则应根据对句子结构的分析和对全句的理解,推断而认准测试的语法点,再根据括号中所给出的词,将其正确的语法形式填入空格。本节测试的语法点主要是指四大实词的语法要点,其语法范围主要包括:动词的各种时态、被动语态、虚拟语气、非谓语动词(动词不定式、动名词、现在分词和过去分词)的变化和运用等;名词单、复数形式,以及主谓语一致等;形容词和副词的比较级和最高级等。

(三) 常考语法知识

1. 动词的时态与语态

动词常用的时态有八种,各种时态中被动语态的构成是不一样的。

时态	主动语态	被动语态
一般现在时	do / does	is / am / are + done
一般过去时	did	was / were + done
现在进行时	am / is / are + doing	am / is / are + being + done
现在完成时	have / has + done	has / have + been + done
一般将来时	will / shall / be going to + do	will / shall / be going to + be + done
过去进行时	was / were + doing	was / were + being + done
过去完成时	had + done	had + been + done
过去将来时	would / should / be going to + do	would / should / be going to + be + done
含有情态动词	can / may / must + do	can / may / must + be done

2. 虚拟语气

虚拟语气是以动词的特殊形式来说明句中所叙述的内容不是事实,或是不可能发生的事情,而是一种愿望、建议或是与事实相反的一种假设。虚拟语气通常出现在各种主从复合句中。其构成如下:

假设类型	条件从句的谓语	主句谓语
与现在事实相反	动词的过去式(be 用 were 而不用 was)	would(could, might,第一人称可用 should)+动词原形
与过去事实相反	had+ -ed 分词	would(could, might,第一人称可用 should)+have + -ed 分词
与将来事实相反	were to + 动词原形或用过去式 (be 用 were 而不用 was)	would(could, might,第一人称可用 should)+动词原形
与将来事实可能相反	should + 动词原形	would(第一人称可用 should)+动词原形

3. 非谓语动词

在句子中不是谓语的动词叫做非谓语动词。非谓语动词主要包括不定式、动名词、分词(现在分词和过去分词),即非谓语动词除了不能独立作谓语外,可以承担句子的任何成分。

非谓语动词与谓语动词的不同点有:非谓语动词可以有名词作用(如动词不定式和动名词),在句中作主语、宾语、表语;非谓语动词可以有形容词作用(如动词不定式和分词),在句中作定语、表语或宾语补足语;非谓语动词可以有副词作用(如动词不定式和分词),在句中作状语;非谓语动词在句中不能单独作谓语,它不受主语的人称和数的限制。谓语动词在句中作谓语,受主语的人称和数的限制。

三种非谓语动词的主要区别:

非谓语动词		区别
不定式		常表示一次性动作;表示将要发生的动作;一般表目的;倾向于动作性。
动名词		表示多次的、反复的、习惯性的动作;倾向于名词性。
分词	现在分词	表示正在进行的动作;表示主动意义;一般表原因或伴随的状况。
	过去分词	表示已发生过的动作;表示被动意义;一般表原因或伴随的状况。

4. 主谓一致

(1) 语法一致原则。语法上一致就是谓语动词和主语在单、复数形式上保持一致。需要注意的是:主语为单数名词或代词,尽管后面跟有 with, together with, except, but, like, as well as, rather than, more than, no less than, besides, including 等引起的短语,谓语动词仍用单数形式;若主语为复数,谓语动词用复数形式。

(2) 逻辑意义一致原则。逻辑意义一致就是谓语动词的数必须和主语的意义一致(因有时主语形式为单数,但意义为复数;有时形式为复数,但意义为单数)。常见的单词有:family, committee, crew, jury, staff, board, panel, government 等。当这些名词在句中强调的是整体时,谓语动词用单三形式,如果它们在句中强调的是各个成员、个体,谓语动词则用单数形式。表示"时间、重量、长度、价值"等的名词的复数作主语时,谓语动词通常用单数形式,这是由于作主语的名词在概念上是一个整体。

(3) 就近一致原则。在英语句子中,有时谓语动词的人称和数与最近的主语保持一致。当两个主语由 either... or, neither... nor, whether... or..., not only... but also 连接时,谓语动词和邻近的主语保持一致。there be 句型 be 动词的单复数取决于其后的主语。如果其后是由 and 连接的两个主语,则应与靠近的那个主语保持一致。

三、阅读理解

(一) 试题分析

本部分测试考生从书面文字材料获取信息的能力。短文题材包括社会、文化、常识、科普、经贸、人物和实用性文字。包括 5 个 Task,其中 Task 1 和 Task 2 是一种类型,在短文后有五道选择题;Task 3 是在总结原文的基础上,用简单的词汇填空;Task 4 是连线题;此题会考查某一特殊领域的专业词汇的名称;Task 5 和 Task 3 相似,在读懂文章的基础上,总结并用简单的词汇填空。根据对历年真题的分析,现总结 5 种类型的阅读理解题型如下：

1. 词汇题。考查目的是让考生以上下文内容为参考，尝试理解文中出现的生词。而这个生词的下文往往有对这个词的解释、说明、举例等。

2. 主旨题。这类题最简单的解题方法是把文中每段的首句串起来考虑。若是仅问其中某一段的中心思想，则可将该段的首、尾句加起来考虑。

3. 作者观点、态度题。解题的关键是要看作者在文中用了什么样的口气。若用褒义词，显然是赞成；若用贬义词，显然是反对；若客观陈述，则是中性的立场，不偏不倚。更为明显的一个解题办法，就是寻找文中的转折词，一般转折词后面的文段表明了作者的观点。

4. 细节题。这类题以考查文章中某一个细节问题为入手点。它可能出现在原文中的某一句话中。但是，往往照抄原文的句子并不一定是正确选项。这类题的正确答案，应该是与原文意思和所问问题相符的才对。

5. 推理性问题。既然这类题被命名为推理题，你就不应该指望在原文中搜索出答案，而应该通过自己的理解去推理答案，但切忌凭空瞎想，要忠实原文内容去推理。这类题是阅读理解中最难的一类问题。只有以原文中某句话或某个词语为依据去合理推测才能找到合适的答案。

做英语阅读，需要有量的积累，但是如果只知道一味埋头做题，同样无济于事。做了一定量的题目以后，需要有一个反思总结。要把自己错的题归类出来，属于上面5种题型的哪一种。并将自己的答案与参考答案进行对比，体会出题者的意图和你理解的偏差。

(二) 解题步骤

(1) 快速浏览题干，通过题干先对问题做一些区分。一般来说，出题人在题目的设置方面，都会按照文章的内容来依次设置问题的顺序。问题设置的难度也是由浅入深。所以，大家在第一遍阅读文章时，基本上可以找出1—3小题的答案或是找到问题在文章中出现的位置。细节题可以在第一遍浏览文章的时候，拿铅笔把题干中最具代表性的几个词划出来，为第二遍精读时找寻答案或是思考答案做铺垫。

(2) 看过题干之后，再返回原文阅读，在阅读的过程中不用过于注重对词句的把握，遇到不认识的单词不必作太久地停留，以免影响阅读速度。近些年英语阅读的特点是几乎不出现需要综合跨段的信息情况。因而，理解之后就可以立即返回题目，阅读选项进行选择。

(3) 做完题目应该再快速地浏览一下原文，核对题目。

(三) 解题技巧

1. 扩大阅读视野

所谓阅读视野是指眼睛在"凝视"的瞬间所能接收或覆盖的印刷符号。普通读者眼睛停顿时可接收两个英语单词，阅读能力强的读者一眼可以看四个左右的单词，但能力差的读者一眼只能接收一个或者不到一个的单词。因此，在相等的阅读时间里，视野狭窄的读者所看到的单词要少得多，如果再经常回视，阅读速度肯定快不了。

我们阅读时应该特别注意词的整体性，要把注意力放在句子中较大的单位上，而不要放在一个个孤立的单词上。例如，下面的句子可以分成三个词群，Most paragraphs/ have a topic sentence/ which expresses the central idea.我们不妨将它们作为三个相对独立的整体看待，阅读时，眼睛只要停顿三次而不是十次。

2. 用英语思考

在阅读时,不必把英文翻译成中文,否则将大大地降低阅读速度,从而影响对阅读材料的全面理解。

3. 注意预读

预读是每个读者必须掌握的一项基本阅读技巧。在我们正式阅读一本书之前,首先应该通过预读粗略地估计一下该书写的是什么内容。书籍预读主要包括七个方面:(1)思考标题的含义;(2)速读作者姓名与书籍出版日期;(3)看看封面或书中的照片或插图;(4)速读目录内容;(5)浏览索引或附录;(6)速读作者简介以及前言;(7)浏览书尾的参考书目。

短篇文章预读要相对地简单一些。它主要包括阅读标题、作者姓名以及照片和插图。有些读者不知道预读的重要性,或者觉得它是浪费时间。特别是在做阅读与理解测试题时,时间一紧,就忽略预读,捧起文章就埋头看正文。由于跳过了预读这一重要环节,他们的阅读在相当长的时间内是在盲目地探索中进行的。

4. 增强猜词能力

看文章经常会遇到一些生词。这时,我们不要急于查词典,许多生词的意义都可以猜出来。查词典不但会减慢速度,而且会打断读者的思路,降低阅读效率。猜词义的方法多种多样,最常用的是根据上下文猜测生词的含义。另外我们还可以根据构词法(如前缀、后摄)、同义词、反义词等揣摩某些生词的意思。当然,有不少生词(特别是一些抽象名词)的意思是很难猜出来的。如果它们对理解文章内容无多大妨碍,我们完全可以跳过它,不要把精力过分地放在猜词义上。只见树木不见林的阅读方法是不可取的。

5. 注意把握重点

文章的主旨一般出现在开头和结尾,有时也可能在中间。把握文章的主旨还要注意每段的开头和结尾部分,重点是动词、形容词的把握,并且要重视文中出现的有明显转折词的地方。这样就能快速找出重点,进行定位。

四、英译汉

(一) 试题分析

英译汉主要有两种题型,一种是单句翻译,即一句英文下给出四个中文翻译的选项,要求考生进行选择;另一种是段落翻译,要求考生完整地翻译出一则篇幅较短的文字。在这两种题型中, 第二种题型考查考生的英语综合水平, 而第一种题型则比较注重答题技巧,具体如下:1.英译汉选择题型共四题,总分值8分,每小题2分。每小题的选项中,有一个选项所做出的翻译与题目所给出的英文内容是最符合的,如选择该答案,可得2分。剩余的三个选项中,仍有两个选项可以得分,但是这两个选项与上述最佳选项相比,在某些内容上有偏差或错误。根据选项给出的翻译与原文内容之间差别的不同程度,选择这两个选项中较佳的一项可得1.5分,另外一项可得1分。如选择翻译效果最差的选项不得分。

(二) 解题技巧

1. 了解英汉两种语言的差异

当考生面临英译汉的问题时,往往不了解不同语言的差异,即使知道了是什么意思,却无法用另一种语言表达出来。英汉两种语言之间并不存在一对一关系,在翻译中要变被动翻译为主动翻译,要学会两种语言之间进行变通,所谓直译和意译,区别并不大,关键是用一种变通的方法把意思表达出来就可以了。

2. 从答案中推敲生词的意思

如果题目中出现了比较生僻的单词,考生可以从选项中所给的对应的汉语意思推敲英语单词的含义,并结合整句话的含义进行选择。

3. 分析句子结构

在做英译汉题的过程中,如果搞不清楚句子结构,很难做出正确的选择。分析句子结构时,要注意分清主从句。其次,要理解句子的意义,不仅要弄清句子表面的意义,还要理解在特定的语言环境中的意义,也要特别注意句子中的代词和所指代的意义。另外,要注意句子中包含的短语和固定结构,这也往往是考点。

4. 运用排除法

在这一类翻译选择题中,排除法的使用会起到相当大的作用,当考生无法从常规角度做出最佳选择时,排除法也不失为一种好方法。

(三) 具体翻译方法

1. 分译法

如果英语句子是比较复杂的主句套从句,而汉语中没有与之一一对应的翻译,因此,要翻译出来让人看懂,就必须将其拆开,分译成各个简单的部分。

2. 转译法

很多被动语态如果机械地翻译成被动语态,可能会让人看了觉得别扭,因此需要转为主动语态。此外,还有否定转译等各种情况。

3. 添减词法

由于英汉两种语言的差异,在英文看上去比较正常的句子,译成汉语时,如果不或增或减一些词可能无法把英文的原意表达出来,这样就需要适当地运用添减词法。

4. 单复数译法

主要是指根据具体情况把英语中的单复数用汉语明确地表达出来。

5. 时态的译法

英语中有专门表示时态的句子结构,而汉语则没有,因此,有时必须加一些表示时间的副词,如"着、了、在"等。

6. 代词的译法

为了表达清楚,代词一般需要转译成名词,即把其所指代的意义译出。

7. 人名地名的译法

人名地名以前一般采用音译法,现在一般采用保留的方式,所以知道的可以译出来,不知道的就保持原文。

五、写作

（一）题型分析

本部分要求考生在 25 分钟内写出一篇不少于 80 词的短文。根据高职高专考试大纲要求，写作主要测试考生套写应用性短文、商务信函、履历、合同、通知、请帖等实用性文字的能力。写作考试旨在测试考生的综合能力，其中包括词汇、句型、语法、运用英语逻辑组织短文的能力以及对应用文基本格式、基本用途等的了解。要求文章切题，思想表达正确，意义连贯，文理基本通顺，无重大语法错误。

（二）写作评分原则及标准

作文评分主要从表达和语言两方面来考虑。分数可以分为四个等级，即：

1. 11 分：内容完整，表达清楚；语言上仅有很少的错误。
2. 8 分：内容较完整，表达尚清楚；有一些语言错误，可以有个别句子结构上的错误。
3. 5 分：内容大体完整，表达可以被勉强理解；有较多的语言错误，包括少量严重错误。
4. 2 分：内容不完整，但是没有离题；表达上有较大的困难；语言有很多错误，包括少量严重错误。

（二）写作技巧

既然作文评分主要是从表达和语言两方面来考虑，写作时就应先从这两方面总体把握，力争语言优美，表达清晰，条理清楚。下面拟就各种文体做一简要介绍：

1. 书信

书信是日常生活中常用的文体，是用以交涉事宜、传达信息、交流思想、联络感情、增进了解的重要工具。书信一般可分为商务信件或公函和私人信件两大类。值得注意的是，英语书信的写法与汉语书信有一些明显区别，应特别加以区分。英语书信通常包括下面几个组成部分：信端、信内地址、称呼、正文、结束语、签名、附件、再启等。所以写作的时候应该注意书信的格式和分类，注意审题，按要求作答。

2. 履历

履历是另外一种总结你工作经历的方式，跟简历很类似。这类题目一般会以填表的形式出现。所以只需按照要求用规范的语言表达清楚即可。

3. 合同

标准英文合同通常可以分为前言(Preamble)、正文(Habendum)、证明部分(Attestation)、附录(Schedule)四大部分组成。合同为法律的一部分，因此要求语言准确，不能有任何模糊不清或表达错误的地方。所以写作的时候务必注意语言的精确和格式的正确。其实这类题只要多积累一些素材便可以得心应手，因为一般都有模式可以套用，所以应注意平时的积累。

4. 通知

通知是上级对下级、组织对成员布置工作、传达情况或告诉公众某种情况的一种实用性文体。一般有固定的格式，语言清晰简练。所以写作时应注意这些特点。

模拟试题

模拟试题（一）

Part I　　　　Listening Comprehension　　　（15 minutes）

Directions: *This part is to test your listening ability. It consists of 3 sections.*

Section A

Directions: *This section is to test your ability to understand short dialogues. There are 5 recorded dialogues in it. After each dialogue, there is a recorded question. Both the dialogues and questions will be spoken only once. When you hear a question, you should decide on the correct answer from the 4 choices marked A), B), C) and D) given in your test paper. Then you should mark the corresponding letter on the Answer Sheet with a single line through the center.*

Example:　*You will hear:*

You will read: A) New York City.　　　B) An evening party.

C) An air trip.　　　　D) The man's job.

From the dialogue we learn that the man is to take a flight to New York. Therefore, ***C)An air trip*** *is the correct answer. You should mark C) on the Answer Sheet with a single line through the center.*

[A] [B] [C] [D]

Now the test will begin.

1. A) 9:30.　　　　B) 10:30.　　　　C) 8:30.　　　　D) 8:00.

2. A) At a shop.　　B) In a restaurant. C) At a hotel room.　　D) At a railroad station.

3. A) Sunny.　　　B) Windy.　　　C) Rainy.　　　D) Cloudy.

4. A) For the food. B) For the service. C) For the environment. D) For the distance.

5. A) Upset.　　　B) Dissatisfied.　　C) Happy.　　　D) Enjoyable.

Section B

Directions: *This section is to test your ability to understand short conversations. There are 2 recorded conversations in it. After each conversation, there are some recorded questions. Both the conversations and questions will be spoken two times. When you hear a question, you should decide on the correct answer from the 4 choices* *marked A), B), C) and D) given in your test paper. Then you should mark the corresponding letter on the Answer Sheet with a single line through the center.*

Conversation 1

6. A) A blue sweater in size ten.　　　B) A blue sweater in size eleven.

　C) A black sweater in size ten.　　　D) A black sweater in size eleven.

7. A) She is going to meet her friend.

　B) She is going to expecting her friend.

　C) She is going to take part in a party with her friend.

　D) She is going to take part in a party with the man.

Conversation 2

8. A) South.　　　B) North.　　　C) West.　　　D) East.

9. A) Three rooms.　　B) Four rooms.　　C) Two rooms.　　D) Five rooms.

10. A) 1,000 yuan.　　B) 800 yuan.　　C) 900 yuan.　　D) 700 yuan.

Section C

Directions: *This section is to test your ability to comprehend short passages. You will hear a recorded passage. After that you will hear five questions. Both the passage and the questions will be read two times. When you hear a question, you should complete the answer to it with a word or a short phrase (**in no more than 3 words**). The questions and incomplete answers are printed in your test paper. You should write your answers on the Answer Sheet correspondingly. Now listen to the passage.*

11. What is the sign of a smile?

　A smile is a strong sign of a friendly and _____ and a willingness to communicate.

12. What is the probable result when you smile at someone?

　That person will usually _____.

13. What is the most common form of first contact between two people?

　In many cultures the most common form of first contact between two people is a _____.

14. How should we react at the first time of contact?

　We should be the first to _____ in greeting, and couple this with a friendly "hello", a nice smile, and your name.

15. What can direct eye contact show?

　It shows you are listening to the other person and that you want to _____ her.

Part II　　　　　　　Structure　　　　(15 minutes)

Directions: *This part is to test your ability to construct grammatically correct sentences. It consists of 2 sections.*

Section A

Directions: *In this section, there are 10 incomplete sentences. You are required to complete each one by deciding on the most appropriate word or words from the 4 choices marked A), B), C) and D). Then you should mark the corresponding letter on the Answer Sheet with a single line through the center.*

16. Mike was walking along the street _____ he ran into an old friend.

    A) when   B) who   C) which   D) whom

17. Although their lives changed, they _____ continued writing to one another.

    A) ever   B) never   C) still   D) rather

18. _____ the novel last year, I'm looking forward to seeing the film.

    A) having read   B) reading   C) to read   D) having to read

19. Michael put me in a _____ position when we talked about the matter that day.

    A) real difficulty   B) really difficulty   C) really difficult   D) real and difficult

20. She is looking forward to _____ you. Please write to her soon.

    A) hearing from   B) hearing of   C) writing to   D) writing for

21. You _____ leave now, because there is an all-night bus.

    A) mustn't   B) don't have to   C) aren't able to   D) can't

22. Although he lives alone in the countryside, he doesn't feel _____ .

    A) alone   B) on his own   C) himself   D) lonely

23. It _____ be quite late now, we should go and catch the last bus.

    A) can   B) must   C) would   D) may

24. The star has been playing basketball _____ he was a boy.

    A) during   B) when   C) since   D) as

25. My little son has not learned how to _____ the time yet.

    A) see   B) know   C) understand   D) tell

Section B

Directions: *There are 10 incomplete statements here. You should fill in each blank with the proper form of the word given in brackets. Write the word or words in the corresponding space on the Answer Sheet.*

26. "I'm sorry." he said (sincere) _____ .

27. Unhealthy people must be stopped from (smoke) _____ .

28. She spends one hour (watch) _____ TV every day.

29. Keep (quietly) _____ ! They are listening to the teacher.

30. Would you please say it again more (loud) _____ ?

31. Keep on (work) _____ hard, or you'll fall behind other students.

32. I've been to Shanghai (two) _____ .

33. Thank you for (lend) _____ me the bike.

34. Tom did (bad) _____ than Mike in the exam.

35. After ten minutes' rest, he went on (work) _____.

Part Ⅲ   Reading Comprehension   (40 minutes)

Directions: *This part is to test your reading ability. There are 5 tasks for you to fulfill. You should read the reading materials carefully and do the tasks as you are instructed.*

Task 1

Directions: *After reading the following passage, you will find 5 questions or unfinished statements, numbered 36 to 40. For each question or statement there are 4 choices marked A), B), C) and D). You should make the correct choice and mark the corresponding letter on the Answer Sheet with a single line through the center.*

Every town in the United States has a post office. Some are very small, and you may also find them in the corner of a shop. Others are larger buildings. They are open five days a week and on Saturday mornings. From Monday through Friday they are usually open from 8:30 a.m. to 4:30 p.m..

If you know how much the postage (邮资) is for your letter, you can buy stamps at any window. In some post offices you can buy stamps from machines. Stamps are sold many different prices, from one cent to many dollars. If you are not sure how much postage is for your letter, you may ask the man or the woman in the post office for help. He or she will give you the stamps you need. If you are sending your letter far away, you should use airmail envelopes (航空信封). Remember that postage will be more expensive for a letter to be sent outside the country.

At a post office you can also buy postcards. A postcard is cheaper than a letter. Usually the price of postage for a postcard is about half that of a letter. The postcards that you buy at a post office do not have pictures. However, also they are not to be sent outside the country.

36. The passage tells us that we can find _____ easily in the United States of America.

   A) post offices   B) large buildings

   C) small shops   D) different banks

37. The post offices in the United States are open _____.

   A) seven hours a day   B) six hours a day

   C) five hours a day   D) eight hours a day

38. If you are not sure how much postage is for your letter, you can _____.

   A) go and buy stamps from the machine in the post office

   B) get in touch with somebody you know in the post office

C) ask the man or the woman in the post office for help

D) buy the stamps at any window

39. The price of postage for _____ is more expensive.

A) a beautiful postcard　　　　　　　　B) a letter written on envelope

C) a letter by airmail　　　　　　　　　D) a postcard with pictures

40. The passage tells us something about _____ in the USA.

A) the post　　　B) the postage　　　C) letters　　　D) postcards

Task 2

Directions: *This task is the same as Task 1. The 5 questions or unfinished statements are numbered 41 to 45.*

Do you know why different animals or pests have their special colors? Colors in them seem to be used mainly to protect themselves.

Some birds like eating locusts（蝗虫）, but birds cannot easily catch them. Why? It is because locusts change their colors together with the change of the colors of crops. When crops are green, locusts look green. But as the harvest time comes, locusts change to the same brown color as crops have. Some other pests with different colors from plants are easily found and eaten by others. So they have to hide themselves for lives and appear only at night.

If you study the animal life, you'll find the main use of coloring is to protect themselves. Bears, lions and other animals move quietly through forests. They cannot be easily seen by hunters. This is because they have the colors much like the trees.

Have you ever found an even more strange act? A kind of fish in the sea can send out a kind of very black liquid（液体）when it faces danger. While the liquid spreads over, its enemies cannot find it. And it immediately swims away. So it has lived up to now though it is not strong at all.

41. From the passage we learn that locusts _____.

A) are small animals

B) are easily found by birds

C) are dangerous to their enemies

D) change their colors to protect themselves

42. How can pests with different colors from plants keep out of danger?

A) They run away quickly.

B) They have the colors much like their enemies.

C) They hide themselves by day and appear at night.

D) They have to move quietly.

43. Bears and lions can keep safe because _____.

A) they have the colors much like the trees　B) they move quietly

C) they like brown and grey colors　　　　　D) they live in forests

44. Why can the kind of fish live up to now?

   A) Because it is very big and strong.

   B) Because the liquid it sends out can help it escape from its enemies.

   C) Because the liquid it sends out can kill its enemies.

   D) Because it swims faster than any other fish.

45. Which is the best title for this passage?

   A) The Change of Colors for Animals and Pests.

   B) Colors of Different Animals and Pests.

   C) The Main Use of Colors for Animals and Pests.

   D) Some Animals and Pests.

Task 3

Directions: *The following is a job advertisement. After reading it, you are required to complete the outline below it （No. 46 through No. 50）. You should write your answers briefly (**in no more than 3 words**) on the Answer Sheet correspondingly.*

Live-in Caregiver

Terms of Employment: Permanent, Full Time, Shift, Day.

Salary: $1,800 monthly for 44 hours per week.

Education: Completion of high school, Completion of college/CEGEP/vocational or technical training

Credentials (certificates, licenses, memberships, courses, etc.): First Aid Certificate

Experience: 2 years to less than 3 years

Languages: Speak English, read English, write English

Specific Skills: Prepare and serve nutritious meals, Perform light housekeeping and cleaning duties

Work Location Information: Work in employer's/client's home, Urban area

Essential Skills: Oral communication

Other Information: The live-in caregiver looks after a 81 years old lady. Accommodation will be provided for $336/month

Employer: Johnson Lee

How to Apply: Please apply for this job only in the manner specified by the employer. Failure to do so may result in your application not being properly considered for the position.

By phone: between 14:30 and 20:00 (780) 484-9918

Advertised until: 2009/08/04

A job advertisement

Position offered: __46__

Qualifications: 1. __47__ certificate.

               2. required language: __48__

Responsibilities: to take care of a __49__ years old lady.

Time of contact: between __50__

Task 4

Directions: *The following is a list of different scenes. After reading it, you are required to find the items equivalent to （与…相同的）those given in Chinese in the table below. Then you should find out the corresponding letters in brackets on the Answer Sheet, numbered 51 to 55.*

A —— bamboo garden   B —— walkway plaza

C —— outdoor cafe   D —— hanging bridge

E —— feature stepping stone   F —— river wild

G —— Japanese garden   H —— rock sculpture

I —— tree battle formation   J —— golf clubhouse

K —— garden on the Yangtze Delta   L —— entrance to shopping center

M —— children playground   N —— swimming pool

O —— exercise plaza   P —— central plaza

Examples: (P) 中心广场   (M) 儿童乐园

51. (　) 野趣小溪	(　) 健身广场
52. (　) 竹园	(　) 儿童乐园
53. (　) 吊桥	(　) 江南园林
54. (　) 日艺园	(　) 高尔夫球会所
55. (　) 趣味树阵	(　) 特色踏步

Task 5

Directions: *The following is a News report. After reading it, you should give brief answers to the 5 questions (No. 56 through No. 60) that follow. The answers (**in no more than 3 words**) should be written after the corresponding numbers on the Answer Sheet.*

Hello, welcome to "This Week's Sports". It will be 9:00 a.m. when the Los Angeles Lakers and Philadelphia 76ers tip off the NBA Finals tonight in Los Angeles. But the early hour has not discouraged students at Beijing University from organizing a special viewing party to watch the game live. The young Chinese basketball fans will be joining an estimated

2.5 billion viewers worldwide who will be turning in to the games, making up the biggest global audience for any basketball event in the history of the game.

More than 90 broadcasters from international networks have set up operations at Staples Center for tonight's opening joust (比赛). Among them are CCTV from China, Supersport cable channel from Greece, DSF from Germany, Canal Plus from France, NHK from Japan, and Israel's Channel 5. Coming to the Finals for the first time are MTV from Lebanon and ITV from Korea. Broadcasters will give their local viewers play-by-play accounts of the game in 41 languages, including Arabic, Bosnian, Cantonese, Japanese, Korean, Maltese and Mandarin.

This year is by far the biggest international audience for the Finals. The number of countries signing on for the NBA Finals has risen from 100 seven years ago to 295 this year.

56. Which are the two opposing teams?

_____.

57. What has the students of Beijing University done to watch the game?

They have organizing a _____ to watch the game.

58. How many viewers worldwide have been estimated?

_____.

59. Where will this Final joust hold?

At the _____ of Los Angeles.

60. How many broadcasters from international networks are there in the center?

_____.

Part IV   Translation — English into Chinese   （25 minutes）

Directions: *This part, numbered 61 through 65, is to test your ability to translate English into Chinese. After each of the sentences numbered 61 to 64, you will read four choices of suggested translation. You should choose the best translation and mark the corresponding letter on your Answer Sheet. And for the paragraph numbered 65, write your translation in the corresponding space on the Translation / Composition Sheet.*

61. My income is now twice as much as I used to earn two years ago.

 A）我现在的收入是两年前的两倍。

 B）我现在的收入比两年前多两倍。

 C）我现在的收入是我习惯收入的两倍。

 D）我现在的收入比习惯收入多了两倍。

62. I could have eaten as much again if the doctor had not told me to go on a diet.

 A）如果医生没有告诉我节食的话我可以吃很多。

 B）如果医生没有告诉我节食的话我还可以再吃这么多。

C) 如果医生没有告诉我继续吃饭的话我还可能再吃这么多。

D) 如果医生没有告诉我节食的话我会再吃一顿饭。

63. As I view these once familiar surroundings, images of myself as a child there came to mind.

A) 在我看到这些熟悉的场景那一刻,我就想起了我孩提时代住在那的样子。

B) 当我看到这些我曾经熟悉的环境时,我想起了我孩提时代住在那是个什么模样。

C) 当我看到这些曾经熟悉的场景时,我想起了我孩提时的模样。

D) 当我看到那些熟悉的环境时,作为孩童的我就对自己有了一个初步的印象。

64. Scott arrived at the South Pole on January 17th, only to find that someone had got there before him.

A) 斯科特在1月17号到达南极,发现已经有人在那里驻扎了。

B) 斯科特在1月17号到达南极,很遗憾地发现只有他一个人到达。

C) 斯科特在1月17号到达南极,仅仅发现已经有人在他之前到达。

D) 斯科特在1月17号到达南极,结果发现已经有人在他之前到达那里。

65. The grandest of these ideals is an unfolding American promise that everyone belongs, that everyone deserves a chance that no insignificant person was ever born. Americans are called to enact this promise in our lives and in our laws. And though our nation has sometimes halted, and sometimes delayed, we must follow no other course.

Part V　　　　　Writing　　　　（25 minutes）

Directions: *This part is to test your ability to do practical writing. You are required to write an email according to the following information given in Chinese. You should include all the points listed in the following table. Remember to write the email on the Translation / Composition Sheet.*

说明:假设你是学校学生会主席。你负责为留校过新年的同学筹划新年期间的北京之行,为期7天,请你给北京长青旅行社的赵林发一封电子邮件,联系相关事宜。要点如下:

1. 希望能够派车接送;

2. 需要一名非常熟悉北京的导游;

3. 请求告知旅行日程及就餐、旅馆、费用等情况;

4. 你的联系方式:电子邮箱地址 *luckyxiaodong@163.com* 或电话号码 135××××3421

Words for reference:

旅馆住宿 accommodation;旅行日程安排 itinerary;长途客车 coach

模拟试题(二)

Part I　　　　Listening Comprehension　　　（15 minutes）

Directions: *This part is to test your listening ability. It consists of 3 sections.*

Section A

Directions: *This section is to test your ability to understand short dialogues. There are 5 recorded dialogues in it. After each dialogue, there is a recorded question. Both the dialogues and questions will be spoken only once. When you hear a question, you should decide on the correct answer from the 4 choices marked A), B), C) and D) given in your test paper. Then you should mark the corresponding letter on the Answer Sheet with a single line through the center.*

Example: *You will hear:*

You will read: A) New York City. 　　　　　　B) An evening party.

　　　　　　　　C) An air trip. 　　　　　　　　D) The man's job.

From the dialogue we learn that the man is to take a flight to New York. Therefore, **C) An air trip** *is the correct answer. You should mark C) on the Answer Sheet with a single line through the center.*

[A] [B] [C] [D]

Now the test will begin.

1. A) They like the salad very much. 　　B) They are fed up of the salad.
　　C) They have nothing else to eat. 　　D) They love their mother very much.
2. A) Apple. 　　　B) Banana. 　　　C) Orange. 　　　D) Grape.
3. A) He doesn't like cola. 　　　　　　B) He doesn't like to eat medicine.
　　C) He would like a cup of cola. 　　D) He would like a cup of coffee.
4. A) Once a week. 　　B) Never. 　　C) Once a month. 　　D) Once a year.
5. A) Football. 　　　B) Tennis. 　　　C) Swimming. 　　　D) Basketball.

Section B

Directions: *This section is to test your ability to understand short conversations. There are 2 recorded conversations in it. After each conversation, there are some recorded questions. Both the conversations and questions will be spoken two times. When you hear a question, you should decide on the correct answer from the 4 choices marked A), B), C) and D) given in your test paper. Then you should mark the corresponding letter on the Answer Sheet with a single line through the center.*

Conversation 1

6. A) Strangers.　　　B) Friends.　　C) Relatives.　　　D) Coworkers.

7. A) She wanted to sit by the window.　　B) She wanted to sit by the aisle.

　C) She couldn't bear the smoke.　　D) She wanted to talk with the man.

Conversation 2

8. A) Before 6:00 p.m.　　　　B) After 6:00 p.m.

　C) Anytime that day.　　　　D) Anytime.

9. A) Mr. James Potter.　　　　B) Mr. James Potter's boss.

　C) Mr. James Potter's secretary.　　D) Mr. James Potter's friend.

10. A) Mr. James Potter works for Sun Electronics.

　B) Mr. Martin Richard works for ABC company.

　C) Mr. Martin Richard is wanted on the phone but he is not available.

　D) Mr. James Potter is wanted on the phone but he is not available.

Section C

Directions: *This section is to test your ability to comprehend short passages. You will hear a recorded passage. After that you will hear five questions. Both the passage and the questions will be read two times. When you hear a question, you should complete the answer to it with a word or a short phrase (**in no more than 3 words**). The questions and incomplete answers are printed in your test paper. You should write your answers on the Answer Sheet correspondingly. Now listen to the passage.*

11. How do people feel about doctor's income?

　Many people in the United States think that doctors are _____.

12. Why can't people have their medical care they need?

　They haven't got _____ to pay for it.

13. How much will a visit to the doctor's office cost?

　A visit to a doctor's office costs people from _____ dollars.

14. What is the reason for the high medical cost mentioned in the article?

　_____ is the reason for the high medical cost.

15. What is the method to lower the cost of medical care?

　The method to lower costs would be to have medical schools that are _____.

Part Ⅱ　　　　Structure　　　　（15 minutes）

Directions: *This part is to test your ability to construct grammatically correct sentences. It consists of 2 sections.*

Section A

Directions: *In this section, there are 10 incomplete sentences. You are required to complete each one by deciding on the most appropriate word or words from the 4 choices marked A), B), C) and D). Then you should mark the corresponding letter on the Answer Sheet with a single line through the center.*

16. — Clare, can you smell something _____ ?

    — Oh, My God! It must be the rice.

    A) burns   B) to burn   C) burning   D) to be burning

17. _____, here's coming a heavy-truck.

    A) Look up   B) Look out   C) Look on   D) Look round

18. _____ a larger sense, our outlook is determined by the culture in which we live.

    A) To   B) In   C) From   D) For

19. This meat tasted _____ somewhat like beef.

    A) of   B) at   C) on   D) /

20. Kate wondered what the result was, but I refused to tell her until she _____ the novel.

    A) finishes   B) have finished   C) had finished   D) finished

21. We have just dined on the flesh of _____ killed fish.

    A) fresh   B) freshly   C) freshed   D) freshing

22. Mr. Li had an American style and he _____ like an American.

    A) thought   B) thinks   C) thinking   D) has thought

23. As a Chinese, he felt uncomfortable and _____ in England.

    A) out of the place B) out of the position C) out of place   D) out of position

24. Not until several months later _____ I realize how foolish I had been then.

    A) have   B) had   C) did   D) do

25. I greatly appreciate _____ the opportunity to study abroad two years ago.

    A) giving   B) have been given C) give   D) having been given

Section B

Directions: *There are 10 incomplete statements here. You should fill in each blank with the proper form of the word given in brackets. Write the word or words in the corresponding space on the Answer Sheet.*

26. I saw a wallet (lie) _____ on the ground on my way home.

27. They enjoy (take) _____ a walk after supper.

28. Linda is busy (get) _____ ready for tomorrow's exam.

29. Xiao Li is the (tall) _____ one of the two.

30. Who has the (many) _____ books, Kate, Rose, Mary?

31. It's (danger) _____ to cross the road now.

32. The ground is (cover) _____ with heavy snow.

33. It is a (sun) _____ day. Let's go out for a walk.

34. Edison was a great (science) _____ in the world.

35. We are all (surprise) _____ at the news.

Part III　　　　Reading Comprehension　　　（40 minutes）

Directions: *This part is to test your reading ability. There are 5 tasks for you to fulfill. You should read the reading materials carefully and do the tasks as you are instructed.*

Task 1

Directions: *After reading the following passage, you will find 5 questions or unfinished statements, numbered 36 to 40. For each question or statement there are 4 choices marked A), B), C) and D). You should make the correct choice and mark the corresponding letter on the Answer Sheet with a single line through the center.*

Americans with small families own a small car or a large one. If both parents are working, they usually have two cars. When the family is large, one of the cars is sold and they will buy a van (房车).

A small car can hold four persons and a large car can hold six persons but it is very crowded. A van hold seven persons easily, so a family three children could ask their grandparents to go on a holiday travel. They could all travel together.

Mr. Hagen and his wife had a third child last year. This made them sell a second car and buy a van. Their sixth and seventh seat are used to put other things, for a family of five must carry many suitcases (衣箱) when they travel. When they arrive at their grandparents' home, the suitcases are brought into the two seats can then carry the grandparents.

Americans call vans motor homes. A motor home is always used for holidays. When a family is traveling to the mountains or to the seaside, they can live in their motor home for a few days or to the seaside, they can live in their motor home for a few days or weeks. All the members of a big family can enjoy a happier life when they are traveling together. That is why motor homes have become very popular. In America there are many parks for motor homes.

36. From the passage, a van is also called _____.

　　A) a motor car　　B) a motor home　　　C) a motor bike　　D) a big truck

37. Before Mr. Hagen and his wife bought a van, they _____.

　　A) sold their old house　　　　　　　B) moved to their grandparents' house

　　C) built a new place for a van　　　　D) sold their second car

38. A motor home is usually owned by a family with _____.

　　A) a baby　　　　　　　　　　　　　B) much money

　　C) more than two children　　　　　　D) interest in vans

39. Americans usually use motor homes _____.

    A) to travel with all the family members for holiday

    B) to do some shopping with all the family members

    C) to visit their grandparents at weekends

    D) to drive their children to school every day

40. Motor homes have become popular because _____.

    A) they can take people to another city when people are free

    B) they can let families have a happier life when they go out for their holidays

    C) some people think motor homes are cheap

    D) big families can put more things in motor homes

Task 2

Directions: *This task is the same as Task 1. The 5 questions or unfinished statements are numbered 41 to 45.*

Charles R. Drew was a medical student at Columbia University in New York. Before he graduated, he wrote an article on blood bank — that is, the storing of blood. Up till then, a lot of people had died from lose of blood because there was no such thing as a blood bank.

When the United States entered the Second World War, it became necessary to set up blood banks. Dr. Drew served as the head of the Red Cross's first blood bank.

When the Red Cross started blood banks to collect and store blood for men wounded in the battle, black Americans gave blood along with the whites. At first their blood was not accepted. Later, blood from blacks was accepted but stored in a different place from "white" blood. Although the head doctors insisted that there was no difference at all between the blood of blacks and whites, the Red Cross, with the support of the government, continued to separate black blood from white.

After the war Dr. Drew was driving with three other doctors to attend a meeting in a southern state. In North Carolina their car went into a ditch（水沟）and Dr. Drew was badly hurt. He had lost a lot of blood by the time a passing car took him to the nearest hospital. "We don't take in blacks." They said. He had to be taken to the colored hospital. On the way Dr. Drew died because he had lost too much blood.

41. What does the phrase "blood bank" (Line 2, Para. 1) mean?

    A) A place where blood is stored.　　 B) A place where blood is sold.

    C) A place where blood is borrowed.　 D) A place where you can use blood.

42. When the Red Cross started blood banks _____.

    A) white Americans would not give their blood

    B) black Americans were unwilling to give their blood

    C) no one was able to give his blood

    D) both the white and the black gave blood

43. The nearest hospital Dr. Drew had been taken to after the accident was for _____.

    A) blacks only　　　　　　　　　 B) whites only

    C) both whites and blacks　　　　　 D) the colored

44. Which of the following statement is TRUE according to the passage?

   A) The government thought that blood from blacks was as good as that of whites.

   B) The head doctors insist that there was difference between the blood of blacks and whites.

   C) The government thought that blood from blacks was different from that of whites.

   D) The Red Cross will not save blacks' life.

45. The life story of Dr. Drew was _____ one.

   A) an interesting   B) a strange   C) a sad   D) a funny

Task 3

Directions: *The following is memo. After reading it, you are required to complete the outline below it (No. 46 through No. 50). You should write your answers briefly (**in no more than 3 words**) on the Answer Sheet correspondingly.*

Memo

To: All employees of the Personnel Department

From: Cloye, secretary of the Personnel Department

Subject: Farewell Party for Miss Banbe

Date: Nov. 12, 2009

Our colleague Miss Banbe is going to go abroad next month. His leaving is really a pity to us all as she is such an amiable woman who is always ready to help others, such an honest woman who has won trust and respect from around her, and such a humorous woman who can often add pleasure to our work. We have decided to hold a farewell party for her.

We are going to use the assembly room of our department for the party. I have organized several programs for entertainment, but they are not enough. So if anyone is willing to give performances, please let me know as soon as possible. Besides, our general manager and manager will be present, too.

All the colleagues of the Personnel Department are invited to attend the party which is scheduled on November 20, and will begin at 7 o'clock in the evening. By the way, all suggestions on the party are welcome.

Memo

   Subject: ___46___ for Miss Banbe.

   Reason for the party: Miss Banbe will ___47___ next month.

   Place: The ___48___ of our department.

   Attendants: All the colleagues of the Personnel Department, our manager and

       ___49___ Time of the party: on ___50___ at 7 o'clock in the evening.

Task 4

Directions: *The following is a list of terms used in traffic. After reading it, you are required*

to find the items equivalent to （与…相同的） those given in Chinese in the table below. Then you should find out the corresponding letters in brackets on the Answer Sheet, numbered 51 to 55.

A —— traffic regulation   B —— mark car stop

C —— traffic post   D —— single line

E —— carriage-way   F —— speed limit

G —— no through traffic   H —— passing bay

I —— restricted waiting   J —— caution animals

K —— silent zone   L —— driving without license

M —— slight impact   N —— hit-run driver

O —— traffic jam   P —— public car only

Examples: (H) 让车道   (I) 不准滞留

51. ( ) 只停公用车	( ) 禁止通行
52. ( ) 肇事逃跑司机	( ) 车行道
53. ( ) 交通拥挤	( ) 轻微碰撞
54. ( ) 限速	( ) 无证驾驶
55. ( ) 单行线	( ) 停车标志

Task 5

Directions: *The following is a Guide of reading. After reading it, you should give brief answers to the 5 questions (No. 56 through No. 60) that follow. The answers (**in no more than 3 words**) should be written after the corresponding numbers on the Answer Sheet.*

If you wish to become a better reader, here are four important points to remember about rate and speed of reading:

1. Knowing why you are reading and what you are reading to find out will often help you to know whether to read rapidly or slowly.

2. Some things should be read slowly throughout. Examples are directions for making or doing something, arithmetic problems, science and history books, which are full of important information. You must read such things slowly to remember each important step and understand each important idea.

3. Some things should be read rapidly throughout. Examples are simple stories meant for enjoyment, news, and letters from friends, items, or bits of news from local, or hometown paper telling what is happening to friends and neighbors.

4. In some of your readings, you must change your speed from fast to slow as you go along. You need to read certain pages rapidly and then slow down and do more careful readings when you come to important ideas which must be remembered.

56. In which aspects can this guide help you to become a better reader?

It will help you to remember the _____ of reading.

57. What should be depended on to judge your reading speed?

We should know what you are reading and your _____ in reading something.

58. What should one take up if one wants to be relaxed by reading?

One should take up _____.

59. Why should we read certain books slowly and carefully?

Because we should remember each _____ and understand each important idea.

60. When should we change your reading speed?

We should change the reading speed when we come to _____ which must be remembered.

Part Ⅳ　Translation — English into Chinese　（25 minutes）

Directions: *This part, numbered 61 through 65, is to test your ability to translate English into Chinese. After each of the sentences numbered 61 to 64, you will read four choices of suggested translation. You should choose the best translation and mark the corresponding letter on your Answer Sheet. And for the paragraph numbered 65, write your translation in the corresponding space on the Translation / Composition Sheet.*

61. With our GDP growing steadily, economists are all very optimistic about the prospects of our economic development.

A）通过对经济发展前景的预测,经济学家很乐观地指出我国经济会稳步增长。

B）我国国内生产总值稳步增长使经济学家对我国经济发展的前景持乐观态度。

C）随着我国国内生产总值稳步增长,经济学家们对我国经济发展的前景持乐观态度。

D）随着我国国内生产总值稳步增长,经济学家们很高兴地预见了我国经济发展的前景。

62. The wide use of Internet has changed the way we used to discover new friends and new ideas.

A）因特网的大量使用改变了人们曾经发现新朋友和新观点的方法。

B）因特网的普及改变了人们以往寻找新朋友和新观点的方式。

C）因特网的普及广泛地改变了人们习惯的交朋友和发现新观点的方式。

D）因特网的广泛运用,大大地改变了人们和朋友交流新观点的方式。

63. Senior Net provides the opportunity for some American seniors to express their feelings.

A）老年网为美国的一些老年人提供了表达自己情感的机会。

B）美国的老年人有创作自己的老年网的机会。

C）高级网站为美国的上层社会提供了表达自己情感的机会。

D）老年人网站为美国的一些老年人提供了表达自己观点的机会。

64. Selling styles differ in many ways, but we should know their fundamental difference.

A）面对不同的销售风格,我们必须找到根本的差异。

B）销售风格在很多方面有差异,但我们应该知道其根本的差异。

C）买卖的风格不同,其根本差异就不同。

D）销售风格在很多方面有差异,但我们应该知道其基础是什么。

65. In 2008, the international oil price has experienced the culmination（顶点）and the lowest through the past five years. Sinopec（中石化）performance in this dramatic（剧烈的）wave went through ups and downs. That it revealed the truth of China's petrochemical enterprises in the face of fluctuations to deal with international oil prices is immature. The impact of oil prices on the national economy has a special transmission mechanism（机制）.

Part V　　　　　　　Writing　　　　（25 minutes）

Directions: *This part is to test your ability to do practical writing. You are required to write a RESUME according to the following information in Chinese. The FIVE MAIN TOPICS of the RESUME has been written for you. Remember to write the RESUME on the Translation / Composition Sheet.*

说明：求职简历

内容：

Sany，女，1981 年 7 月 20 日出生，身体健康，未婚；地址：北京市海淀区学院路 38 号；邮政编码：100191，电话：010-67××××92

求职目标： 谋求一个能够充分发挥本人管理经验的职位，并可根据表现而获得晋升的机会

学习经历： 1996—1998　北京市 101 中学

　　　　　　1998—2001　北京大学

工作经历： 2001—2002　南方电子公司经理助理

　　　　　　2003—2008　北京进出口贸易公司经理助理

专长： 英语

Words for reference:

1. 个人基本情况应包括：name, date of birth, sex, health, family status, address, home number, e-mail

2. 发挥本人的专业 display one's specialty in

3. 晋升机会 advancement opportunity

下面是简历的五大部分的标题。填写其他内容时，请注意基本格式！

Resume
Personal Data:
Job Objective:
Education:
Work Experience:
Specialty:

模拟试题(三)

Part I   Listening Comprehension   (15 minutes)

Directions: *This part is to test your listening ability. It consists of 3 sections.*

Section A

Directions: *This section is to test your ability to understand short dialogues. There are 5 recorded dialogues in it. After each dialogue, there is a recorded question. Both the dialogues and questions will be spoken only once. When you hear a question, you should decide on the correct answer from the 4 choices marked A), B), C) and D) given in your test paper. Then you should mark the corresponding letter on the Answer Sheet with a single line through the center.*

Example: *You will hear:*

You will read: A) New York City.   B) An evening party.

C) An air trip.   D) The man's job.

From the dialogue we learn that the man is to take a flight to New York. Therefore, **C) An air trip** *is the correct answer. You should mark C) on the Answer Sheet with a single line through the center.*

[A] [B] [C] [D]

Now the test will begin.

1. A) Nov. 28th.   B) Nov. 30th.   C) Nov. 18th.   D) Nov. 31st.

2. A) He'd like to go swimming with the girl.

B) He'd like to go home and watch TV.

C) He is going to go home to help his mother with the housework.

D) He'd like to visit her mother.

3. A) At 5:15.   B) At 5 o'clock.   C) At 5:45.   D) At 5:10.

4. A) Mr. Zhang must be very popular among his students.

B) Mr. Zhang is not a good teacher.

C) The man is one of Mr. Zhang's favorite students.

D) The man likes Mr. Zhang's class very much.

5. A) Work full time in a shop.

B) Work part time in a shop.

C) Work part time in a restaurant.

D) Work full time in a restaurant.

Section B

Directions: *This section is to test your ability to understand short conversations. There are 2 recorded conversations in it. After each conversation, there are some recorded questions. Both the conversations and questions will be spoken two times. When you hear a question, you should decide on the correct answer from the 4 choices marked A), B), C) and D) given in your test paper. Then you should mark the corresponding letter on the Answer Sheet with a single line through the center.*

Conversation 1

6. A) For money.   B) For experience.

   C) For promotion.   D) Both for money and experience.

7. A) Language skill.   B) Computer skill.

   C) Communication skill.   D) Writing skill.

Conversation 2

8. A) Nov. 7th.   B) Nov. 8th.   C) Nov. 10th.   D) Nov. 13th.

9. A) 100 yuan a night.   B) 150 yuan a night.

   C) 200 yuan a night.   D) 250 yuan a night.

10. A) One single room.   B) Two single rooms.

    C) One double room.   D) Two double rooms.

Section C

Directions: *This section is to test your ability to comprehend short passages. You will hear a recorded passage. After that you will hear five questions. Both the passage and the questions will be read two times. When you hear a question, you should complete the answer to it with a word or a short phrase (**in no more than 3 words**). The questions and incomplete answers are printed in your test paper. You should write your answers on the Answer Sheet correspondingly. Now listen to the passage.*

11. What is the image of "cowboy" in the movie?

    The cowboy is the _____ of many movies.

12. What can "cowboy" symbolize?

    It is a symbol of _____.

13. What is cowboy's job?

    The cowboy's job was to _____.

14. How many days will a cattle drive last?

    A cattle drive usually took _____.

15. How many hours can cowboys ride a day?

    Cowboys rode for _____ a day.

Part Ⅱ　　　　　　　Structure　　　　　　（15 minutes）

Directions: *This part is to test your ability to construct grammatically correct sentences. It consists of 2 sections.*

Section A

Directions: *In this section, there are 10 incomplete sentences. You are required to complete each one by deciding on the most appropriate word or words from the 4 choices marked A), B),C) and D). Then you should mark the corresponding letter on the Answer Sheet with a single line through the center.*

16. — I'm sorry,I'm late.

　　— _____, Lin.

　　A) You're welcome.　　B) Go ahead.　　C) Don't mention it.　　D) No problem.

17. In _____ novel *Little Princess*, Little Princess is _____ brave girl.

　　A) a; the　　　　　　B) the; a　　　　　　C) the; the　　　　　　D) a; a

18. I got caught in the rain and my clothes _____.

　　A) has ruined　　　　　　　　　　B) had ruined

　　C) has been ruined　　　　　　　　D) had been ruined

19. In dangerous places,you _____ take care of your child.

　　A) can　　　　　　B) may　　　　　　C) must　　　　　　D) will

20. Although _____ my opinion, Pro. Wang didn't come up with his own.

　　A) against　　　　B) on　　　　　　C) for　　　　　　D) in

21. _____ that she didn't do a good job, I don't think I am abler than her.

　　A) To have said　　　B) Having said　　C) To say　　　　D) Saying

22. He was free from school, _____ he did his homework.

　　A) after which　　　B) after that　　　C) in which　　　D) in that

23. It doesn't matter who solve the problem; what _____ is how to solve the problem.

　　A) counts　　　　　B) applies　　　　C) stresses　　　　D) functions

24. _____ I don't know much about internet, I find it is really useful.

　　A) As　　　　　　B) Since　　　　　C) If　　　　　　D) While

25. Ann _____ the piano hard for long and now she is a successful pianist.

　　A) practices　　　　B) is practicing　　C) has practiced　　D) practiced

Section B

Directions: *There are 10 incomplete statements here. You should fill in each blank with the proper form of the word given in brackets. Write the word or words in the corresponding space on the Answer Sheet.*

26. It rained (heavy) _____ yesterday afternoon.

27. It was my (luck) _____ day. My bike broke down half way to school and I was late for class.

28. The girl (wear) _____ a light green skirt today.

29. (travel) _____ by train is much cheaper than by air.

30. Does her mother (leave) _____ home at seven every morning?

31. She draws the picture very (wonderful) _____.

32. This is the (twin) _____ room.

33. Shall we (meet) _____ at the school gate?

34. Jim always (finish) _____ his homework before supper.

35. I enjoy (listen) _____ to music after a long time's study.

Part III　　　　Reading Comprehension　　　（40 minutes）

Directions: *This part is to test your reading ability. There are 5 tasks for you to fulfill. You should read the reading materials carefully and do the tasks as you are instructed.*

Task 1

Directions: *After reading the following passage, you will find 5 questions or unfinished statements, numbered 36 to 40. For each question or statement there are 4 choices marked A), B), C) and D). You should make the correct choice and mark the corresponding letter on the Answer Sheet with a single line through the center.*

What makes one person more intelligent than another? What makes one person a genius, like the brilliant Albert Einstein, and another person a fool? Are people born intelligent or stupid, or is intelligence the result of where and how you live? These are very old questions and the answers to them are still not clear.

We know, however, that just being born with a good mind is not enough. In some ways, the mind is like a leg or an arm muscle（肌肉）. It needs exercise. Mental（done with the mind）exercise is particularly important for young children. Many child psychologists（心理学家）think that parents should play with their children more often and give them problems to think about. The children are then more likely to grow up bright and intelligent. If, on the other hand, children are left alone a great deal with nothing to do, they are more likely to become dull and unintelligent.

Parents should also be careful with what they say to young children. According to some psychologists, if parents are always telling a child that he or she is a fool or an idiot, then the child is more likely to keep doing silly and foolish things. So it is probably better for parents to say very positive（helpful）things to their children, such as "That was a very clever thing you did." or "You are such a smart child."

36. What does the word "intelligent" (Line 1, Para. 1) mean?

    A) Great.   B) Handsome.   C) Clever.   D) Busy.

37. According to the author, what is particularly important for young children?

    A) Born with a good mind.   B) Body exercise.

    C) Mental exercise.   D) Muscle.

38. A child _____ is more likely to grow up bright and intelligent.

    A) whose parents are clever

    B) often left alone with nothing to do

    C) born with a good mind

    D) often guided by his parents to play and think

39. It is better for parents _____.

    A) to praise and encourage their children more often

    B) to be hard on their children

    C) to leave their children alone with nothing to do

    D) to give their children as much help as possible

40. Which of the following is NOT true according to the article?

    A) Parents play an important part in their children's growth.

    B) The less you use your mind the duller you may become.

    C) Intelligence is obviously the result of where and how you live.

    D) What makes a person bright or stupid is still under discussion.

Task 2

Directions: *This task is the same as Task 1. The 5 questions or unfinished statements are numbered 41 to 45.*

    You might observe that Americans are always talking. Silence makes most Americans uncomfortable. So they would rather talk about the weather than encounter a lapse(中止) in conversation. Generally speaking Americans are friendly to everyone.

    However, don't mistake friendliness for friendship. Most Americans have many acquaintances (熟人) but few close friends. The people you are friendly with during the first semester (学期) may not necessary stay in touch when classes are over. Each semester brings new acquaintances. Friendships take time to grow. Americans are open and they trust relationships that develop slowly. Young Americans are very friendly and they like to talk to all kinds of people. They smile easily and laugh quite often. But don't mistake friendliness for physical attraction. Because a person is friendly, he or she is not necessarily interested in dating you. Even if someone accepts a date, it doesn't mean that the person is ready for an intimate (亲密的) relationship. In short, interpersonal relationships in any culture are difficult and require the use for judgment in every new situation.

41. Americans are always talking because _____.

    A) they are friendly to everyone

    B) silence makes them uncomfortable

C) they want to build intimate relationship with you

D) they know much about weather

42. Most Americans _____.

    A) have many close friends

    B) believe that friendship develop quickly

    C) trust that friendship develop slowly

    D) will keep in touch with people when classes are over

43. When an American smiles to you, it means that _____.

    A) he is attracted by you

    B) he wants to date with you

    C) he is ready for an intimate relationship

    D) he is friendly to you

44. What does the passage mainly tell us?

    A) Americans like to talk to different people.

    B) Americans enjoy talking to others.

    C) Americans believe it takes time to develop friendship.

    D) Americans are generally friendly to people.

45. What can you infer from the passage?

    A) Americans don't like to make friends with people.

    B) Friendship with Americans doesn't last long.

    C) It is not easy to build intimate relationship with Americans.

    D) Friendliness and friendship are not the same.

Task 3

Directions: *The following is an invitation letter. After reading it, you are required to complete the outline below it (No. 46 through No. 50). You should write your answers briefly (**in no more than 3 words**) on the Answer Sheet correspondingly.*

Dear Professor Mike Whitney,

We are very glad to hear that you are attending an international conference in Beijing. We are writing this letter to inquiry the possibility of inviting you to deliver a lecture on American literature for our postgraduate students on the evening of March 15.

We have long been noticed that you have done a lot of substantial and creative work in this field. Two of your books have become textbooks for our students for several years. So all of us believe your lecture will benefit our students and teaching staff alike.

If you can manage to come, please tell us the number of your flight and we will meet you at the airport. If you can't make it, please also let us know.

We are looking forward to your coming.

Sincerely yours,

Xie Li

Invitation

People invited: ___46___ .

Information about the professor: 1. Professor Whitney has done a lot of creative job in ___47___ field.

　　2. Two of his books have become ___48___ for students.

　　3. He is attending an ___49___ in Beijing.

The purpose of the invitation: to give a lecture for ___50___ on the evening of March 15.

Task 4

Directions: *The following is a list of computer terms. After reading it, you are required to find the items equivalent to （与…相同的） those given in Chinese in the table below. Then you should find out the corresponding letters in brackets on the Answer Sheet, numbered 51 to 55.*

A —— Internet Key Exchange　　　　　B —— Virtual Private Network

C —— Single User Account　　　　　　D —— Request To Send

E —— Local Area Network　　　　　　 F —— Privacy Preference Project

G —— Internet Protocol　　　　　　　 H —— File Transfer Protocol

 I —— Data Terminal Equipment　　　　J —— Flow-control

K —— Clear to Send　　　　　　　　　L —— Call Control Manager

M —— Read-only Memory　　　　　　　N —— Compact Disc

O —— Random Access File　　　　　　 P —— Random Access Memory

Examples: (F)个人隐私安全平台　　　　(A)因特网密钥交换协议

51. (　) 流控制	(　) 需求发送
52. (　) 清除发送	(　) 只读光盘
53. (　) 虚拟局域网	(　) 局域网
54. (　) 单用户账号	(　) 激光唱盘
55. (　) 拨号控制管理	(　) 网际协议

Task 5

Directions: *The following is an introduction to trade fair. After reading it, you should give brief answers to the 5 questions (No. 56 through No. 60) that follow. The answers (**in no more than 3 words**) should be written after the corresponding numbers on the Answer Sheet.*

A trade fair (trade show or expo) is an exhibition (展览) organized so that companies in a specific industry can showcase and demonstrate (展示) their latest products, service, study activities of rivals and examine recent trends and opportunities. Some trade fairs are open to the public, while others can only be attended by company representatives (members of the trade) and members of the press, therefore trade shows are classified as either "Public" or "Trade Only". They are held on a continuing basis in virtually all markets and normally attract companies from around the globe. For example, in the U.S. there are currently over 2,500 trade shows held every year, and several online directories have been established to help organizers, attendees, and marketers identify appropriate events. Consequently, cities often promote trade shows as a means of economic development.

An increasing number of trade fairs are happening online, and these events are called virtual (虚拟的) tradeshows. They are increasing in popularity (流行) due to their relatively low cost and because there is no need to travel whether you are attending or exhibiting.

56. What is the function of a trade fair?

It can help companies to _____ their latest products and other information.

57. What kinds of trade shows are there in the real world?

There are _____ and Trade Only.

58. Who can attend the Trade Only?

Company representatives and _____ can attend the Trade Only.

59. Why do cities often promote trade shows?

Cities often promote trade shows as a means of _____.

60. What is the reason for the popularity of the trade fair?

The popularity due to their _____ and save of traveling time.

Part IV   Translation — English into Chinese （25 minutes）

Directions: *This part, numbered 61 through 65, is to test your ability to translate English into Chinese. After each of the sentences numbered 61 to 64, you will read four choices of suggested translation. You should choose the best translation and mark the corresponding letter on your Answer Sheet. And for the paragraph numbered 65, write your translation in the corresponding space on the Translation / Composition Sheet.*

61. We can assume that this meeting is not likely to start on time.

A) 我们假定人们不喜欢按时召开会议。

B) 我们可以承担这次会谈不可能按时进行的责任。

C) 我们可以假定这次会谈不可能按时进行。

D) 我们也已猜想这次会谈很可能不会按时进行。

62. We should consider not only the country's short-term interest but also the long-term interest.

    A) 我们要考虑的不是国家的短期利益,而是其长期利益。

    B) 我们不仅要考虑国家的短期利益,也要考虑国家的长期利益。

    C) 我们不仅要考虑国家的短暂利益,也要考虑其长久利益。

    D) 我们不仅要考虑国家近期的兴趣,也要考虑未来的兴趣。

63. Because of his outstanding achievement in sale this year, he has been assured of a new flat by his boss.

    A) 他今年因销售了一套新楼层而工作出色。

    B) 由于他今年销售作得好,所以被允许住进新房。

    C) 由于他今年出色的成就,他有了一套新住宅。

    D) 由于他今年的销售工作出色,老板奖励他一套新房。

64. Even the college-trained employees should improve their communication skills.

    A) 即使是大学毕业的雇员也应该证明他们有交流能力。

    B) 即使是受过大学教育的应聘者也需要提高他们的交际能力。

    C) 即使受过大学教育的雇员也需要改进他们的交际能力.

    D) 即使是在职雇员也应该通过大学教育提高他们的交际能力。

65. Originally, shooting was only a tool for survival, and it wasn't a sporting event until the 19th century. In 1896 it became an event of the Olympic Games for the first time. And then it was suspended from 1904 to 1928, and returned to the Olympics in 1932. Women were allowed to join in Olympic shooting competitions in 1968 for the first time. There were only 3 shooting events in the 1896 Olympics, but now it contains 17 events.

Part V   Writing   (25 minutes)

Directions: *This part is to test your ability to do practical writing. You are required to write a speech according to the following information in Chinese. Remember to write the speech on the Translation / Composition Sheet.*

说明:假设你是四川大学的老师,你将在开学典礼上向一年级的新生致辞。

内容:请你根据下面的提示写一篇演讲稿,针对大学的学习生活提出几点要求,并适当阐述其重要性。

    1. 合理安排学习和生活;

    2. 同学之间关系融洽;

    3. 积极参加校园社团活动。

Words for reference:

大学一年级新生 freshman;社团 society

注意:演讲稿必须包括所有提示要点,但不要逐条译成英语。

模拟试题（四）

Part I　　　　Listening Comprehension　　　（15 minutes）

Directions: *This part is to test your listening ability. It consists of 3 sections.*

Section A

Directions: *This section is to test your ability to understand short dialogues. There are 5 recorded dialogues in it. After each dialogue, there is a recorded question. Both the dialogues and questions will be spoken only once. When you hear a question, you should decide on the correct answer from the 4 choices marked A), B), C) and D) given in your test paper. Then you should mark the corresponding letter on the Answer Sheet with a single line through the center.*

Example: *You will hear:*

You will read: A) New York City.　　　　　　B) An evening party.

　　　　　　　　C) An air trip.　　　　　　　D) The man's job.

From the dialogue we learn that the man is to take a flight to New York. Therefore, **C**) ***An air trip*** *is the correct answer. You should mark C) on the Answer Sheet with a single line through the center.*

[A] [B] [C̶] [D]

　　　Now the test will begin.

1. A) 1 dollar.　　　B) 60 cents.　　　C) 1.20 dollars.　　　D) 1.50 dollars.

2. A) He tried calling the woman but failed.

　 B) He had no time to call the woman.

　 C) He called the woman but she was out.

　 D) He doesn't know the number of the woman.

3. A) 10:45.　　　B) 10:30.　　　C) 10:15.　　　D) 10 o'clock.

4. A) In his office.　　B) At the dining room.　C) At home.　　D) In the restaurant.

5. A) 18 years old.　　B) 15 years old.　　C) 20 years old.　　D) 21 years old.

Section B

Directions: *This section is to test your ability to understand short conversations. There are 2 recorded conversations in it. After each conversation, there are some recorded questions. Both the conversations and questions will be spoken two times. When you hear a question, you should decide on the correct answer from the 4 choices marked A), B), C) and D) given in your test paper. Then you should mark the corresponding letter on the Answer Sheet with a single line through the center.*

Conversation 1

6. A) He went to visit his grandma in the countryside.

   B) He went for a picnic with his friend in the park.

   C) He stayed at home and doing nothing.

   D) He climbed the mountain with his friend in the city.

7. A) She has to accompany with her grandma.

   B) She has to prepare things for the picnic.

   C) She has a lot of housework to do.

   D) She has got a bad cold.

Conversation 2

8. A) Selling bike.　　B) Selling books.　　C) Ad in *Campus Daily*.　　D) *Campus Daily*.

9. A) 10 yuan for the first 30 words.　　B) 10 yuan for the first 20 words.

   C) 50 fen for the first 30 words.　　D) 50 fen for the first 20 words.

10. A) Miss Berne Li.　　B) Mr. Berne Li.　　C) Mr. David.　　D) Miss David.

Section C

Directions: *This section is to test your ability to comprehend short passages. You will hear a recorded passage. After that you will hear five questions. Both the passage and the questions will be read two times. When you hear a question, you should complete the answer to it with a word or a short phrase (**in no more than 3 words**). The questions and incomplete answers are printed in your test paper. You should write your answers on the Answer Sheet correspondingly. Now listen to the passage.*

11. Which two countries are the leading ones in apple production besides the United States?

   They are _____.

12. In which three aspects are apples different from each other?

   Apples are different in color, _____.

13. What are the colors of apples?

   The color of the apple may be red, _____.

14. How tall can apple trees grow?

   Apple trees may grow as tall as _____.

15. Why do apple trees grow best in areas that have cold winters?

   Because the _____ is good for the tree.

Part II　　　　　　Structure　　　　　(15 minutes)

Directions: *This part is to test your ability to construct grammatically correct sentences. It consists of 2 sections.*

Section A

Directions: *In this section, there are 10 incomplete sentences. You are required to complete each one by deciding on the most appropriate word or words from the 4 choices marked A), B), C) and D). Then you should mark the corresponding letter on the Answer Sheet with a single line through the center.*

16. Hanna is a brave rider, but she rides _____ of my colleagues.

    A) more bravely   B) the most bravely   C) less bravely   D) the least bravely

17. The information on the Internet gets around much more rapidly than _____ in the newspaper.

    A) it   B) those   C) that   D) one

18. I have worked very hard for the exam, but the result doesn't quite _____.

    A) find out   B) give out   C) hand out   D) work out

19. — Could you put on your earphone?

    — _____. Is it disturbing you?

    A) Take it easy   B) I'm sorry   C) Not a bit   D) It depends

20. When _____ difficult problems, we should often take an optimistic attitude.

    A) faced   B) being faced   C) facing   D) having faced

21. The No. 938 bus _____ to Beijing, and not to Tianjin.

    A) is gone   B) gone   C) goes   D) has gone

22. Children don't need to be made _____. Interest is the best teacher.

    A) to learn   B) learning   C) to have learned   D) learn

23. It was John _____ changed her mind so soon.

    A) why   B) how   C) that   D) when

24. No one has _____ been able to know who she is.

    A) still   B) yet   C) already   D) just

25. Environmental protection _____ everyone's support.

    A) calls for   B) calls forth   C) calls off   D) calls up

Section B

Directions: *There are 10 incomplete statements here. You should fill in each blank with the proper form of the word given in brackets. Write the word or words in the corresponding space on the Answer Sheet.*

26. Some foods can be kept longer if they are put in an airtight (contain) _____.

27. Lucy (go) _____ to the cinema once a month.

28. After answering the phone, Jane continues (watch) _____ TV.

29. The little boy (study) _____ very hard, so he often gets high marks in all his subjects.

30. My little sister always asks me (help) _____ her put on clothes.

31. Mr. Smith (have) _____ two daughters and one son.

32. Look, the mother bird (feed) _____ her babies in the tree.

33. Tony, the telephone (ring) _____ . Please answer it quickly.

34. All goods are on sale in that shop. Let's go and do some (shop) _____ .

35. My grandfather always (read) _____ newspapers before breakfast.

Part III　　　　　Reading Comprehension　　　（40 minutes）

Directions: *This part is to test your reading ability. There are 5 tasks for you to fulfill. You should read the reading materials carefully and do the tasks as you are instructed.*

Task 1

Directions: *After reading the following passage, you will find 5 questions or unfinished statements, numbered 36 to 40. For each question or statement there are 4 choices marked A), B), C) and D). You should make the correct choice and mark the corresponding letter on the Answer Sheet with a single line through the center.*

People who are hit by lightning and survive often have long-term effects. These may include memory loss, sleep disorders, muscle pain and depression.

Experts tell people to seek the safety of a building or a hard-top vehicle（运输工具） anytime they hear thunder, even if it is not raining. They say lightning can strike as far as sixteen kilometers from any rainfall. Lightning can travel sideways. And at least ten percent of lightning happens without any clouds overhead that you can see.

People who are outdoors should make sure they are not the tallest thing around. Bend low to the ground, but do not lie down. And do not stand near a tree or any tall subject. Get away from water and anything made of metal. A car is safe, but do not touch any metal inside.

Safety experts say people in buildings should stay away from anything with wires or pipes that lead to the outside. The National Weather Service says if you plan to <u>disconnect</u> any electronic equipment, do so before the storm arrives. Do not use a wired telephone. Do not use water. All these can carry electricity.

Some people think a person struck by lightning carries an electrical charge（电荷） afterward. Experts say this is not true. It is safe to begin emergency treatment.

Each year about four hundred people in the United States are struck by lightning. Last year forty four people died. The average is close to seventy. The National Weather Service says that is more than the number of people killed by severe storms.

36. According to the passage, which of the following is NOT true?

　A) Lightning can happen even if there is no cloud.

　B) Lightning won't do harm to people's health.

C) Lightning can travel sideways.

D) Lightning can strike very far.

37. The underlined word "disconnect" (Para. 4) refers to "＿＿＿＿＿＿".

A) cut out   B) interrupt   C) cut off   D) disturb

38. Which of the following mustn't you do in order to seek lightning safety?

A) Hide in a building.   B) Sit in a car.

C) Bend low to the ground.   D) Lie under a tall tree.

39. Which of the following object do not carry electricity?

A) Wired telephone.   B) Water.

C) Pipes that lead to the outside.   D) Person struck by lightning.

40. Which of the following is the main idea of the passage?

A) The latest information about lightning.

B) Some common knowledge about lightning safety.

C) How lightning comes into being.

D) Where we should hide in case of lightning.

Task 2

Directions: *This task is the same as Task 1. The 5 questions or unfinished statements are numbered 41 to 45.*

When animals make long journeys across places where there is no food or shelter, such as deserts or oceans, it is very important that they should be able to find their way accurately.

Birds find their way by the stars at night and by the sun during the day. People thought that this was impossible. Then some scientists made an experiment. They put some migrating birds （候鸟） in cages inside a planetarium （天象图）. When the operator turned the artificial sky （人造天空） round, the birds began to fly to the sides of the cage. Every time he moved it, the birds moved to a new position. Scientists discovered that they always flew toward the direction in which they would have flown if the sky had been real. This proved that they could see the stars and respond to them.

Many animals, especially birds, have a very precise sense of time, which is called their "internal clock". In cloudy weather, birds delay setting off on long journeys, but if the cloud lasts for a long time, they must go at last, to complete their migration in time. In such conditions, they are able to steer （引导） by following the magnetic field （磁场） of the earth. We could say that they have their own special compass inside them, which tells the right direction to go.

Most migrating animals travel in groups, sometimes in very large numbers. This makes it more likely that they will find the right way, especially when the group has experienced animals which have made the journey before.

41. What was proved by the experiment mentioned in the passage?

    A) Birds find their way by the stars at night and by the sun during the day.

    B) Birds can tell the differences between real sky and artificial sky.

    C) Birds can see the stars and would move when the stars change position.

    D) Birds always fly to the sides of the cage.

42. The phrase "internal clock" means _____.

    A) a clock that is built inside the bird   B) a clock that tells correct time

    C) an exact sense of direction   D) an accurate sense of time

43. When the cloud lasts for a long time, birds are able to _____.

    A) delay setting off on journey

    B) guided by the magnetic field of the earth

    C) use their "internal clock" to arrive in time

    D) tell the right direction by the "internal clock"

44. How do most migrating animals travel?

    A) They travel together in large numbers.

    B) They travel independently.

    C) They travel on daytime.

    D) They travel with those who have made the journey before.

45. What is the passage mainly about?

    A) How animals sense the time.

    B) How animals find their way in migration.

    C) Why animals like to travel in groups.

    D) How scientists find the secret of birds.

Task 3

Directions: *The following is the introduction of a person. After reading it, you are required to complete the outline below it (No. 46 through No. 50). You should write your answers briefly (**in no more than 3 words**) on the Answer Sheet correspondingly.*

Vera Wang has become a significant figure in the American fashion industry in a relatively short period of time. She has no formal design training because her father wouldn't let her go to art school and wanted her to concentrate on more "practical subjects". After earning a degree in liberal arts, Vera worked as an editor at *Vogue* for 17 years and as a design director of Ralph Lauren for two years. In 1990 she opened her first boutique （时尚精品店）on Madison Avenue in New York, in a less expensive line of ready-to-wear bridal and evening dresses. She chose bridal wear for she wanted to build a fashion company starting with one market and then expand into others. She became a household name in 1994 when she designed stylish costumes （时尚束装）for figure skater Nancy Kerrigan to wear in the Winter Olympics.

Vera Wang herself is a very good skater and she had Olympic dreams too. But that dream was crushed when she did not win at the National Figure Skating Championships in 1968. However her love for the sport never ceased. "I want to make an artistic contribution to the sport," she said. "I don't know if designing costumes for Nancy has been good in terms of actual sales, but it has been tremendous foe name recognition."

What do you know about Vera Wang?

Hobby: ___46___

Education: a degree in ___47___

Working experience: 1. ___48___ at Vogue for 17 years.

2. ___49___ of Ralph Lauren for two years.

Achievement: in 1994 she became a household name when she designed ___50___ for figure skate Nancy Kerrigan to wear in the Winter Olympics.

Task 4

Directions: *The following is a list of terms about law. After reading it, you are required to find the items equivalent to （与…相同的）those given in Chinese in the table below. Then you should find out the corresponding letters in brackets on the Answer Sheet, numbered 51 to 55.*

A —— false imprisonment
B —— interview a client
C —— court acceptance fee
D —— cause of action
E —— local counsel
F —— defense lawyer
G —— point of defense
H —— property tenancy
I —— appear in court
J —— statement of the parties
K —— revocation of lawyer license
L —— investigative record
M —— legal opinions
N —— court announcement
O —— expert conclusion
P —— pending case

Examples: (L)调查笔录　　　　　　(K)吊销执业证

---

51. ( ) 非法禁锢	( ) 法律意见书
52. ( ) 当事人陈述	( ) 案由
53. ( ) 辩护要点	( ) 辩护律师
54. ( ) 法院公告	( ) 案件受理费
55. ( ) 待决案件	( ) 会见当事人

Task 5

Directions: *The following is an apology letter. After reading it, you should give brief answers to the 5 questions (No. 56 through No. 60) that follow. The answers (**in no more than 3 words**) should be written after the corresponding numbers on the Answer Sheet.*

Dear Cindy,

Kindly excuse me for my not being able to attend your graduation ceremony next Wednesday as I have promised.

You know, there will be a meeting of great importance to my company next week in Beijing. But the person who was originally appointed to it is now seriously ill in hospital. And I have been asked to take his place to attend the meeting and make a speech on behalf of my company. On one hand, it is a task assigned by my boss out of his trust in me. On the other hand, I do regard it as an opportunity to both display and enhance my abilities. So I am afraid I cannot be present at your graduation ceremony.

Though I have decided to send you a gift to celebrate your graduation, I really regret that I cannot give you my sincere congratulations on the spot, for I know any gift can never parallel a warm word spoken personally by a family member. I do feel terribly sorry. Please forgive me.

Yours,

Jocy

56. What is the purpose of the letter?

To ask Cindy's ＿＿＿＿＿＿ for not attending her graduation ceremony.

57. Why can't the originally appointed person attend the meeting?

The person originally appointed was ＿＿＿＿＿＿ in hospital.

58. Why can't Jocy attend Cindy's graduation ceremony?

She has to take the sick colleague's place to attend the meeting and ＿＿＿＿＿＿ on behalf of the company.

59. How does Jocy regard this opportunity of attending the meeting?

She regards it as an opportunity to both ＿＿＿＿＿＿ her ability.

60. What is Jocy regretful for?

She is regretful that she can't give her ＿＿＿＿＿＿ on the spot.

Part IV　Translation — English into Chinese　（25 minutes）

Directions: *This part, numbered 61 through 65, is to test your ability to translate English into Chinese. After each of the sentences numbered 61 to 64, you will read four choices of suggested translation. You should choose the best translation and mark the corresponding letter on your Answer Sheet. And for the paragraph numbered 65, write your translation in the corresponding space on the Translation / Composition Sheet.*

61. The larger the city, the more essential the measures for environment protection.

　　A）城市越大，环境保护的措施就越是必不可少。

　　B）为了把城市变大，我们必须从基础入手保护环境。

C) 城市越大,环境保护的措施就越基本。

D) 城市越大,环境保护措施是必不可少的。

62. Automobiles must have certain safety devices such as seat belts and good brakes.

    A) 汽车应有一定的安全性,要有安全带和好的刹车。

    B) 汽车有了安全带和好的刹车就是安全的。

    C) 汽车应有安全装置,比如安全带和好的刹车。

    D) 汽车必须有安全带和好的刹车这两个安全装置。

63. According to the observation of some scientists, we will be short of energy in the near future.

    A) 按照科学家的观察,在将来我们将缺少能源。

    B) 据科学家观察,不久的将来我们面临能源危机。

    C) 按照一些科学家的说法,我们在将来会面临能源短缺。

    D) 据科学家观察,人的寿命会因能源问题而变短。

64. It is considered impolite in China to first-name one's seniors.

    A) 在中国,直呼长辈的姓被认为是不礼貌的。

    B) 在中国,给长辈起外号是不礼貌的。

    C) 在中国,直呼长辈的名字被认为是不礼貌的。

    D) 在中国,直呼领导的名字是不礼貌的。

65. First of all, eyes have to rest when it works two hours later. Then you should insist doing eyes exercises twice a day. It is good for eyes to look farther some times. Don't read in a bed or driving cars or the place where is dark. Don't read under the sun. If there are something in your eyes, don't rub, you should flush with the boiled and cooled water. If it hasn't reason, you must ask for doctors. If you must narrow the eyes to see things clearly, then you should wear glasses.

Part V   Writing   (25 minutes)

Directions: *This part is to test your ability to do practical writing. You are required to write an announcement according to the following information in Chinese. Remember to write the announcement on the Translation / Composition Sheet.*

说明:假如你是公司人事部经理,急需聘一位秘书,请你用英文以"Secretary Wanted"为题目写一则招聘启事。

内容:

1. 该工作主要包括两部分:一是安排经理的工作日程;二是接待工作。

2. 希望该应聘者满足下列要求:

    ① 具备良好的交流沟通能力;② 有一定文字基础;③ 感兴趣的应聘者请在本周内与公司人事部联系。

注意:1. 词数100左右;

    2. 不要逐字翻译,要组成一篇通顺连贯的短文。

模拟试题（五）

Part I   Listening Comprehension   （15 minutes）

Directions: *This part is to test your listening ability. It consists of 3 sections.*

Section A

Directions: *This section is to test your ability to understand short dialogues. There are 5 recorded dialogues in it. After each dialogue, there is a recorded question. Both the dialogues and questions will be spoken only once. When you hear a question, you should decide on the correct answer from the 4 choices marked A), B), C) and D) given in your test paper. Then you should mark the corresponding letter on the Answer Sheet with a single line through the center.*

Example: *You will hear:*

You will read: A) New York City.   B) An evening party.

                      C) An air trip.   D) The man's job.

*From the dialogue we learn that the man is to take a flight to New York. Therefore, **C) An air trip** is the correct answer. You should mark C) on the Answer Sheet with a single line through the center.*

                                                [A] [B] [C] [D]

Now the test will begin.

1. A) Mike.   B) Mike's mother.   C) The man.   D) The cook.
2. A) At a hospital.   B) At a shop.   C) At a bar.   D) At home.
3. A) He has never been to the place.   B) He has never heard of the place.
   C) He forgot the direction.   D) He is not familiar with the place.
4. A) To visit his sister.   B) To eat out with the woman.
   C) To see a movie with his sister.   D) To eat out with his sister.
5. A) He is a pretty lazy man.   B) He doesn't like gym.
   C) He doesn't want a guest pass.   D) He will join the woman.

Section B

Directions: *This section is to test your ability to understand short conversations. There are 2 recorded conversations in it. After each conversation, there are some recorded questions. Both the conversations and questions will be spoken two times. When you hear a question, you should decide on the correct answer from the 4 choices marked A), B), C) and D) given in your test paper. Then you should mark the corresponding letter on the Answer Sheet with a single line through the center.*

Conversation 1

6. A) To live in the suburbs.   B) To live in the city.
   C) To work in New York.   D) To have some changes.

7. A) He doesn't want to live in the city.

   B) He likes to eat tomatoes.

   C) He's afraid that her daughter can't adapt to the city life.

   D) He will adopt the woman's advice.

Conversation 2

8. A) Open an account.   B) Deposit money.

   C) Change money.   D) Withdraw money.

9. A) U.S. dollars.   B) Russian roubles.

   C) Japanese yen.   D) Hong Kong dollars.

10. A) Change money.   B) Deposit money.

    C) Complete a form.   D) Fond out the exchange rate.

Section C

Directions: *This section is to test your ability to comprehend short passages. You will hear a recorded passage. After that you will hear five questions. Both the passage and the questions will be read two times. When you hear a question, you should complete the answer to it with a word or a short phrase (**in no more than 3 words**). The questions and incomplete answers are printed in your test paper. You should write your answers on the Answer Sheet correspondingly. Now listen to the passage.*

11. What festival is the most important one in China?

    _____ is the most important festival in China.

12. What do families do in the evening before this festival?

    They _____ and have a big meal.

13. What is the most traditional food on this festival?

    _____ are the most traditional food.

14. Why do children like this festival?

    Because they can have _____ and wear new clothes.

15. How long will this festival last?

    It lasts about _____ long.

Part II   Structure   (15 minutes)

Directions: *This part is to test your ability to construct grammatically correct sentences. It consists of 2 sections.*

Section A

Directions: *In this section, there are 10 incomplete sentences. You are required to complete each one by deciding on the most appropriate word or words from the 4 choices marked A), B),C) and D). Then you should mark the corresponding letter on the Answer Sheet with a single line through the center.*

16. Kate is a beautiful girl, she _____ her mother more than her father.

　　A）looks out　　　　B）makes out　　C）gets across　　D）takes after

17. He has worked very hard in this term and _____ he will pass the final exam.

　　A）eventually　　　B）yet　　　　　C）finally　　　　D）accordingly

18. We should not overstate the influence of super stars, they are _____ common people.

　　A）nothing but　　B）anything but　　C）above all　　D）rather than

19. The plane will _____ in half an hour.

　　A）break off　　　B）take off　　　C）write off　　D）picked up

20. Mr. Zhou is _____ an excellent professor.

　　A）even so　　　　B）ever so　　　C）ever such　　D）so far

21. This new school principal will take _____ the next week.

　　A）place　　　　　B）effect　　　C）post　　　　D）office

22. I _____ a letter from my sister yesterday.

　　A）accepted　　　B）received　　C）took up　　　D）excepted

23. We must plan _____ the future.

　　A）in relation to　B）in excess of　C）in contrast to　D）in favor of

24. The secretary is very diligent; _____ she can't get admission of the boss.

　　A）however　　　B）therefore　　C）so　　　　D）although

25. Drink more water and you will _____ very soon.

　　A）get over　　　B）get off　　　C）hold back　　D）hold up

Section B

Directions: *There are 10 incomplete statements here. You should fill in each blank with the proper form of the word given in brackets. Write the word or words in the corresponding space on the Answer Sheet.*

26. This kind of (produce) _____ is popular in the market.

27. You can put an (advertise) _____ in the newspaper to sell your old car.

28. Children usually enjoy playing in the (amuse) _____ park because there are many interesting things to do there.

29. Little birds are (spread) _____ their wings and flying in the sky happily.

30. — Do you enjoy (ski) _____, John?

　　— Yes, I do.

31. Smoking is (harm) _____ to your health, so you had better give it up.

32. Why not (tell) _____ your difficulty to me? I may be able to help you.

33. Mother (wash) _____ dishes after each dinner.

34. Don't cover my mouth; I can hardly (breathe) _____.

35. The villagers found a lot of (fossil) _____ of unknown animals in that area last week.

Part Ⅲ　　Reading Comprehension　　（40 minutes）

Directions: *This part is to test your reading ability. There are 5 tasks for you to fulfill. You should read the reading materials carefully and do the tasks as you are instructed.*

Task 1

Directions: *After reading the following passage, you will find 5 questions or unfinished statements, numbered 36 to 40. For each question or statement there are 4 choices marked A), B), C) and D). You should make the correct choice and mark the corresponding letter on the Answer Sheet with a single line through the center.*

On February 14th many people in the world celebrate an unusual holiday. St. Valentine's Day, a special day for lovers. Valentines are cards usually red and shaped like hearts with messages of love written on them. Lovers send these cards to each other on that day, often without signing their names.

The origin of this holiday is uncertain but according to one story it gets its name from a Christian named Valentine who lived in Rome during the 3rd century A.D. His job was to perform marriages for Christian couples. Unfortunately the Emperor of Rome didn't allow Christian marriages. So they had to be performed in secret. Finally Valentine was arrested and put into prison. While he was in prison he fell in love with the daughter of the prison guard. After one year the Emperor offered to release Valentine if he would stop performing Christian marriage. Valentine refused and so he was killed on February, 270 A.D. Before he was killed Valentine sent a love letter to the daughter of the guard. He signed the letter "from your Valentine". That was the first Valentine.

Today tens of millions of people send and receive Valentines on St. Valentine's Day. Whether it is an expensive heart-shaped box of chocolates from a secret admirer or a simple hand-made card from a child, a valentine is a very special message of love.

36. People send Valentines to each other to _____.

    A) celebrate Valentine's birthday

    B) prove this holiday is unusual

    C) show their love and affection

    D) send messages of friendship

37. According to the passage, the holiday gets its name from _____.

    A) a place of interest named Valentine   B) a Christian named Valentine

    C) an emperor named Valentine   D) a card sent to Valentine

38. Christian marriage had to be performed in secret because _____.

    A) Christian marriage is illegal

    B) the couple is not old enough to get married

    C) their parents didn't allow the marriage

    D) the Emperor of Rome didn't allow Christian marriages

39. The Emperor offered to release Valentine on condition that _____.

    A) Valentine stop performing Christian marriage

    B) Valentine get married with the daughter of the prison guard

    C) Valentine do not perform marriage secretly

    D) Valentine quit his job

40. What is the passage mainly about?

    A) The love story of valentine.

    B) An unusual holiday.

    C) How do people celebrate the holiday?

    D) The possible origin of St. Valentine's Day.

Task 2

Directions: *This task is the same as Task 1. The 5 questions or unfinished statements are numbered 41 to 45.*

    Scientists have created a tomato that can grow on salty water. The plant is the first crop of its kind ever produced in the world.

    Its significance can not be overestimated (高估). The new technology can help mankind solve the problem of feeding its ever-expanding population. It is estimated that by 2025 the world population will amount to more than 9 billion, an increase of 3 billion over 2000. Each day 240,000 more people are born, ready to be fed like the rest of us. Unfortunately, not all the land on Earth can be used to grow crops for humans. About 24.7 million acres of the problem is irrigation (灌溉). When farmers water their crops, salts in the water also enter the soil. Over time, salts such as sodium (钠) and calcium (钙) build up to such a point that they severely harm the growth of crops. Salts destroy most plants' ability to draw up water through their roots.

    But, the new variety of tomato produced by American and Canadian scientists can store salts in its leaves so that the fruit doesn't taste salty. Researchers hope this technology will enable areas of poor-quality land to become productive (多产的). And they can feed some of the world's growing population.

41. The world "significance" (Para. 2) means _____.

    A) importance   B) quality   C) price   D) quantity

42. What kind of problem can be solved by the new technology?

    A) It can help mankind solve the problem of planting tomatoes.

    B) It can help mankind solve the problem of watering.

    C) It can help mankind solve the problem of salt.

    D) It can help mankind solve the problem of feeding its population.

43. What is the population of the world in 2000 according to the passage?

    A) About 9 billion.   B) About 6 billion.

    C) About 3 billion.   D) About 5 billion.

44. Why do salts left in the soil harm the growth of crops?

    A) They are poisonous to the plant.

    B) They contain sodium and calcium.

    C) They upset most plant's ability to draw up water through their roots.

    D) They destroy the soil's ability to water plant.

45. The fruit of the new tomato doesn't taste salty because _____.

    A) The new kind of tomato doesn't need to be watered.

    B) The new kind of tomato can store salts in its leaves.

    C) The new kind of tomato can store salts in its roots.

    D) The new kind of tomato is planted with special water.

Task 3

Directions: *The following is a News Report. After reading it, you are required to complete the outline below it (No. 46 through No. 50). You should write your answers briefly (**in no more than 3 words**) on the Answer Sheet correspondingly.*

On the afternoon 14:28 of May 12, 2008, an earthquake measuring 8.0 on the Richter scale(里氏震级) hit Sichuan Province, a mountainous region in Western China. By the next day, the death toll stood at 69,000, with another 18,000 still missing. Over 15 million people live in the affected area, including almost 4 million in the city of Chengdu. Nearly 2,000 of the dead were students and teachers caught in schools that collapsed.

News Report

Type of disaster: __46__

Time: the afternoon 14:28 of May 12, 2008

Place: __47__

Number of people killed: __48__

Number of people missing : __49__

Number of people live in affected area: __50__

Task 4

Directions: *The following is a list of occupations. After reading it, you are required to find the items equivalent to (与…相同的) those given in Chinese in the table below. Then you should find out the corresponding letters in brackets on the Answer Sheet, numbered 51 to 55.*

A —— Administration Staff		B —— Bond Trader	
C —— Computer Engineer		D —— Export Sales Manager	
E —— General Manager / President		F —— Insurance Actuary	
G —— Manager for Public Relations		H —— Marketing Executive	
I —— Office Assistant		J —— Application Engineer	
K —— Business Controller		L —— Electrical Engineer	
M —— Financial Controller		N —— Import Liaison Staff	
O —— Legal Adviser		P —— Market Analyst	

Examples: (D) 外销部经理   (I) 办公室助理

51. (　) 销售主管		(　) 财务主任	
52. (　) 法律顾问		(　) 进口联络员	
53. (　) 总经理		(　) 证券交易员	
54. (　) 行政人员		(　) 公关部经理	
55. (　) 应用工程师		(　) 业务主任	

Task 5

Directions: *The following is a weather report. After reading it, you should give brief answers to the 5 questions (No. 56 through No. 60) that follow. The answers (**in no more than 3 words**) should be written after the corresponding numbers on the Answer Sheet.*

A storm in Changchun, capital of Northeast China's Jilin Province, claimed four lives on Sunday. The storm lasted about three minutes from around 8∶00 p.m. the winds reached speeds of over a hundred miles an hour, causing serious damage and a widespread power failure.

And for today's weather: a fine day is in store nearly everywhere, with the best of the sunshine in southern and central areas of China. A pleasant day, then, with long sunny periods developing. Light winds. These will be light with a maximum temperature of 22 degrees Celsius （摄氏温度）. Looking at the outlook for the next few days, it will become mostly cloudy with heavy showers moving in from the west.

56. When did the storm started?

It started _____.

57. How damaging was the storm?

It caused four deaths and serious damage including a _____.

58. What is the general weather condition for today?

_____.

59. What is the temperature today?

_____ Celsius.

60. What is the weather outlook for the next few days?

Cloudy with _____.

Part IV　Translation — English into Chinese　（25 minutes）

Directions: *This part, numbered 61 through 65, is to test your ability to translate English into Chinese. After each of the sentences numbered 61 to 64, you will read four choices of suggested translation. You should choose the best translation and mark the corresponding letter on your Answer Sheet. And for the paragraph numbered 65, write your translation in the corresponding space on the Translation / Composition Sheet.*

61. In whatever culture, people must be faced with the necessity of clothing, eating, living and commuting.

A) 在世界各地，人都要解决衣、食、住、行的问题。

B) 不管在哪种文化里，人们都要面对衣、食、住、行的问题。

C) 不管文化程度如何，人们都要面对衣、食、住、行的问题。

D) 不管在哪种文化里，人们都认为衣、食、住、行是必要的。

62. Bewilderment and frustration that the new environment has brought about can easily impair one's self-confidence.

A）人在新环境中感受到的困惑和挫折会使一个人丧失自信。

B）陌生环境带来的困惑和挫折会击败一个人的自信。

C）困惑和挫折很容易削弱一个在新环境中的人的自信。

D）陌生的环境带来的困惑和挫折很容易削弱一个人的自信。

63. We must have an adequate knowledge of culture so as to interpret how people from another country behave and speak.

A）掌握足够的文化背景知识有助于我们理解不同国家的人的言语行为。

B）掌握足够的文化背景知识的目的是理解不同国家的人的言语行为。

C）我们必须掌握足够的关于文化的知识,这样才能理解他们的言语行为。

D）我们必须掌握足够的文化背景知识,这样才能翻译各国不同的语言文字。

64. I think that Susana is by far the most active member of our group.

A）我认为苏珊娜是我们组里较为积极的成员。

B）我认为苏珊娜远远不是我们组里的积极分子。

C）我认为苏珊娜是离我们组最远的积极分子。

D）我认为苏珊娜是我们组里最最积极的成员。

65. School rules:

1. Students should be wearing your school badges（校章）and uniforms.

2. School starts at 7:30 in the morning and finishes at 4:30 in the afternoon. Don't be late or leave early.

3. Do some cleaning after school to keep the school clean.

4. Those who go to school by bike should apply for a bike permit.

Part V   Writing   （25 minutes）

Directions: *This part is to test your ability to do practical writing. You are required to write a notice according to the following information in Chinese. Remember to write the notice on the Translation / Composition Sheet.*

说明:请以班主任的名义写一份通知,2010 年 3 月 2 日发出。

内容如下:

1. 时间:3 月 7 日晚上 7 点。

2. 地点:4 号楼 401 房间。

3. 事由:对上学期的总结以及对下学期的计划。

4. 参加人员:全体同学。

5. 要求:带笔记本,按时到场,做好记录。

第3章

专家预测试题

专家预测试题（一）

Part I　　　　Listening Comprehension　　　　（15 minutes）

Directions: *This part is to test your listening ability. It consists of 3 sections.*

Section A

Directions: *This section is to test your ability to understand short dialogues. There are 5 recorded dialogues in it. After each dialogue, there is a recorded question. Both the dialogues and questions will be spoken only once. When you hear a question, you should decide on the correct answer from the 4 choices marked A), B), C) and D) given in your test paper. Then you should mark the corresponding letter on the Answer Sheet with a single line through the center.*

Example: *You will hear:*

You will read: A) New York City.　　　　B) An evening party.

C) An air trip.　　　　D) The man's job.

From the dialogue we learn that the man is to take a flight to New York. Therefore, ***C)An air trip*** *is the correct answer. You should mark C) on the Answer Sheet with a single line through the center.*

[A] [B] [C] [D]

Now the test will begin.

1. A) He doesn't like pork.　　　　　　　B) He never eats pork in this restaurant.

C) He wants to have a change.　　　　D) He has no appetite.

2. A) She brought the man the wrong dish.

B) She wanted to change the dish he had ordered.

C) She kept the man waiting for too long a time.

D) She brought the dish to the wrong customer.

3. A) About 10 years.　　B) About 8 years.　　　C) About 20 years. D) About 12 years.

4. A) Send a document to Mr. Baker's office.　　B) Send a document to Mr. White's office.

C) Send newspaper to Mr. White's office.　　D) Send newspaper to Mr. Baker's office.

5. A) Red.　　　　　　B) White.　　　　　　C) Black.　　　　D) Blue.

Section B

Directions: *This section is to test your ability to understand short conversations. There are 2 recorded conversations in it. After each conversation, there are some recorded questions. Both the conversations and questions will be spoken two times. When you hear a question, you should decide on the correct answer from the 4 choices marked A), B), C) and D) given in your test paper. Then you should mark the corresponding letter on the Answer Sheet with a single line through the center.*

Conversation 1

6. A) 24 dollars.　　B) 15 dollars.　　C) 20 dollars.　　D) 25 dollars.

7. A) First class ticket on the express.　　B) Second class ticket on the express.

   C) First class ticket on the regular.　　D) Second class on the regular.

Conversation 2

8. A) His car broke down.

   B) He forgot the telephone number.

   C) He was late for the appointment.

   D) He couldn't remember the name of the restaurant.

9. A) At the garage.　　B) At home.　　C) In the park.　　D) In the restaurant.

10. A) Over an hour.　　　　　　　　　B) Half an hour.

   C) Less than half an hour.　　　　D) Less than an hour.

Section C

Directions: *This section is to test your ability to comprehend short passages. You will hear a recorded passage. After that you will hear five questions. Both the passage and the questions will be read two times. When you hear a question, you should complete the answer to it with a word or a short phrase (**in no more than 3 words**). The questions and incomplete answers are printed in your test paper. You should write your answers on the Answer Sheet correspondingly. Now listen to the passage.*

11. At what time is the air the freshest in the day?

   The air is never as fresh as early _____.

12. Why do early rising help us in our study?

   Because we learn more quickly in the morning, and find it _____.

13. How can we work well according to the author?

   In order to work well, we should have _____.

14. What should we prepare before our work?

   We should wash _____ and eat our breakfast properly.

15. What is the main idea of this passage?

   The main idea is that early rising is _____ in more than one way.

Part Ⅱ   Structure   （15 minutes）

Directions: *This part is to test your ability to construct grammatically correct sentences. It consists of 2 sections.*

Section A

Directions: *In this section, there are 10 incomplete sentences. You are required to complete each one by deciding on the most appropriate word or words from the 4 choices marked A）, B）,C) and D）. Then you should mark the corresponding letter on the Answer Sheet with a single line through the center.*

16. The old lady had a _____ escape when she pass across the road in front of the bus.

   A）close   B）short   C）narrow   D）fine

17. Li Hua is the monitor of the class, so he should _____ charge of this matter.

   A）take   B）hold   C）make   D）get

18. It isn't quite _____ that he will change his mind.

   A）sure   B）right   C）exact   D）certain

19. They _____ the dust by having double windows.

   A）put down   B）shut out   C）cut short   D）taken off

20. As soon as the child was _____, their mother got them out of bed and into the bathroom.

   A）woke   B）waken   C）wake   D）awake

21. _____ for your help we could not have finished it in time.

   A）In spite of   B）But for   C）Because of   D）As for

22. Officers are entitled _____ travel first class.

   A）for   B）with   C）to   D）of

23. The difficulty lies _____ their lack of money.

   A）in   B）to   C）on   D）with

24. I'm going to the supermarket. _____, what is the time now?

   A）As a result   B）By the way   C）On the whole   D）In a word

25. These apples are fresher than _____ in that shop.

   A）anyone   B）the others   C）that   D）the ones

Section B

Directions: *There are 10 incomplete statements here. You should fill in each blank with the proper form of the word given in brackets. Write the word or words in the corresponding space on the Answer Sheet.*

26. The weather forecast says the weather of tomorrow will be as (bad) _____ as that of today.

27. There (be) _____ a lot of sunshine in Hainan all year around.

28. People go to Happy Valley for (funny) _____.

29. Jenny (do) _____ some cleaning every weekend.

30. That young man is very (diligence) _____ , so everyone like working with him.

31. Have you found your (lose) _____ watch?

32. Thank you for (make) _____ English fun.

33. Wind power are being used to generate (electronic) _____ .

34. Have fun (watch) _____ the movie.

35. My computer has just (attack) _____ by an unknown virus.

Part III　　　　　Reading Comprehension　　　(40 minutes)

Directions: *This part is to test your reading ability. There are 5 tasks for you to fulfill. You should read the reading materials carefully and do the tasks as you are instructed.*

Task 1

Directions: *After reading the following passage, you will find 5 questions or unfinished statements, numbered 36 to 40. For each question or statement there are 4 choices marked A), B), C) and D). You should make the correct choice and mark the corresponding letter on the Answer Sheet with a single line through the center.*

In some countries video games are fast becoming a social problem. They are banned in the Philippines and Indonesia. In Japan, those who are under 15 years old are forbidden to use the public machines at night. City elders across the United States are campaigning (呼吁) to restrict their numbers, while the Hong Kong government is proposing to license (批准) their operation. These video games are causing children to waste their money on them. Even adults are lured (诱惑) into spending working hours playing them.

In Singapore, the battle of man against the machines takes place in licensed amusement centers (娱乐中心), mostly located in shopping centers. According to one estimated, each establishment can make between $250 and $1,500 a day. The schoolchildren in uniforms there are not allowed into these centers. However, one cannot help noticing that the majority of those who are often found in these places are youngsters. Many of them are schoolchildren who have changed out of their uniforms. Some play for the fun of it, others have turned them into a form of gambling (赌博), and some are hopelessly addicted to (沉迷) them.

Now kids and adults alike play these games in the privacy of their homes. Video game sets have invaded (进入) most homes. The question that must be asked is: Have they any education value?

36. In Singapore, the battle of man against the machines takes place in _____ .

　　A) licensed amusement centers　　　　B) banned amusement centers

　　C) government building　　　　　　　D) school square

37. How can schoolchildren go into the amusement centers in Singapore?

　　A) They are allowed to go into such places.　B) They pretended to be adult.

　　C) They changed out of their uniforms.　　　D) They put on their uniforms.

38. Various governments are taking actions on video games because _____.

A) schoolchildren waste time and money on them

B) they can easily be turned into a form of gambling

C) they are becoming a social problem, affecting both adults and children

D) too many adults spend working hours playing them

39. We can learn from the passage that _____.

A) placing video game machine inside amusement centers is not really effective in discouraging youngsters from using them

B) schoolchildren in uniforms are not allowed into amusement centers in many countries

C) people, regardless of their age, are crazy about video games

D) those who are under 15 years old are allowed to use the machine during the day in many countries

40. The speaker's attitude towards video games is _____.

A) positive　　　　B) negative　　　C) doubtful　　　D) indifferent

Task 2

Directions: *This task is the same as Task 1. The 5 questions or unfinished statements are numbered 41 to 45.*

We know mosquitoes very well. Mosquitoes fly everywhere. They can be found almost all over the world, and there are more than 2,500 kinds of them.

No one likes the mosquito. But the mosquito may decide if she loves you. She? Yes, she. The male mosquito doesn't bite! Only the female mosquito bites because she needs blood to lay eggs. She is always looking for things or people she wants to bite. If she likes what she finds, she bites. But if she doesn't like your blood, she will turn to someone else for more delicious blood. Next time a mosquito bites you, just remember you are chosen. You're different from the others!

If the mosquito likes you, she lands on your body without letting you know. She bites you so quickly and quietly that you may not feel anything different. After she bites, you will have an itch（痒）on your body because she puts something from her mouth together with your blood. When the itch begins, she has flown away.

And then what happens? Well, after her delicious dinner, the mosquito feels tired. She wants to find a place to have a good rest. There, in a tree or on a wall, she begins to lay eggs, hundreds of eggs.

41. Only the female mosquito bites because _____.

A) the male mosquito doesn't have the ability

B) she needs blood to lay eggs

C) female mosquitoes are stronger than male

D) male mosquitoes are more friendly to people

42. Which of the following is NOT true?

A) Only the female mosquito bites.

B) No one likes the mosquito.

C) Mosquitoes will bite everyone.

D) Mosquitoes lands on your body without letting you know.

43. If a mosquito wants to bite you, it means _____.

    A) she is very tired   B) she likes your blood

    C) she wants to lay eggs on you   D) she is hungry

44. From the passage we know that _____.

    A) you will notice at once when a mosquito lands on your body

    B) you can feel something different when the mosquito bites you

    C) after she bites, you will have an itch (痒) on your body

    D) when you felt the itch you can catch the mosquito

45. After the delicious dinner, the mosquito will _____.

    A) continue biting you

    B) turn to someone else for more delicious blood

    C) lay eggs on your body

    D) have a rest and lay eggs on a wall or a tree

Task 3

Directions: *The following is a resume. After reading it, you are required to complete the outline below it (No. 46 through No. 50). You should write your answers briefly (**in no more than 3 words**) on the Answer Sheet correspondingly.*

Resume

Name: Lidia

Sex: Female

Address: Room 602, Dormitory Building 12, Peking University, Beijing.

Date of Birth: June 16, 1983

Telephone: (010) 97××××56, 133××××6745

E-mail: *axiaodongi@gmail.com*

Hobbies: swimming, tennis, Internet surfing, dancing

Foreign Languages: English

Objective: To work as a regional sales representative who is responsible for sales activity and coordination

Education:

    2002—Present   Studying at Peking University Bachelor of Arts in finance

    1999—2002   Studying at Haidian No. 1 High School

    1996—1999   Studying at Changhong No. 7 Junior High School

Work Experience:

          Student Teacher, Yucai High School; Tutor, New Oriental Learning Center; Assistant Coach, New Star Swim Team.

Special Skills and Technical Qualifications:

I am professionally trained in finance and economics.

In addition to Mandarin, I can speak, write and read English fluently.

Lidia is applying for a position as a ___46___. Lidia was graduated from Peking University and her major is ___47___. When she was in the university, she had a lot of work experiences when she studied in the university. She worked as ___48___ in Yucai High School. She also worked as a tutor in New Oriental Learning Center, and she was the assistant coach of the New Star ___49___. When she was in the university, she liked swimming, tennis, surfing the Internet and ___50___.

Task 4

Directions: *The following is a list of terms about the press. After reading it, you are required to find the items equivalent to （与…相同的） those given in Chinese in the table below. Then you should find out the corresponding letters in brackets on the Answer Sheet, numbered 51 to 55.*

A —— editorial office   B —— free-lancer
C —— off the record   D —— back alley news
E —— copy editor   F —— full position
G —— investigative reporting H —— opinion poll
I —— press conference   J —— faxed photo
K —— in-depth reporting   L —— accredited journalist
M —— contributing editor   N —— covert coverage
O —— invasion of privacy   P —— man of the year

Examples: （C）不宜公开报道   （E）文字编辑

51. ( ) 编辑部	( ) 深度报道
52. ( ) 自由撰稿人	( ) 特派记者
53. ( ) 民意测验	( ) 隐性采访
54. ( ) 调查性报道	( ) 传真照片
55. ( ) 新闻发布会	( ) 年度新闻人物

Task 5

Directions: *The following is an argument. After reading it, you should give brief answers to the 5 questions （No. 56 through No. 60）that followed. The answers （**in no more than 3 words**）should be written after the corresponding numbers on the Answer Sheet.*

Exam-oriented or Quality-oriented

At present there exists side by side two contradictory educational systems: the traditional exam-oriented system and the new quality-oriented one, which leads to a heated nationwide discussion as to which is preferable.

The exam-oriented educational pattern is the inevitable （不可避免的）result of the existing exam assessment （评估）system. In order to climb into the "ivory tower" or work for their degrees, students are cramming data and facts only for exams and forget all the information right after the exams. What's worse, when students become interested in testing techniques, they gradually lose their freedom and creativity. As a result, they always bury themselves in multiple choices and never attach importance to practical ability and originality (独创性).

  In contrast, the quality-oriented educational pattern stresses the creativity of students and their all-round development. Students are not expected to memorize information mechanically and passively as computers. Instead, they are encouraged to do some creative work actively and independently as the programmers of computers. In this pattern, what students aim at is no longer their academic performances, but their practical abilities.

  No doubt, what the new quality-oriented pattern aims to train and bring up are not merely learners successful in studies, but responsible citizens fit in health, rich in knowledge and competent in their work. Therefore, it's high time we reformed our existing exam assessment system and adopted the new one.

56. Which two educational systems exist at present?

  The _____ system and the quality-oriented system.

57. What is the shortcoming of traditional exam-oriented pattern?

  It made students neglect the _____ and originality.

58. What does the quality-oriented pattern stress?

  It stresses the creativity of students and their _____.

59. What is the aim of the new quality-oriented pattern?

  It aims to train students to be responsible, knowledgeable and _____.

60. What is the author's attitude towards the two educational patterns?

  The author prefers the _____ system.

Part IV Translation — English into Chinese （25 minutes）

Directions: *This part, numbered 61 through 65, is to test your ability to translate English into Chinese. After each of the sentences numbered 61 to 64, you will read four choices of suggested translation. You should choose the best translation and mark the corresponding letter on your Answer Sheet. And for the paragraph numbered 65, write your translation in the corresponding space on the Translation / Composition Sheet.*

61. There are so many books that I really don't know which one to choose.

 A）那儿书这么多,我真不知道挑了哪本。

 B）那儿书这么多,我真不知道挑哪本。

 C）我真不知道可挑的书这么多。

 D）我挑了这么多书,真不知道哪本书好。

62. I'm the least ambitious of all the students here.

 A）我与这儿所有的同学一样没有雄心。

 B）我是这儿所有同学中最没有雄心的。

 C）我是这儿所有同学中干有雄心的事最少的。

 D）我是这儿没有雄心的同学之一。

63. At the international conference, the famous scientist gave an excellent report based on his recent experiment.

A) 在国际会议上,这位著名科学家根据他最近的实验结果做了精彩的报告。

B) 在国际会议上,这位著名科学家宣读了他最近实验的精彩报告。

C) 在国际会议上,这位著名科学家以他的精彩报告为基础,做了实验。

D) 这位著名科学家以最近的国际会议为基础,宣读了精彩的实验报告。

64. Whether we like it or not, the world we live in has changed a great deal in the last hundred years, and it is likely to change even more in the next hundred.

A) 无论我们是否喜欢这个世界,它都在过去的一百年间发生了巨大的变化,而其在未来会有更大的变化。

B) 无论我们是否愿意,我们的生活在过去一百年间已经变化了许多,而且在未来一百年里可能变化更多。

C) 无论我们是否愿意,我们的生活方式令这个世界改变了很多,而且在未来还会有更大的变化。

D) 无论我们是否愿意,我们生活的世界在过去一百年间已经变化了许多,而且在未来的一百年里可能变化更多。

65. We have learned from the letter that your company has produced and exported a variety of textile machinery to us. According to the letter, it seems that there may be some negligence (疏忽) in the delivery time, we are arranging our representative in Paris to go to your company to check the material in the next week.

Part V　　　　　　　　Writing　　　　　　　（25 minutes）

Directions: *This part is to test your ability to do practical writing. You are required to write a note according to the following information in Chinese. Remember to write the note on the Translation / Composition Sheet.*

说明:假如你是要出国深造,公司答应派车送你去机场。你在临行前一天写了张便条提醒李秘书。

内容:

1. 请检查明天的车是否落实,提醒司机;

2. 你之所以要确定一下,是因为太早不好叫出租车;

3. 感谢费心,并感谢一年来的关心;

4. 在公司的一年来,生活愉快、难忘,很可能再来;

5. 留下一些资料,希望对公司有用。

专家预测试题（二）

Part I Listening Comprehension （15 minutes）

Directions: *This part is to test your listening ability. It consists of 3 sections.*

Section A

Directions: *This section is to test your ability to understand short dialogues. There are 5 recorded dialogues in it. After each dialogue, there is a recorded question. Both the dialogues and questions will be spoken only once. When you hear a question, you should decide on the correct answer from the 4 choices marked A), B), C) and D) given in your test paper. Then you should mark the corresponding letter on the Answer Sheet with a single line through the center.*

Example: *You will hear:*

You will read: A) New York City.　　　B) An evening party.

　　　　　　　　C) An air trip.　　　　　D) The man's job.

*From the dialogue we learn that the man is to take a flight to New York. Therefore, **C)An air trip** is the correct answer. You should mark C) on the Answer Sheet with a single line through the center.*

[A] [B] [C̶] [D]

Now the test will begin.

1. A) She will go on foot. 　　　　　B) She will take two turnings.
   C) She will go by bus. 　　　　　 D) Not mentioned.
2. A) Husband and wife. 　　　　　 B) Waiter and customer.
   C) Boss and employee. 　　　　　 D) Father and daughter.
3. A) At a shop. 　　B) In a restaurant. 　　C) At home. 　　　D) At sport meets.
4. A) Pop music. 　　B) Rock music. 　　C) Classical music. 　　D) Country music.
5. A) She thinks it's too crazy to wear red. 　　B) She thinks red is not fashionable.
   C) She has no enough money. 　　D) She thinks red is too bright for her.

Section B

Directions: *This section is to test your ability to understand short conversations. There are 2 recorded conversations in it. After each conversation, there are some recorded questions. Both the conversations and questions will be spoken two times. When you hear a question, you should decide on the correct answer from the 4 choices marked A), B), C) and D) given in your test paper. Then you should mark the corresponding letter on the Answer Sheet with a single line through the center.*

Conversation 1

6. A) She has a quiz at that time.

   B) She has to do her homework.

   C) She has an important exam at that time.

   D) She has an important meeting at that time.

7. A) He will hold the party on time.　　　B) He will hold the party ahead of time.

   C) He will put off the time.　　　D) He will cancel the party.

Conversation 2

8. A) The pet's shop.　　B) The station.　　C) The hospital.　　D) The cinema.

9. A) The love between cats and dogs.　　B) The friendship between cats and dogs.

   C) The fight between cats and dogs.　　D) The cooperation between cats and dogs.

10. A) Wonderful.　　B) Violent.　　C) Horrible.　　D) Common.

Section C

Directions: *This section is to test your ability to comprehend short passages. You will hear a recorded passage. After that you will hear five questions. Both the passage and the questions will be read two times. When you hear a question, you should complete the answer to it with a word or a short phrase （**in no more than 3 words**）. The questions and incomplete answers are printed in your test paper. You should write your answers on the Answer Sheet correspondingly. Now listen to the passage.*

11. Who is Washington's father?

    His father is a _____.

12. When did the war break out between America colonies and England?

    The war broke out in _____.

13. When did Washington become the first president of the U.S.A.?

    He became the first president of the U.S.A. _____.

14. What won Washington great respect?

    His wisdom and _____ won him great respect

15. Why was the new capital of the U.S.A. named Washington D.C.?

    The new capital of the U.S.A. was named Washington D.C. _____ him.

Part II　　　　　　Structure　　　　（15 minutes）

Directions: *This part is to test your ability to construct grammatically correct sentences. It consists of 2 sections.*

Section A

Directions: *In this section, there are 10 incomplete sentences. You are required to complete each one by deciding on the most appropriate word or words from the 4 choices marked A), B), C) and D). Then you should mark the corresponding letter on the Answer Sheet with a single line through the center.*

16. If you do it _____, do it well.

    A) above all   B) in all   C) at all   D) after all

17. Time is limited and I can _____ finish my work in time.

    A) almost   B) even   C) nearly   D) hardly

18. _____, I will stick to my dream.

    A) Somehow   B) Anyhow   C) Somewhat   D) Anywhere

19. You can't _____ him in his knowledge of physics.

    A) equal   B) agree   C) help   D) match

20. Tom thought that the summer holiday ends _____ too soon.

    A) all   B) only   C) very   D) so

21. Scott _____ the first prize in his class.

    A) hit   B) bitten   C) beaten   D) won

22. I have promised Linda not to give _____ the secret.

    A) away   B) in   C) out   D) up

23. Tomas is kind, humorous, clever and _____ he is diligent.

    A) in general   B) above all   C) after all   D) in all

24. I can speak French, but only _____.

    A) little   B) few   C) a little   D) a few

25. Children have a variety of interests. Some like sports; some like music; _____ like literature.

    A) the others   B) others   C) the other   D) other

Section B

Directions: *There are 10 incomplete statements here. You should fill in each blank with the proper form of the word given in brackets. Write the word or words in the corresponding space on the Answer Sheet.*

26. Hurry up, or you (be) _____ late.

27. Many (store) _____ in China sell mooncakes that day.

28. I think this one is bigger and (cheap) _____ than that one.

29. Today I have to (walk) _____ home.

30. The farmers in China don't use animals (do) _____ farm work any more.

31. My hair is too long. I want to have it (cut) _____.

32. All the trees (plant) _____ last summer.

33. Different (country) _____ have different weather.

34. I am afraid I can't go. I have to do some (clean) _____ at home.

35. He (read) _____ a book when the telephone rang.

Part III   Reading Comprehension   （40 minutes）

Directions: *This part is to test your reading ability. There are 5 tasks for you to fulfill. You should read the reading materials carefully and do the tasks as you are instructed.*

Task 1

Directions: *After reading the following passage, you will find 5 questions or unfinished statements, numbered 36 to 40. For each question or statement there are 4 choices marked A), B), C) and D). You should make the correct choice and mark the corresponding letter on the Answer Sheet with a single line through the center.*

Isn't it surprising that scientists have a better understanding of how many stars there are in the galaxy（银河系）than how many species there are on Earth? Their estimates of global species diversity vary from 2 to 100 million species. Most people agree on an estimate of somewhere near 10 million and yet only 1.75 million have actually been named. Current knowledge of species diversity is limited. This problem becomes more serious because there is a lack of a central database or list of the world's species.

New species are still being discovered — even new birds and mammals(哺乳动物).On average, about three new species of birds are found each year, and since 1990, 10 new species of monkeys have been discovered. Other groups are still far from being completely described: an estimated 40 percent of freshwater fishes in South America have not yet been classified.

Scientists were started in 1980 by the discovery of a huge diversity of insects in tropical forests. In one study of just 19 trees in Panama, 960 new species of beetles were discovered.

As scientists begin investigating other little-known ecosystem, like the soil and the deep sea, "surprising" discoveries of species become commonplace. There is nothing strange about this, though, since as many as a million undescribed species are believed to live in the deep sea. And one gram of a small-sized piece of land might hold 90 million bacteria(菌类) and other microbes（微生物）. How many species these communities contain is still anyone's guess.

36. Which of the following is true?

A) Scientists have a sound knowledge about the diversity of species.

B) Scientists don't know much about the number of stars in the galaxy.

C) Scientists show more interest in stars in the galaxy than in species on Earth.

D) Scientists don't agree on the number of species in the world.

37. How many species are there on Earth according to most scientists?

A) About 2 million.　　　　　　　　B) About 10 million.

C) About 100 million.　　　　　　　D) About 1.75 million.

38. In which of the following groups is the discovery of new species not mentioned in the passage?

A) Birds.　　　　B) Monkeys.　　　　C) Trees.　　　　D) Freshwater fish.

39. What can you learn from the passage?

A) The soil and the deep sea belong to communities that haven't been fully explored.

B) It is surprising news wherever new species are discovered in the deep sea.

C) About 90 million species are believed to live in the deep sea.

D) A million species in the deep sea have been discovered and named.

40. Which of the following best reveals the main idea of the passage?

A) Surprising discoveries of new species are commonplace.

B) The mystery of the deep sea and the soil remains to be uncovered.

C) Knowledge of global species diversity is still limited.

D) Estimates of global species diversity vary among scientists.

Task 2

Directions: *This task is the same as Task 1. The 5 questions or unfinished statements are numbered 41 to 45.*

　　The expensive shops in a famous arcade (有拱廊的街道) near Piccadilly were just opening. At this time of the morning, the arcade was almost empty. Mr. Taylor, the owner of a jewellery shop was admiring a new window display. Two of his assistants had been working busily since 8 o'clock and had only just finished. Diamond necklaces and rings had been beautifully arranged on a background of black velvet (丝绒). After gazing at the display for several minutes, Mr. Taylor went back into his shop.

　　The silence was suddenly broken when a large car, with its headlights on and its horn blaring (喇叭响声), roared down the arcade. It came to stop outside the jeweller's. One man stayed at the wheel, two others with black stockings over their faces jumped out and smashed the window of the shop with iron bars. While this was going on, Mr. Taylor was upstairs. He and his staff began throwing furniture out of the window. Chairs and tables went flying into the arcade. One of the thieves was struck by a heavy statue, but he was too busy helping himself to diamonds to notice any pain. The raid (袭击) was all over in three minutes, for the men scram-bled back into the car and it moved off at an unbelievable speed. Just as it was leaving, Mr. Taylor rushed out and ran after it throwing ashtrays (烟灰缸) and vases, but it was impossible to stop the thieves. They had got away with thousands of pounds worth of diamonds.

41. Who is the Mr. Taylor?

　　A) He is the owner of a famous Piccadilly arcade.

　　B) He is the owner of Piccadilly's famous arcade.

　　C) He is the owner of a jewellery shop.

　　D) He is the assistant of a jewellery shop.

42. While Mr. Taylor was admiring the new window display _____.

　　A) his two assistants were arranging jewellery in the window

　　B) some thieves were arranging

　　C) he was standing inside his shop

　　D) his staff were finishing their work for the day

43. How many thieves are there in the robbery?

　　A) 2.　　　　　B) 3.　　　　　C) 4.　　　　　D) 5.

44. While the robbery was going on _____.

　　A) Mr. Taylor and his staff fight with the robbers downstairs

　　B) Mr. Taylor and his staff stayed upstairs

　　C) Mr. Taylor and his staff called the police immediately

　　D) Mr. Taylor and his staff throwing furniture out of the window upstairs

45. Which of the following statements is NOT true according to the passage?

　　A) The raid lasted for a long time.

　　B) The robbery happened in the morning.

　　C) One of the thieves was struck by a heavy statue.

　　D) Thieves had got away with thousands of pounds worth of diamonds.

Task 3

Directions: *The following is a notice. After reading it, you are required to complete the outline below it（No. 46 through No. 50）. You should write your answers briefly （**in no more than 3 words**）on the Answer Sheet correspondingly.*

Notice

　　The Student Union has decided to hold a Chinese speech contest to celebrate the coming National Day. The maximum time（最长时间）of each speaker is eight minutes. We will invite seven experts to serve as judges. Every speaker will be judged from three aspects: script（文字材料）, eloquence（口才）, and the reaction of the audience. The results will be announced immediately.

　　All the participants are required to hand in their request form before September 12th. The preliminary contest（初赛）falls on September 18th in the school library. The final contest will be held on September 30th in the cinema of our university.

The Student Union

Sept. 2nd, 2005

Chinese Speech Contest

Purpose: to celebrate the coming ___46___

Judges: ___47___

Aspects to be judged: script, eloquence, and the ___48___

Time of the preliminary contest: ___49___

Place of the final contest: ___50___ of our university

Task 4

Directions: *The following is a list of terms about finance. After reading it, you are required to find the items equivalent to (与…相同的) those given in Chinese in the table below. Then you should find out the corresponding letters in brackets on the Answer Sheet, numbered 51 to 55.*

A —— Unit Trust		B —— Unlisted Security	
C —— Upside Risk		D —— Value-at-risk	
E —— Venture Capital		F —— Weak Holdings	
G —— Withdrawal Plan		H —— Withholding Tax	
I —— Working Capital		J —— Sector Fund	
K —— Seed Financing		L —— Sell Short	
M —— Senior Debt		N —— Separate Listing	
O —— Shareholder Value		P —— Shell Company	

Examples: (M) 优先债务　　　　　　(D) 风险值

51. (　　) 提款计划　　　　　　(　　) 上调风险

52. (　　) 周转资金　　　　　　(　　) 空壳公司

53. (　　) 卖空　　　　　　　　(　　) 股东价值

54. (　　) 产业基金　　　　　　(　　) 单位信托

55. (　　) 独立上市　　　　　　(　　) 短期持股

Task 5

Directions: *The following is an application letter. After reading it, you should give brief answers to the 5 questions (No. 56 through No. 60) that followed. The answers (**in no more than 3 words**) should be written after the corresponding numbers on the Answer Sheet.*

Dear Mr. Cavendish,

I am writing to apply for the position as the general assistant that you recently advertised in newspaper. I take keen interest in the post because I find that my major and experiences well meet the requirements you stated in the advertisement.

Being interested in management and English, I pursued my graduate study in the direction of Public Relations in Sichuan International Studies University, and got a Master's Degree in 2005. I was a top student through the three academic years, as can be shown in the enclosed resume and reports. After graduation, I ever have been a tour guide in a travel agency. As Shanghai is my hometown and I love it very much, I have decided to move back and so I venture to apply for the position in your company.

If I were favored with an interview, I would be most grateful. Please contact me at 139××××2398. Thank you for your consideration.

Best wishes.

Yours sincerely

56. Where does the applicant see the advertisement?

The applicant founds it _____.

57. What position does the person applying for?

The person is applying for a position of _____.

58. What is the applicant's major in university?

The applicant's major is _____.

59. Where is the applicant's hometown?

_____.

60. How to contact the applicant?

By _____.

Part Ⅳ　Translation — English into Chinese　（25 minutes）

Directions: *This part, numbered 61 through 65, is to test your ability to translate English into Chinese. After each of the sentences numbered 61 to 64, you will read four choices of suggested translation. You should choose the best translation and mark the corresponding letter on your Answer Sheet. And for the paragraph numbered 65, write your translation in the corresponding space on the Translation/Composition Sheet.*

61. Anyway, even if one wanted to, one couldn't put the clock back to an earlier age.

A）无论如何，人们也无法找回失去的岁月。

B）不管他怎么做，也无法将时钟拨回到早先的时代。

C）不管怎样，即使有人想这么做，他也无法将时钟拨回到早先的时代。

D）不管怎样，即使有人想这么做，他也无法使自己退回到年轻的时候。

62. Sometimes, evidence of intelligence can be seen in attempts to deceive.

A）有时，动物的智能可以从其欺骗的企图中得以证明。

B）有时，动物的智能可以从其欺骗的行为中得以证明。

C）有时，动物试图欺骗来证明它们有智能。

D）有时，动物用它们的智能来试图欺骗。

63. No modestly educated adult can fail to be upset by such an experience.

A）没有略受教育的成年人会为这样的经历难过。

B）略受教育的成年人没有谁不会为这样的经历难过。

C）略受教育的成年人都不会为这样的经历难过。

D）不是所有受过教育的成年人都会为这样的经历难过。

64. I'd like you to describe to my friend your exciting adventures in Africa as you have described them to me.

A）我想让你把我描述给你的非洲冒险经历讲给我朋友听。

B）我想让你把我和你在非洲的刺激冒险经历描述给我的朋友听。

C）我想让你像我一样,把非洲的刺激冒险经历描述给我的朋友。

D）我想让你像给我描述的那样,给我的朋友描述你在非洲的刺激的冒险经历。

65. Energy shortage is a very serious problem in the world. Many people worry that energy resources will be exhausted if we use them in an unchecked way. This will cause serious problems and even crisis and jeopardize the survival of mankind. The problem can be solved in one way or another. One is to conserve and save our energy. Another way is to develop new energy resources.

Part V   Writing   （25 minutes）

Directions: *This part is to test your ability to do practical writing. You are required to write a introduction according to the following information in Chinese. Remember to write the introduction on the Translation / Composition Sheet.*

说明:假如你是学校外事办的负责人,你要向来你校参观的市领导介绍学校的情况。

具体信息

1. 学校情况:地区最大的大学,10 个学院,一个图书馆,两个教学区;

2. 教师:40 位教授,200 多位教师,30%的教师到国外学习过;

3. 学生:15,000 名学生;

4. 学生情况:学习 4 年,一年两个学期,2/3 的课堂学习,1/3 的实践活动;

5. 学校生活:丰富多彩,经常有各种竞赛。

历年真题

2009 年 6 月真题

Part I   Listening Comprehension   (15 minutes)

Directions: *This part is to test your listening ability. It consists of 3 sections.*

Section A

Directions: *This section is to test your ability to understand short dialogues. There are 5 recorded dialogues in it. After each dialogue, there is a recorded question. Both the dialogues and questions will be spoken only once. When you hear a question, you should decide on the correct answer from the 4 choices marked A), B), C) and D) given in your test paper. Then you should mark the corresponding letter on the Answer Sheet with a single line through the center.*

Example: *You will hear:*

 You will read: A) New York City.   B) An evening party.

　　　　　　 C) An air trip.   D) The man's job.

From the dialogue we learn that the man is to take a flight to New York. Therefore, **C)** *An air trip is the correct answer. You should mark C) on the Answer Sheet with a single line through the center.*

[A][B][C][D]

　　 Now the test will begin.

1. A) In a restaurant.   B) In a hospital.
　 C) At a post office.   D) At a railway station.

2. A) He will go to the concert.   B) He has been to the concert.
　 C) He is not interested in the concert.   D) He can't go to the concert.

3. A) $2.   B) $12.   C) $7.   D) $14.

4. A) He's going to find a job.   B) He's going to go abroad.
　 C) He's going to study for a degree.   D) He's going to do a part-time job.

5. A) Husband and wife.   B) Nurse and patient.
　 C) Teacher and student.   D) Boss and employee.

Section B

Directions: *This section is to test your ability to understand short conversations. There are 2* *recorded conversations in it. After each conversation, there are some recorded questions. Both the conversations and questions will be spoken two times. When you hear a question, you should decide on the correct answer from the 4 choices marked A), B), C) and D) given in your test paper. Then you should mark the corresponding letter on the Answer Sheet with a single line through the center.*

Conversation 1

6. A) To be a teacher.　　　　　B) To take care of animals.
　　C) To work as a secretary.　　D) To further her study.

7. A) To work in an office.　　　B) To be an animal doctor.
　　C) To go abroad.　　　　　　D) To be a salesman.

Conversation 2

8. A) She lost her data.
　　B) She broke the disc.
　　C) She bought a computer of a wrong model.
　　D) She couldn't get her computer working.

9. A) Buy a computer for her.　　B) Go to the store with her.
　　C) Lend her some money.　　　D) Replace the disc for her.

10. A) To show the receipt.　　　　B) To call the store first.
　　C) To pay some more money.　　D) To bring the instruction manual.

Section C

Directions: *This section is to test your ability to comprehend short passages. You will hear a recorded passage. After that you will hear five questions. Both the passage and the questions will be read two times. When you hear a question, you should complete the answer to it with a word or a short phrase (**in no more than 3 words**). The questions and incomplete answers are printed in your test paper. You should write your answers on the Answer Sheet correspondingly. Now listen to the passage.*

11. When was the customer survey conducted?
　　It was conducted _____.

12. How did customers feel about the products of the company?
　　The products were quite _____.

13. What did customers complain in the survey?
　　It took _____ to settle their complaints.

14. How did customers feel about the service staff?
　　The service staffs were not always _____.

15. When should the Customer Service Department come up with a plan to improve their service?

　　_____.

Part II   Structure   （15 minutes）

Directions: *This part is to test your ability to construct grammatically correct sentences. It consists of 2 sections.*

Section A

Directions: *In this section, there are 10 incomplete sentences. You are required to complete each one by deciding on the most appropriate word or words from the 4 choices marked A), B), C) and D) given in your test paper. Then you should mark the corresponding letter on the Answer Sheet with a single line through the center.*

16. By the end of this year Mr. Smith _____ in our company for exactly three years.

    A) is working   B) has worked   C) will work   D) will have worked

17. I think that the Great Wall is worth _____ hundreds of miles to visit.

    A) to travel   B) traveling   C) traveled   D) travel

18. The new staff didn't know how to use the system _____ I explained it to him yesterday.

    A) until   B) because   C) if   D) since

19. _____ is reported in the newspapers that the talks between the two companies have not made any progress.

    A) That   B) What   C) It   D) As

20. _____ by the failure of the project, the manager could hardly say a word.

    A) To be shocked   B) Shocked   C) Be shocked   D) Shocking

21. The first question we now discuss is _____ we should go there so early tomorrow.

    A) whether   B) where   C) what   D) whom

22. He was attending a meeting, _____ he would have come to your party yesterday.

    A) unless   B) when   C) but   D) or

23. Enclosed you _____ an application form that you are asked to fill out.

    A) will find   B) find   C) found   D) are finding

24. The auto industry spends large amounts of money on marketing campaigns _____ young adult customers.

    A) attract   B) attracted   C) to attract   D) attracts

25. The advertising company recently hired a designer _____ had once won a prize in a national contest.

    A) whose   B) which   C) whom   D) who

Section B

Directions: *There are 10 incomplete statements here. You should fill in each blank with the proper form of the word given in brackets. Write the word or words in the corresponding space on the Answer Sheet.*

26. Your daughter is (luck) _____ enough to have been admitted to this large company.

27. After an (introduce) _____ by the chairperson, we'll go on with the day's discussion.

28. We must keep the manager (inform) _____ of the advertising campaign.

29. It is suggested that the president of the Union (make) _____ a speech on behalf of all the workers.

30. Having been badly damaged by the earthquake, the city has to be (rebuild) _____ .

31. She described the ancient city in detail because she (live) _____ there for years.

32. The new university graduate is confident of (win) _____ the post as the assistant to the managing director.

33. Successful companies concentrate (much) _____ on selling their products to their existing customers than to their new ones.

34. The local economy depends (heavy) _____ on the exports of manufactured goods.

35. With such a short time (leave) _____ , it's impossible for us to finish this complicated experiment.

Part III   Reading Comprehension   (40 minutes)

Directions: *This part is to test your reading ability. There are 5 tasks for you to fulfill. You should read the reading materials carefully and do the tasks as you are instructed.*

Task 1

Directions: *After reading the following passage, you will find 5 questions or unfinished statements, numbered 36 to 40. For each question or statement there are 4 choices marked A), B), C) and D). You should make the correct choice and mark the corresponding letter on the Answer Sheet with a single line through the center.*

An ebook (also referred to as an electronic book, eBook, or ebook)is a digital version (版本)of a print book that you download and read. But if you want to read an ebook, you must have an Ebook Reader, which is a kind of free software used by your computer. Make sure you have installed the appropriate Reader before you download your ebook from the Internet. The software allows you to turn the words on the screen into the size you like. It also helps you turn pages and change your viewing options (计算机屏幕上的阅读选择). Ebooks are a fun alternative to regular books. You can download them to any computers and create your own library of hundreds of titles. If you load them onto your portable computer, you can take them with you when you travel. Some ebooks are even interactive! Best of all, when you order an ebook, there is no waiting and no shipping charges. The amount of time it takes to download your ebook depends on the speed of your connection and the size of your ebook.

36. From this passage, we learn that an ebook _____.

A) can be found in any library

B) can be read directly from the Internet

C) can be read by any one who has a computer

D) can be read when special software is installed

37. The Ebook Reader is used for _____.

A) reading an ebook you've downloaded

B) turning a print book into a digital version

C) downloading an ebook from the Internet

D) copying an ebook onto a portable computer

38. From this passage, we can learn that _____.

A) you can read an ebook on a laptop when you travel

B) you can order an ebook using the Ebook Reader

C) the ebooks ordered have to be shipped to you

D) it takes a lot of trouble reading an ebook

39. Which of the following statements is TRUE?

A) An ebook is ordered in the same way as a print book is.

B) The size of the words in an ebook cannot be changed.

C) The downloading time is decided by the ebook's size.

D) There is less fun reading an ebook than a print book.

40. The passage is mainly about _____.

A) a better way to download an Ebook   B) a new kind of book — the Ebooks

C) the new version of Ebooks   D) the fun of reading Ebooks

Task 2

Directions: *This task is the same as Task 1. The 5 questions or unfinished statements are numbered 41 to 45.*

Check-in Requirements

Passengers and their baggage must be checked in at least 45 minutes before departure for domestic flights and 60 minutes for international flights. Government-issued photo identification is required for all passengers. Passengers traveling across any international boundary (边界) are responsible for obtaining all necessary travel documents. Passengers may be denied boarding if travel documents are not in order. When check-in requirements are not met, a passenger may be separated from his/her bag. Frontier Airlines will gladly hold the bag in the destination baggage service office for pick-up at the passenger's convenience. Passengers must be at the gate 20 minutes before departure for boarding.

Free Baggage Allowance for Each Ticketed Passenger

Frontier Airlines, Inc. will accept, per ticketed passenger, two free checked bags not to exceed 62 inches and 50 pounds per piece — one carry-on bag and one personal item (purse, laptop, etc.).

NOTE: A ticketed passenger may check one carry-on bag if it is within established limitations. All carry-on items must be put under a passenger seat or in a shared overhead compartment (行李舱).

Excessive (超重) Baggage Charges

An excess charge will be made for each piece of baggage over the free allowance and for each piece of over-sized or over-weight baggage.

41. An international flight passenger should check in at least _____.

    A) 20 minutes before departure   B) 30 minutes before departure

    C) 45 minutes before departure   D) 60 minutes before departure

42. What is required of all domestic and international passengers for check-in?

    A) An invitation letter.   B) A company's job offer.

    C) An official photo identification.   D) An official immigration permit.

43. How much baggage is a ticketed passenger allowed free of charge?

    A) One piece.   B) Two pieces.   C) Three pieces.   D) Four pieces.

44. What will passengers have to do if their baggage is over the free allowance?

    A) To pay extra money.   B) To carry it themselves.

    C) To ask for special permit.   D) To drop the excessive item.

45. This passage is probably taken from _____.

    A) an advertisement of an airline   B) a notice for airline passengers

    C) a schedule of an international flight D) an introduction to an airline company

Task 3

Directions: *The following is an advertisement. After reading it, you are required to complete the outline below it (No. 46 to No. 50). You should write your answers briefly (**in no more than 3 words**) on the Answer Sheet correspondingly.*

Sakura Scholarships offer students the opportunity of taking part in a three-month Japanese language course in the city of Kyoto. The scholarship covers free accommodation, meals and tuition. Return air fares between their country of residence and Osaka are paid, and $1,000 pocket money is also provided.

To apply for one of these Scholarships, you should write a letter of about 300 words, describing your own educational career so far, and giving reasons why you think your education would benefit from participation in the Sakura Scholarship Scheme.

The closing date for application is February 1, 2009. Applicants who have been selected for the short list (入选名单) will receive the notice by March 31. The final selection will be made on the basis of interviews held during May.

Applications are open to all students, regardless of age, sex or nationality, and are also open to people who are not currently full-time students.

Please apply to Ms. Kyoto Matsumoto, Sakura Scholarship Scheme, Sakura Trading Co, 200 East Avenue, London E97PS.

```
                         Sakura Scholarships
Course offered: Japanese language
Items covered: 1. accommodation, meals and    46
               2.    47    air fares
               3. $1,000    48
Content of application letter: 1. describing the applicant's    49
                               2. giving reasons for taking the course
Deadline for application:    50
```

Task 4

Directions: *The following is a list of medical terms. After reading it, you are required to find the items equivalent to （与…等同）those given in Chinese in the table below. Then you should put the corresponding letters in the brackets on the Answer Sheet, numbered 51 through 55.*

A —— assembly line   B —— packer

C —— forklift   D —— explosive materials

E —— fire extinguisher   F —— loading dock

G —— machine operator   H —— electrical hazard

I —— conveyor belt   J —— safety boots

K —— shipping clerk   L —— time card

M —— warehouse   N —— hard hat

O —— earplug   P —— hand truck

Q —— safety earmuffs

Examples: (F)装载码头   (K)运务员

```
51. (    ) 易爆材料          (    ) 安全耳罩
52. (    ) 工时卡            (    ) 安全靴
53. (    ) 装配线            (    ) 灭火器
54. (    ) 安全帽            (    ) 手推车
55. (    ) 机器操作员         (    ) 输送带
```

Task 5

Directions: *The following is an application letter. After reading it, you should give brief answers to the 5 questions（No. 56 to No. 60）that follow. The answers（**in no more than 3 words**）should be written after the corresponding numbers on the Answer Sheet.*

Dear Ms. Pascal,

    I would appreciate very much an opportunity to meet with you and demonstrate how my unique experience and education could be of particular advantage to your company's future growth.

My practice last summer at Pascal Business Systems helped me focus on my academic and career goals. My fourteen weeks with your company involved me in a whole variety of sales support activities including preparing brochures and catalogs, coordinating trade shows, providing data and information to salespeople in the field, and interacting with customers.

During the past two semesters I have concentrated on developing my electronic publishing and business communication skills. I am confident that I can improve the ways in which Pascal Business Systems provides support for field marketing representatives. This would include designing and maintaining an online catalog which could be coordinated with current inventories(库存清单).

I am available for an interview at your convenience and look forward to an opportunity to discuss ways to improve operations and communications with field locations and sales. Thank you for your kind consideration.

Sincerely,

Lourdes Santiago

56. How long did Lourdes Santiago work at Pascal Business System?

_____.

57. What activities was he involved in when he had his practice in the company?

A whole variety of _____.

58. What special skills did Lourdes Santiago develop during the past two semesters?

He developed electronic publishing and _____.

59. What could he do to help support the field marketing representatives?

By designing and maintaining _____.

60. What is the purpose of the letter?

Lourdes Santiago writes the letter to ask for _____.

Part Ⅳ   Translation — English into Chinese   （25 minutes）

Directions: *This part, numbered 61 through 65, is to test your ability to translate English into Chinese. After each of the sentences numbered 61 to 64, you will read four choices of suggested translation. You should choose the best translation and mark the corresponding letter on your Answer Sheet. And for the paragraph numbered 65, write your translation in the corresponding space on the Translation / Composition Sheet.*

61. For you safety, the electrical appliance can only operate when it has been correctly mounted on a dry and cool base.

A) 你只有在干燥通风的地方操作这一台电子仪器才安稳。

B) 只有在干燥通风的场所才能使电子仪器持续运转。

C) 为了安全起见,本电器设备只有安装在通风阴凉处才能确保其正常运行。

D) 为了安全起见,本电器装置只有正确安装在干燥阴凉的基座上才能运行。

62. Not only does asking questions at a meeting involve you in discussions, it is also a good way to demonstrate your professional knowledge.

A) 会上提问不仅能使你参与到讨论中, 而且还是一种展示你专业知识的好方法。

B) 会上提问不仅可以讨论你所提出的问题, 而且还可以很好地利用你的专业知识。

C) 提问题不仅能使会议讨论你所关注的问题, 还是一种表现你专业技能的好途径。

D) 在会上不仅要提问还要参与讨论, 这是提高你自己专业技能的一种有效方法。

63. People feel that the interdependence of nations, so long talked about by statesmen, is today more than ever a reality.

A) 人们感到, 一直都在谈论的国家的独立, 今天比以往任何时候这个问题都显得重要。

B) 人们感到, 政治家长期谈论的国家间的相互依存, 现在比任何时候都更为实在。

C) 人们感到, 许多国家以前一直关心的独立问题, 现在比以前任何时候都更加现实。

D) 人们感到, 政治家以前认为国家之间要互相依赖, 今天显得比以往更加现实了。

64. The purchaser will not be responsible for any cost or expenses in connection with the packing or delivery of the above goods.

A) 卖主并非没有责任解决上述货物在包装和运输方面出现的问题。

B) 对于上述货物的包装和运输有关费用的任何事宜卖主概不负责。

C) 以上货物在包装和运输方面所产生的有关费用买主均不予过问。

D) 买主概不承担与上述货物的包装和运输有关的任何成本或费用。

65. The city government recognizes that citizens have certain new needs. To better meet your needs, we have made several changes in community facilities in 2009. Three stations for the suburbs have been added to the western train service. Broadband(宽带)cable is now available to all parts of the city. 5, 000 new books were bought for the City Library. Some new facilities at the city hospitals have been installed. Next year, we will try our best to make your life even better.

Part V   Writing   (25 minutes)

Directions: *This part is to test your ability to do practical writing. You are required to write a business letter according to the following information given in Chinese. Remember to do the task on the Translation / Composition Sheet.*

说明: 假设你是某公司人事部职员王林, 为安排一次职工的假期旅行, 向某旅行社写信询问有关事宜。

内容: 1. 询问旅游信息(如: 线路、价格、折扣等);

     2. 告诉对方参加旅游的人数和时间安排;

     3. 索要相关的资料, 特别是行程安排;

     4. 告之联系方式。

Words for reference:

Travel Agency 旅行社

注意信函格式!

2009 年 12 月真题

Part I　　　　Listening Comprehension　　　（15 minutes）

Directions: *This part is to test your listening ability. It consists of 3 sections.*

Section A

Directions: *This section is to test your ability to understand short dialogues. There are 5 recorded dialogues in it. After each dialogue, there is a recorded question. Both the dialogues and questions will be spoken only once. When you hear a question, you should decide on the correct answer from the 4 choices marked A), B), C) and D) given in your test paper. Then you should mark the corresponding letter on the Answer Sheet with a single line through the center.*

Example: *You will hear:*

You will read: A) New York City.　　　　B) An evening party.

　　　　　　　　C) An air trip.　　　　　　D) The man's job.

From the dialogue we learn that the man is to take a flight to New York Therefcre, **C) An air trip** *is the correct answer. You should mark C) on the Answer Sheet with a single line through the center.*

[A] [B] [C] [D]

Now the test will begin.

1. A) A teacher.　　　B) A doctor.　　　C) A secretary.　　　D) A salesman.

2. A) Visiting a company.　　　　　　　B) Meeting with the new manager.

　 C) Looking for the meeting room.　　D) Showing a newcomer around.

3. A) In an office.　　　　　　　　　　B) In a department store.

　 C) In a restaurant.　　　　　　　　D) In a library.

4. A) To attend a conference.　　　　　B) To work in a firm.

　 C) To do some sightseeing.　　　　　D) To visit an exhibition.

5. A) The rise of costs.　　　　　　　　B) The drop of sales.

　 C) The decrease of production.　　　D) The increase of pollution.

Section B

Directions: *This section is to test your ability to understand short conversations. There are 2 recorded conversations in it. After each conversation, there are some recorded questions. Both the conversations and questions will be spoken two times. When you hear a question, you should decide on the correct answer from the 4 choices marked A), B), C) and D) given in your test paper. Then you should mark the corresponding letter on the Answer Sheet with a single line through the center.*

Conversation 1

6. A) All staff.   B) Young workers.

   C) New employees.   D) Department managers.

7. A) 1 week.   B) 2 weeks.   C) 3 weeks.   D) 4 weeks.

8. A) How to operate machines.   C) How to use computers.

   B) How to collect information.   D) How to be a manager.

Conversation 2

9. A) Because there was no access to the Internet.

   B) Because the traffic outside was too noisy.

   C) Because the air conditioner was out of order.

   D) Because there was no hot water in the bath.

10. A) Room 201.   B) Room 203.   C) Room 204.   D) Room 206.

Section C

Directions: *This section is to test your ability to comprehend short passages. You will hear a recorded passage. After that you will hear five questions. Both the passage and the questions will be read two times. When you hear a question, you should complete the answer to it with a word or a short phrase (**in no more than 3 words**). The questions and incomplete answers are printed in your test paper. You should write your answer on the Answer Sheet correspondingly. Now listen to the passage.*

11. What's Peter Johnson's position in the company?

   He is the _____ Manager.

12. What places will the visitors see in the company?

   _____ and the laboratory.

13. How long does it take to look around the laboratory?

   About _____ minutes.

14. What measures are taken to ensure the visitors' safety?

   The visitors are required to wear protective hard hats and _____.

15. What is not allowed to do during the tour?

   _____.

Part II   Structure   (15 minutes)

Directions: *This part is to test your ability to construct grammatically correct sentences. It consists of 2 sections.*

Section A

Directions: *In this section, there are 10 incomplete sentences. You are required to complete each one by deciding on the most appropriate word or words from the 4 choices* *marked A), B), C) and D). Then you should mark the corresponding letter on the Answer Sheet with a single line through the center.*

16. We must find a way to cut prices _____ reducing our profits too much.

    A) without   B) despite   C) with   D) for

17. She didn't know _____ to express her ideas in English clearly in public.

    A) which   B) why   C) what   D) how

18. _____ the weather improves, we will suffer a huge loss in the tourist industry.

    A) As   B) Since   C) While   D) Unless

19. We are happy at the good news _____ Mr. Black has been awarded the Best Manager.

    A) that   B) which   C) what   D) whether

20. It is important that we _____ the task ahead of time.

    A) will fish   B) finished   C) finish   D) shall finish

21. Would you please pass me the book _____ cover is black?

    A) which   B) whose   C) that   D) its

22. _____ in the company for three years, Mark has become experienced in business negotiations.

    A) Having worked   B) Have been working   C) Have worked   D) Worked

23. Not until she arrived at the meeting room _____ she had forgotten to bring the document.

    A) she realized   B) did she realize   C) she did realize   D) does she realize

24. John had never been abroad before, _____ he found the business trip very exciting.

    A) because   B) though   C) so   D) while

25. _____ some students are able to find employment after graduation, others will have to return to school and earn an advanced degree.

    A) Since   B) While   C) Because   D) If

Section B

Directions: *There are 10 incomplete statements here. You should fill in each blank with the proper form of the word given in the brackets. Write the word or words in the corresponding space on the Answer Sheet.*

26. Employees are not allowed (make) _____ personal phone calls in the office.

27. The shop assistant priced the goods before (put) _____ them on the shelf.

28. The purpose of new technology is to make life (easy) _____, not to make it more difficult.

29. The proposal about the annual sales (discuss) _____ at the next board meeting.

30. Since we work in different sections of the company, we see each other only (occasional) _____.

31. Some domestic manufacturers are busy increasing production, losing the chance to develop more (advance) _____ technology.

32. I shall appreciate your effort in (correct) _____ this error in my bank account as soon as possible.

33. If your neighbors are too noisy, then you have a good reason to make your (complain) _____.

34. 30 percent of the students who (interview) _____ yesterday believe they should continue with their education until they have a university degree.

35. Measures should be taken to avoid the negative effect (bring) _____ about by unfair competition.

Part III   Reading Comprehension   (40 minutes)

Directions: *This part is to test your reading ability. There are 5 tasks for you to fulfill. You should read the reading materials carefully and do the tasks as you are instructed.*

Task 1

Directions: *After reading the following passage, you will find 5 questions or unfinished statements, numbered 36 to 40. For each question or statement there are 4 choices marked A), B), C) and D). You should make the correct choice and mark the corresponding letter on the Answer Sheet with a single line through the center.*

Google, the Internet search-engine company, has announced it will give more than twenty-five million dollars in money and investments to help the poor. The company says the effort involves using the power of information and technology to help people improve their lives.

Aleem Walji works for Google.org — the part of the company that gives money to good causes. He said the company's first project will help identify where infectious (传染性的) diseases are developing. In Southeast Asia and Africa, for example, Google.org will work with partners to strengthen early-warning systems and take action against growing health threats.

Google.org's second project will invest in ways to help small and medium-sized businesses grow. Walji says microfinance (小额信贷) is generally small, short-term loans that create few jobs. Instead, he says Google.org wants to develop ways to bring investors and business owners together to create jobs and improve economic growth.

Google.org will also give money to help two climate-change programs announced earlier this year. One of these programs studies ways to make renewable (再生的) energy less costly than coal-based energy. The other is examining the efforts being made to increase the use of electric cars.

The creators of Google have promised to give Google.org about one percent of company profits and one percent of its total stock value every year. Aleem Walji says this amount may increase in the future.

36. The purpose of Google's investments is to _____.

A) help poor people   B) develop new technology

C) expand its own business   D) increase the power of information

37. According to Aleem Walji, the company's first project is to _____.

  A) set up a new system to warn people of infectious diseases

  B) find out where infectious diseases develop

  C) identify the causes of infectious diseases

  D) cure patients of infectious diseases

38. What kind of businesses will benefit from Google.org's second project?

  A) Large enterprises.   B) Corss-national companies.

  C) Foreign-funded corporations.   D) Small and medium-sized businesses.

39. From the fourth paragraph, we learn that Google's money is also invested to help _____.

  A) start more research programs

  B) make more advanced electric cars

  C) develop renewable and coal-based energy

  D) conduct studies related to climate changes

40. From the last paragraph we learn that the investments by Google.org come from _____.

  A) Google's profits and stock value   B) some international IT companies

  C) the company's own interests   D) local commercial banks

Task 2

Directions: *This task is the same as Task 1. The 5 questions or unfinished statements are numbered 41 to 45.*

Your boss holds your future prospects in his hands. Some bosses are hard to get along with. Some have excellent qualifications but no idea when it comes to dealing with people. Of course, not all bosses are like that.

The relationship you have with your boss can be a major factor in determining your rise up the career ladder. Your boss is not only your leader, he is also the person best equipped to help you do the job you are paid to do. He can inform you of company direction that may affect your professional development.

Your boss also needs you to perform at your best in order to accomplish his objectives. He needs your feedback in order to provide realistic and useful reports to upper management. But how does this help you establish a meaningful working relationship with your boss?

The key is communication. Learn and understand his goals and priorities (优先的事). Observe and understand your boss's work style. If he has not been clear with his expectations, ask! Likewise, ask for feedback and accept criticism gracefully. And if he understands that you do not view your job as just something to fill the hours between 9:00 and 5:00, he may be more likely to help you.

In short, getting along with your boss requires getting to know his likes and dislikes and learning to work with his personality and management style.

41. The main idea of the first paragraph is that _____.

  A) bosses are hard to deal with

  B) bosses have good character

C) bosses determine your career future

D) bosses must have similar personality

42. In the second paragraph, "rise up the career ladder" (Line 2) means _____.

    A) going to work abroad   B) changing jobs frequently

    C) being promoted in position   D) pursuing an advanced degree

43. In order to achieve his objectives, your boss expects that you will _____.

    A) do your best in your work   B) show your management skills

    C) get along with your colleagues   D) write reports to upper management

44. The most important factor for establishing a good working relationship with the boss is _____.

    A) high expectations   B) quick feedback

    C) frequent criticism   D) effective communication

45. The best title for the passage might be _____.

A) How to Take Care of Your Boss

B) How to Get Along with Your Boss

C) How to Accept Your Boss's Criticism

D) How to Accomplish Your Boss's Objective

Task 3

Directions: *The following is an announcement. Reading it, you are requited to complete the outline below it (No. 46 to No. 50). You should write your answers briefly (**in no more than 3 words**) on the Answer Sheer correspondingly.*

We welcome you aboard the Eastern Flight and will do our best to make your trip comfortable and enjoyable.

For your safety and convenience

To begin the trip, we would like to draw your attention to some safety-related details. These are also explained on the instruction card in the seat pocket in front of you. Seat belts must remain fastened while the "Fasten seatbelts" sign is on. It is advisable to keep them fastened at all times while seated. All flights are non-smoking. The use of mobile telephones is now allowed when the airplane is on the ground. During the flight the use of CD and DVD players is not allowed.

For your entertainment

To help you enjoy your trip, we provide a range of newspapers. On our MD-11 and Boeing aircraft, we provide music and video programs. On Airbus A321 / 320 / 319, short videos are shown.

Meals and drinks

During most flights we serve you a tasty meal and drinks. Beer, wine and other drinks are served free of charge. Coffee, tea and juice are served free of charge on all domestic (国内的) flights. On domestic flights leaving before nine and on all flights to Northern China, a snack is served.

Eastern Flight Service

Safety and convenience

1) Seat belts: remain ___46___ while the "Fasten seatbelts" sign is on

2) Smoking: not allowed on board

3) Mobile phones: used only when the airplane is ___47___

4) CD and DVD: not allowed to play ___48___

Entertainment provided

1) newspapers

2) music and ___49___ on MD-11 and Boeing aircraft

Meals and drinks on board

1) meals served on most flights

2) coffee, tea and juice served free of charge

3) a snack served on all flights to ___50___

Task 4

Directions: *The following is a list of terms related to Security. After reading it, you are required to find the items equivalent to (与…等同) those given in Chinese in the table below. Then you should put the corresponding letters in the brackets on the Answer Sheet, numbered 51 through 55.*

A —— air traffic control system	B —— armed police
C —— crime prevention	D —— entry requirement
E —— international criminal police organization	F —— level of security
G —— picket line	H —— police station
I —— patrolling vehicle	J —— safety precaution measure
K —— safety control device	L —— security command center
M —— security service	N —— security control center
O —— security personnel	P —— valid documents
Q —— security monitoring and control	

Examples: (M) 保安服务   (G) 警戒线

51. ( ) 空中交通管制系统		( ) 安全预防措施
52. ( ) 巡逻车		( ) 武装警察
53. ( ) 国际刑警组织		( ) 有效证件
54. ( ) 入境要求		( ) 安保人员
55. ( ) 安全保障级别		( ) 安全监控

Task 5

Directions: *The following is a business letter. After reading it, you should give brief answers* *to the 5 questions (No. 56 to No. 60) that follow. The answers (**in no more than 3 words**) should be written after the corresponding numbers on the Answer Sheet.*

Dear Mr. Smith,

I am pleased to offer you the position of the after-sales manager at our company starting on June 16, 2009. I propose that the terms of employment will be those in the attached draft individual employment agreement.

Please note that you are entitled to discuss this offer and to seek advice on the attached proposed agreement with your family, a union, a lawyer, or someone else you trust. If you want some information on your employment rights, you can also contact the Employment Service Office or visit our website.

Also, if you disagree with, or do not understand or wish to clarify anything in this offer, please ring me to discuss any issue you wish to raise.

If you are happy with the proposed terms and wish to accept this offer of employment, please sign the duplicate copy of this letter and return it to me by June 1, 2009. In the event I have not heard from you by that date, this offer will be automatically withdrawn on that date.

I look forward to working with you.

Yours sinecerely,

John Brown

56. What job position is offered to Mr. Smith in the letter?

　　_____.

57. From whom may Mr. Smith seek advice about the proposed agreement?

　　His family, a union, _____, or someone else he trusts.

58. How can Mr. Smith get information about employment rights?

　　By contacting the _____ or visiting its website.

59. When should Mr. Smith return the signed duplicate copy of this letter?

　　By _____.

60. What will happen if the duplicate copy of the letter is not returned by the deadline?

　　This offer will be _____ on that date.

Part Ⅳ　Translation — English into Chinese　（25 minutes）

Directions: *This part, numbered 61 through 65, is to test your ability to translate English into Chinese. After each of the sentences numbered 61 to 64, you will read four choices of suggested translation. You should choose the best translation and mark the corresponding letter on your Answer Sheet. And for the paragraph numbered 65, write your translation in the corresponding space on the Translation / Composition Sheet.*

61. If either party wants to renew the contract, it should submit a written notice to the other party three months prior to the expiration of the contract.

    A) 如果任何一方希望撤销合约,必须将撤销的理由在三个月内通知对方。

    B) 如果合同一方希望重签合同,必须在合同到期三个月内写信通知对方。

    C) 如果任何一方希望更改合同,必须提前三个月向对方书面提交其理由。

    D) 如果合同一方希望续签合同,必须在合同期满前三个月书面通知对方。

62. There is no sign that the world economic crisis will lessen in the next few months, although a certain degree of recovery is in sight.

    A) 尽管没有人认为未来几个月内世界经济危机会消失,但是在一定程度上的复苏是肯定的。

    B) 尽管世界经济复苏的迹象是肯定的,但是未来几个月内经济危机缓和的现象还不很明显。

    C) 尽管已经显现出一定程度的经济复苏,但没有迹象表明世界经济危机在未来几个月会减缓。

    D) 尽管没有人承认未来几个月内世界经济危机触底,但我们肯定会看到世界经济的复苏。

63. Most of the issues concerning personnel management have been solved satisfactorily, only a few of secondary importance remain to be discussed.

    A) 多数有关人员管理的问题顺利地解决了,仅剩下几个问题还需要进行第二次讨论。

    B) 大多数有关人事管事问题已经得到圆满解决,只剩下几个次要的问题还有待于讨论。

    C) 很多有关人员配备问题基本都得到了答复,只有第二个重要问题还未经过讨论。

    D) 第二个重要问题是有关人员调动的问题,这次已经得到妥善解决,不必再次讨论。

64. Only in this way can Chinese enterprises improve their competitiveness and avoid being defeated by their foreign rivals after China's entry into the WTO.

    A) 只有这个方法才能帮助中国企业去参加竞争力,避免在加入世贸组织后被其外国对手所击败。

    B) 只有这样中国企业才能提高竞争力,并且在中国加入世贸组织后不会败给它们的外国对手。

    C) 如果中国企业要想在世贸组织中参加竞争,必须通过这种办法才能击败它们的外国对手。

    D) 中国企业只有通过这种途径来击败外国的对手,才能表明它们在世贸组织中具备竞争力。

65. Thank you, Mr. Black. It's a great honor to be appointed as Overseas Sales Manager. To be honest, this promotion came as quite a surprise to me. I'd like to think it's mainly the contribution of the whole team. I'd like to thank all my colleagues in the company for their support and hard work. Due to their efforts, we've started some overseas projects successfully. Looking to the future, I'd still like to maintain contact with everyone, even though, I'll be working at the management level.

Part V　　　　　　　　Writing　　　　　　　(25 minutes)

Directions: *This part is to test your ability to do practical writing. You are required to write a notice according to the following information in Chinese. Remember to write the notice on the Translation / Composition Sheet.*

说明:根据下面中文信息写一封询问信。

发信人: Mark Zhang

收信人: Mr. Smith

发信日期: 2009 年 12 月 22 日

内容:

1. Mark 在最近的广交会上认识了 Smith 先生;

2. Mark 对 Smith 先生所在公司展出的新款手机很感兴趣;

3. 询问产品的详细信息,包括产品的规格、颜色、价格和功能等;

4. 说明该款手机市场销售前景看好;

5. 希望和对方建立长远的商务关系。

Words for references:

广交会 Guangzhou Trade Fair; 规格 specifications

第5章

参考答案与解析

模拟试题(一)

Part I Listening Comprehension

Section A

1. C 【解析】根据 It leaves at 9:30, but you must check in one hour ahead of departure. 可知,乘客应与 8:30 到达机场。

2. A 【解析】根据男士的话"我想要退这双鞋。"可知,对话发生在商店。

3. C 【解析】根据... you'd better take an umbrella. 可知,有可能要下雨。

4. A 【解析】根据 I think the dishes are very delicious.可知,是因为食物可口。

5. B 【解析】根据 My husband and I have kept waiting for nearly an hour for our meal.可知,女士对他们服务不满意。

Section B

6. D 【解析】根据 But I wear size eleven. I'll take this black sweater.可知,男士最后要的是黑色 11 号的毛衣。

7. C 【解析】根据 But we're going to be late for tonight's party.可知,女士要去参加一个聚会。

8. B 【解析】根据... the bedroom faces east and the living room north.可知,客厅朝向北。

9. B 【解析】由对话可知,公寓里面有 one bedroom,one living room,a small kitchen and a bathroom,所以公寓有四间房。

10. B 【解析】根据 800 yuan 可知,房租是每月 800 元。

Section C

11. open attitude 【解析】本题问的是微笑传递了什么信息。由第一句 A smile is a strong sign of a friendly and open attitude and a willingness to communicate. 可知,微笑传递了友好、开放的态度以及愿意交往的信息。

12. smile back 【解析】由 The result? That person will usually smile back.可知,你的微笑同样会换来别人的微笑。

13. handshake 【解析】由第二段第一句 In many cultures the most common form of first contact between two people is a handshake.可知,在很多国家的文化中,握手是很普遍的交往方式。

14. extend our hand 【解析】由 Be the first to extend your hand in greeting. Couple this with a friendly "hello", a nice smile... 可知,初次见面应该主动伸出双手以示问候。

15. know about 【解析】由最后一句 Direct eye contact shows you are listening to the other person and that you want to know about her.可知,直接的眼神交流意味着你正在倾听对方并且想要了解她。

附:听力原文

Section A

1. **M:** Excuse me, Miss, what time is Flight 298 for Beijing due to depart?

   W: It leaves at 9:30, but you must check in one hour ahead of departure.

   Q: At what time must the passenger arrive at the airport for Flight 298?

2. **M:** I would like to return this pair of shoes.

   W: Do you have a sales slip?

   Q: Where does this conversation most probably take place?

3. **M:** If you really have important things to go out you'd better take an umbrella.

   W: Thank you! I've got the weather forecast.

   Q: What is the weather going to be?

4. **M:** Have you ever been to that restaurant near my home?

   W: Yes, many times. I think the dishes are very delicious.

   Q: Why does the woman often eat in the restaurant?

5. **M:** Is there anything wrong, Miss?

   W: My husband and I have kept waiting for nearly an hour for our meal.

   Q: How did the woman feel about the restaurant's service?

Section B

Conversation 1

M: Is this blue too bright for me?

W: Mmm-hmm. It is a very bright blue. Try this. It's size ten.

M: But I wear size eleven.

W: How about black? It's size eleven.

M: Let me try it on. I'm taking too much of your time.

W: It's seven o'clock. Where's my friend Jack? I was expecting him here at six forty-five.

M: Don't worry. The traffic is very heavy at this hour.

W: I know. But we're going to be late for tonight's party.

M: I'll take this black sweater. I like the color on me. How do you think?

W: I think it looks terrific on you.

Q6. What is the man's final choice for the sweater?

Q7. What is the woman going to do that night?

Conversation 2

M: Good morning. Can I help you?

W: Yes. I wonder if you have a one-bedroom apartment to rent.

M: Let me check. Yes, we have one. It's on Nanjing Street, near a shopping center and a subway station.

W: Sounds nice. Does it face south?

M: Well, the bedroom faces east and the living room north. But it looks out on a beautiful park.

W: Mmm, is the living room large?

M: Yes, it's quite big. And there's a small kitchen and a bathroom as well. It's very comfortable.

W: Well, what's the rent per month?

M: 800 yuan.

W: Mmm, it's more than I have in mind. Let me think it over. I'll call you back in a day or two.

M: Certainly.

Q8. Which direction does the living room face?

Q9. How many rooms are there in the apartment?

Q10. What is the rent per month?

Section C

A smile is a strong sign of a friendly and open attitude and a willingness to communicate. It is a positive, silent sign sent with the hope the other person will smile back. When you smile, you show you have noticed the person in a positive way. The result? That person will usually smile back.

In many cultures the most common form of first contact between two people is a handshake. Be the first to extend your hand in greeting. Couple this with a friendly "hello", a nice smile, and your name and you have made the first step to open the lines of communication. Direct eye contact shows you are listening to the other person and that you want to know about her.

Q11. What is the sign of a smile?

Q12. What is the probable result when you smile at someone?

Q13. What is the most common form of first contact between two people?

Q14. How should we react at the first time of contact?

Q15. What can direct eye contact show?

Part II   Struture

Section A

16. A 【解析】本题考查的是状语从句的用法。根据句意,该题是由连词 when 引导的时间状语从句,故选 A。

17. C 【解析】本题考查对让步状语从句的理解。句意为:尽管他们的生活发生了改变,但他们仍然继续给对方写信。C 符合句意,故选 C。

18. A 【解析】本题考查分词短语作原因状语的用法。句意为:因为去年读过这个故事,所以我期待着观看这部影片。故选 A。

19. C 【解析】本题考查形容词、副词同时修饰名词时的位置。当两类词同时出现修饰名词时离名词最近的应是形容词,形容词前接副词,故选 C。

20. **A** 【解析】本题考查固定搭配的用法。hear from 意为"收到……的来信"。looking forward to 中的 to 为介词,其后的动词应用分词形式,故选 A。

21. **B** 【解析】本题考查情态动词的否定用法。句意为:是说没有必要现在走,故选 B。

22. **D** 【解析】本题考查形容词用法。句意为:尽管他独自住在乡下,但他并不感到孤独。故选 D。

23. **B** 【解析】本题考查情态动词的用法。句意为:现在肯定很晚了,表示推测,故选 B。

24. **C** 【解析】本题考查连词的用法。主句为现在完成进行时。句意为:这位球星从小就一直打篮球。故选 C。

25. **D** 【解析】本题考查对句意的理解。句意为:我的孩子仍然没有学会辨认时间。故选C。

Section B

26. **sincerely** 【解析】本题考查词性转换。这里应用副词来修饰 said,故形容词变副词。

27. **smoking** 【解析】本题考查固定搭配。stop from doing sth. 意为"阻止某人做某事"。

28. **watching** 【解析】本题考查固定搭配。spend (on) doing sth. 意为"花费……做……"。

29. **quiet** 【解析】本题考查词性转换。这里 keep 相当于系动词,其后应接形容词,故副词应变形容词。

30. **loudly** 【解析】本题考查词性转换。这里应用副词来修饰 say,故形容词应变副词。

31. **working** 【解析】本题考查固定搭配。keep on doing sth. 意为"坚持做"。

32. **twice** 【解析】本题考查词性转换。这里应用副词修饰动词,故量词应变副词。

33. **lending** 【解析】本题考查固定搭配。thank for doing sth. 意为"因某事感谢某人"。

34. **worse** 【解析】本题考查形容词比较级的用法。这里的关键词是 than。

35. **working** 【解析】本题考查固定搭配。go on doing sth. 意为"继续做……"。

Part Ⅲ Reading Comprehension

Task 1

【文章概述】 本文介绍了美国邮局的一般业务。其中包括信件的邮递、邮资,以及明信片的购买等问题。

36. **A** 【解析】细节题。根据第一句 Every town in the United States has a post office.可以推断出答案为 A。

37. **D** 【解析】计算题。根据第一段最后一句 From Monday through Friday they are usually open from 8:30 a.m. to 4:30 p.m..计算得知美国邮局的营业时间是每天 8 小时,故选 D。

38. **C** 【解析】细节题。根据第二段第四句 If you are not sure how much postage is for your letter, you may ask the man or the woman in the post office for help.可知,如果你不定你所需的邮费,可以询问邮局的男女职员,故选 C。

39. **C** 【解析】细节题。根据第二段最后一句 Remember that postage will be more expensive for a letter to be sent outside the country.可知,答案为 C。

40. **A** 【解析】综合概括题。可以用排除法选择。B、C、D 选项分别说的是邮资、信件和明信片,都不全面。只有 A 最为全面,总结了文章的大意,故选 A。

Task 2

【文章概述】 本文主要介绍了颜色对于动物生存的不同作用,以及动物的不同生存法则。

41. D 【解析】细节题。根据第二段第二句 It is because locusts change their colors together with the change of the colors of crops.可知,答案为 D。

42. C 【解析】细节题。根据第二段最后一句 So they have to hide themselves for lives and appear only at night.可知,与植物颜色不一样的动物只能选择夜间出行来保护自己。

43. A 【解析】细节题。根据第三段最后一句 This is because they have the colors much like the trees.可知,它们皮肤的颜色和树的颜色一样。

44. B 【解析】细节题。最后一段解释了为什么这种鱼可以存活到现在。原因就是它释放出来的液体使得它的敌人找不到它,这样它就能趁机逃跑。

45. C 【解析】总结归纳题。通读全文可知,本文主要讲述的是颜色对于动物自保所起的不同作用,故选 C。

Task 3

【文章概述】 本文是一则招聘家庭护理的广告。

46. Live-in caregiver 【解析】细节题。由招聘广告的标题 Live-in caregiver 可知,广告提供的是家庭护理的职位。

47. First Aid 【解析】细节题。由广告的第四项要求 Credentials: First Aid Certificate 可知,应聘者要有急救能力的证书。

48. English 【解析】细节题。根据广告的第六项要求 Languages: Speak English, read English, write English 可知,要求的是英语。

49. 81 【解析】细节题。根据广告的 Other Information: the live-in caregiver looks after a 81 years old lady.可知,需要护理的是一位 81 岁的女士。

50. 14:30 and 20:00 【解析】细节题。广告词中关于 How to Apply 一项中提到 By Phone: between 14:30 and 20:00。由此可知,打电话联系的时间是从 14:30 到 20:00。

Task 4

【说明】 这是一组不同地方的名称。

51. F, O 52. A, M 53. D, K 54. G, J 55. I, E

各项的译文:

A —— 竹园		B —— 漫步广场	
C —— 露天咖啡廊		D —— 吊桥	
E —— 特色踏步		F —— 野趣小溪	
G —— 日艺园		H —— 石景雕塑	
I —— 趣味树阵		J —— 高尔夫球会所	
K —— 江南园林		L —— 商业中心入口	
M —— 儿童乐园		N —— 游泳池	

O —— 健身广场　　　　　　　　P —— 中心广场

Task 5

【文章概述】　本文是一则关于"湖人"和"76 人"两队的对抗赛的新闻报道。

56. Lakers vs 76ers　【解析】细节题。根据新闻报道第一段第二句 It will be 9:00 a.m. when the Los Angeles Lakers and Philadelphia 76ers tip off the NBA Finals tonight...可知,是"湖人"和"76 人"两队对抗。

57. special viewing party　【解析】细节题。根据报道第一段第三句 But the early hour has not discouraged students at Beijing University from organizing a special viewing party to watch the game live.可知,答案为 special viewing party。

58. 2.5 billion　【解析】细节题。根据报道第一段... an estimated 2.5 billion viewers world-wide who will be turning in to the games... 可知,大约有 25 亿人观看。

59. Staples Center　【解析】细节题。根据报道第二段第一句... from international networks have set up operations at Staples Center for tonight's opening joust.可知,比赛地点在洛杉矶斯坦普斯中心球馆。

60. more than 90　【解析】细节题。根据报道第二段第一句 More than 90 broadcasters from international networks...可知,有 90 多家国际网络电台参与了直播。

Part Ⅳ　Translation — English into Chinese

61. A—B—C—D　【解析】本题的翻译要点是 twice as much as (是……的两倍)和 used to do(过去常常)。译文 A 在准确地理解原文的基础上,用通顺、流畅的中文表达了原意;译文 B 中"多了两倍"是误译;译文 C 中"习惯"为误译;译文 D 完全误解了原文的意思,是错译。

62. B—A—D—C　【解析】本题的翻译要点是 again(再一次)和 go on a diet (节食)。译文 A 基本准确地翻译了全文,但是"吃很多"还不够准确;译文 B 在准确地理解原文的基础上,用通顺、流畅的中文表达了原意;译文 C 完全误解了原文的意思,是错译;译文 D 中"再吃一顿饭"为误译。

63. B—A—C—D　【解析】译文 A 基本译出了原文的意思,但用词不够准确;译文 B 在准确地理解原文的基础上,用通顺、流畅的中文表达了原意;译文 C "孩提时的模样"属于误译;译文 D 完全误解了原文的意思,属于错译。

64. D—C—A—B　【解析】译文 A "驻扎"为误译;译文 B 完全误解了原文的意思,属于错译;译文 C 基本译出了原文的意思,但用词不够准确;译文 D 在准确地理解原文的基础上,用通顺、流畅的中文表达了原意。

65.【参考译文】这些理想中最伟大的理想是正在慢慢实现的美国的承诺,这就是:每个人都有自身的价值,每个人都有成功的机会,每个人天生都会有所作为的。美国人民肩负着一种使命,那就是要竭力将这个诺言变成生活中和法律上的现实。虽然我们的国家过去在追求实现这个承诺的途中停滞不前甚至倒退,但我们仍将坚定不移地完成这一使命。

Part V Writing

解题步骤:

第一步:审题

1. 题型:提纲作文;

2. 文体:应用文。

第二步:框架分析

1. 信件格式:①在信的右上角写上写信人的信息。先写姓名,再写地址。地址的写法是由小到大,门牌、街道、邮编、市、省、国家;

②在刚刚写好的地址下面左起写收信人的信息,格式同上;

③再隔一两行顶格是收信人的称呼;

④称呼下隔两行,开始写正文;

⑤正文结束后,是结束语;

⑥写信人的签名在右下角;

⑦最后是日期,月/日/年。

2. 点出每个要点。

第三步:写作思路

1. 说明信件的主要内容;

2. 注意信件的格式。

第四步:关键词和词组

　　organize a trip to Beijing, a seven-day tour during the Spring Festival, accommodation, etc.

第五步:落笔成文

Linda
Shanghai University

Miss Zhao,

　　I'd like you to organize a trip to Beijing for my classmates. I have here a group of students studying in Shanghai University, who want to go on a seven-day tour during the Spring Festival. I hope we can have a coach which will take us to Beijing and then bring us back to Shanghai. We also need a guide who knows Beijing well. I would be very grateful if you can work out an itinerary as soon as possible and tell me about our accommodation, meals as well as how much each of us has to pay. If you have any information, please either email me to *luckyxiaodong@163.com* or call me at 135××××3421.

　　Looking forward to your early reply.

Yours Truly,
Linda

模拟试题(二)

Part I Listening Comprehension

1. A 【解析】根据 Can you make more for us? 可知,他们很喜欢吃妈妈做的沙拉。

2. B 【解析】根据 Next to banana. 可知,他最喜欢香蕉。

3. A 【解析】根据 I think it tastes like medicine. 可知,男士不喜欢喝可乐。

4. B 【解析】根据 No. I enjoy meeting friends at weekends. 可知,他在周末根本不看电视节目,而是和朋友聚会。

5. C 【解析】根据 As for me, swimming is my favorite sport. 可知,他最喜欢游泳。

Conversation 1

6. A 【解析】由录音对话可知两人是在旅行当中因为座位问题认识的,并相互作了自我介绍,故选 A。

7. C 【解析】根据 I just changed my seat. A man next to me was smoking, and smoke really bothers me. 可知,女士是因为受不了烟味而换的座位。

Conversation 2

8. C 【解析】根据 He can reach me... anytime today on my mobile. 可知,可以在当天任何时间给他打手机。

9. C 【解析】根据 Good afternoon. ABC company. May I help you? 可知,接电话的应该是该公司的秘书。

10. D 【解析】根据 I'm afraid Mr. James Potter isn't available right now. 可知,有人打电话找 Mr. James Potter,但他不方便接电话。

11. overpaid 【解析】根据 Many people in the United States think that doctors are overpaid. 可知,很多人认为医生的薪酬过高。

12. enough money 【解析】根据 It is impossible to pay for the medical care they need. 可知,因为每次去医院的花费都在 15 到 50 美元之间,所以大家支付不起医院的费用。

13. fifteen to fifty 【解析】根据 A visit to a doctor's office costs people from fifteen to fifty dollars. 可知,每次的花费在 15 到 50 美元之间。

14. High tuition 【解析】根据 Because high tuition is one cause of high costs... 可知,医疗费用高的原因之一就是医学专业学费高的问题。

15. free or have low tuition 【解析】根据 ... one way to lower costs would be to have medical schools that are free or have low tuition. 可知,降低或免除医学专业的学费是解决问题的办法。

附:听力原文

Section A

1. **W:** Where is the salad I made this morning?

   M: We ate it, mom. Can you make more for us?

   Q: What can we learn from the conversation?

2. **W:** I hear you like apple best.

   M: Next to banana.

   Q: What does the man like best?

3. **W:** Mike, do you want a cola?

   M: Cola? I think it tastes like medicine.

   Q: What did the man mean?

4. **W:** Do you watch sports programs on weekend?

   M: No. I enjoy meeting friends at weekends.

   Q: How often does the man watch sports programs on weekend?

5. **W:** I'm fond of playing football and tennis.

   M: As for me, swimming is my favorite sport.

   Q: Which sport does the man like?

Section B

Conversation 1

W: Excuse me. Is this seat taken?

M: No, it's not taken.

W: Oh, thank you.

M: Oh, let me help you with this.

W: Oh, thank you.

M: Do you want to sit by the window?

W: No, no, no. I like the aisle seat better. You can sit by the window.

M: My name is Mike Gerard Hogan. Pleased to meet you.

W: I'm Elsa Tobin. How do you do?

M: Do you live in New York?

W: No, no. I'm from Florida.

M: I am, too. But didn't you just get on?

W: No, no. I just changed my seat. A man next to me was smoking, and smoke really bothers me.

Q6. What is the most probable relationship between the two speakers?

Q7. Why did the woman changed her seat?

Conversation 2

W: Good afternoon. ABC company. May I help you?

M: Yes, may I speak to Mr. James Potter, please?

W: I'm afraid Mr. James Potter isn't available right now. Would you like to leave a message?

M: This is Martin Richard with Sun Electronics. It's very important that he returns my call this afternoon.

W: Does he have your office number and your mobile phone number?

M: I think so, but let me give them to you again.

W: Okay.

M: My office number is 714-888-3765; my cell phone number is 909-333-8739. He can reach me at my office number before 6:00 p.m. or anytime today on my mobile.

W: Very well, I'll give him your message as soon as he returns to the office.

Q8. At what time can Mr. James Potter call Martin Richard on his mobile?

Q9. Who might be the person that has answered the phone call?

Q10. What can be learned from the telephone conversation you've just heard?

Section C

The cost of medical care in the United States is very high. The time and money that doctors spend on their medical education are probably one reason for this problem.

A visit to a doctor's office costs people from fifteen to fifty dollars. It is impossible to pay for the medical care they need. Many people in the United States think that doctors are overpaid. Most doctors, however, disagree. They say that they were required to study medicine for a long time. Tuition for many years of medical education costs a lot of money. And young doctors need a lot of money for their work. So, they charge people high prices for medical care. Therefore it is possible that the high cost of medical care in America is unnecessary. Because high tuition is one cause of high costs, one way to lower costs would be to have medical schools that are free or have low tuition.

Q11. How do people feel about doctor's income?

Q12. Why can't people have their medical care they need?

Q13. How much will a visit to the doctor's office cost?

Q14. What is the reason for the high medical cost mentioned in the article?

Q15. What is the method to lower the cost of medical care?

Part II Struture

Section A

16. C **【解析】**本题考查分词的用法。句意为：你能闻到什么糊了吗？正在散发糊味用 burning,故选 C。

17. B **【解析】**本题考查 look 词组的意思。look up 意为"向上看；查阅"；look out 意为"当心"；look on 意为"旁观"；look round 意为"环顾"。

18. B **【解析】**本题考查介词搭配。 in a larger sense 意为"从广义上讲",比较符合文意。

19. D **【解析】**本题考查动词的使用。taste 作及物动词时,表示"品尝",作系动词时,表示"尝上去……";但后面均不能跟介词 of。而 taste 不能与 on, at 构成短语,故选 D。

20. C **【解析】**本题考查时态。根据上下文逻辑,在凯特看完小说了之后,我才告诉她结局是什么。所以此处应该为过去完成时,故选 C。

21. B 【解析】本题考查词语修饰。kill 是动词,前面的修饰语应为副词,故选 B。

22. A 【解析】本题考查时态。句中 and 为并列连词,因此前后两句的时态应该保持一致,故选 A。

23. C 【解析】本题考查短语的使用。句意为:作为一个中国人,他感觉在英国他很不舒服,感觉自己与周围的环境格格不入。out of place 意为:"格格不入"。

24. C 【解析】本题考查倒装的用法。not until 在句首时,该句谓语动词部分倒装。

25. D 【解析】本题考查动名词的用法。appreciate 后要用动名词作宾语,此处是两年前给的机会,还要考虑使用动名词完成时。又因动作与主语之间是被动关系,句子应用被动语态,故选 D。

Section B

26. lying 【解析】本题考查非谓语动词形式。在这里用现在分词形式表示一种状态。

27. taking 【解析】本题考查固定短语。enjoy 后跟动名词形式,所以应把 take 改成 taking。

28. getting 【解析】本题考查固定搭配。be busy doing sth. 意为"忙于做某事"。

29. taller 【解析】本题考查比较级。这里是两者之间的比较,应用比较级。

30. most 【解析】本题考查最高级。这里是三者之间的比较,应用最高级。

31. dangerous 【解析】本题考查词性转换。这里系动词后缺少一个形容词,所以应将名词(danger)变成形容词(dangerous)。

32. covered 【解析】本题考查动词的被动语态。这里 the ground 是被雪覆盖,所以应用 covered。

33. sunny 【解析】本题考查词性转换。这里需要一个形容词来修饰名词 day,所以应将名词 sun 变成形容词 sunny。

34. scientist 【解析】本题考查名词的运用。从句意上看 Edison 是个人,所以应将 science(科学)变成 scientist(科学家)。

35. surprised 【解析】本题考查固定短语。be surprised at 意为"对……吃惊"。

Part Ⅲ Reading Comprehension

Task 1

【文章概述】 本文主要讲述了在美国房车的用途以及它给人们的生活带来了种种便利。

36. B 【解析】细节题。根据第四段第一句 Americans call vans motor homes.可知,美国人称其为移动居住车,即 motor home,故选 B。

37. D 【解析】细节题。第三段第二句 This made them sell a second car and buy a van.可知,在他们买房车之前,Hagen 夫妇先卖掉了自己的二手车,故选 D。

38. C 【解析】推理题。根据 When the family is large, one of the cars is sold and they will buy a van.我们得知人口多的家庭更适合买房车,故选 C。

39. A 【解析】细节题。根据最后一段第二句 A motor home is always used for holidays.可知,美国人经常用房车去旅行度假,故选 A。

40. B 【解析】细节题。根据 All the members of a big family can enjoy a happier life when they are traveling together.可知,房车之所以盛行是因为当一家人外出旅行,家人都可以很开心,故选 B。

Task 2

【文章概述】 本文讲述了查尔斯德鲁医生的人生经历。医学出身的德鲁创建了血库。这为当时处于二战中的美国提供了巨大的帮助,挽救了无数人的生命。但当时美国存在种族歧视的问题,所以身为黑人的德鲁医生而后因意外事故却被白人专用医院拒绝而死亡。

41. A 【解析】细节题。根据第一段第二句... blood bank — that is, the storing of blood.可知,血库就是存血的地方,故选 A。

42. D 【解析】细节题。根据... black Americans gave blood along with the whites.可知,黑人和白人都捐血了。

43. B 【解析】推断题。根据最后一段第四句 We don't take in blacks.可知,医院不收黑人,由此推断医院只为白人服务。

44. C 【解析】细节题。根据... with the support of the government, continued to separate black blood from white.可知,政府认为黑人的血与白人的血不一样,故选 C。

45. C 【解析】总结归纳题。通读全文,我们可以得知,德鲁医生是血库的创建人,拯救了无数人的生命,但最后当自己需要输血时,却因为自己是黑人而被医院拒绝,耽误了时间而最终死亡。由此我们可以推断 C 为正确选项。

Task 3

【文章概述】 本文是一则关于给同事开欢送会的备忘录。

46. Farewell Party 【解析】细节题。从备忘录中的 Subject 一项可以得知这次聚会是为 Miss Banbe 举行送行会。

47. go abroad 【解析】细节题。从备忘录的正文内容第一句 Our colleague Miss Banbe is going to go abroad next month.可知,聚会的原因是 Miss Banbe 下个月将要出国了。

48. assembly room 【解析】细节题。根据 We are going to use the assembly room of our department for the party.可知,聚会是在人事部门的会议室举行。

49. general manager 【解析】细节题。根据... our general manager and manager will be present, too.可知,除了全体人事部门的员工、经理外还有总经理。

50. November 20 【解析】细节题。根据... party is scheduled on November 20, and will begin at 7 o'clock in the evening.可知,聚会在 11 月 20 号举行。

Task 4

【说明】 本文是关于交通的一系列用语。

51. P, G   52. N, E   53. O, M   54. F, L   55. D, B

各项的译文:

A —— 交通规则   B —— 停车标志

C —— 交通岗	D —— 单行线
E —— 车行道	F —— 限速
G —— 禁止通行	H —— 让车道
I —— 不准滞留	J —— 当心牲畜
K —— 寂静地带	L —— 无证驾驶
M —— 轻微碰撞	N —— 肇事逃跑司机
O —— 交通拥挤	P —— 只停公用车

Task 5

【文章概述】 本文提供了关于如何成为一个好的读者的建议,并指出一个好的读者应该时刻注意阅读速度。

56. rate and speed 【解析】细节题。根据指南的第一句 If you wish to become a better reader, here are four important points to remember about rate and speed of reading. 可知,本指南是在阅读速度上给读者以帮助。

57. purpose 【解析】细节题。根据指南的第一点 Knowing why you are reading and what you are reading to find out will often help you to know whether to read rapidly or slowly. 可知,要判断阅读速度,首先要知道你读的是什么以及读书的目的。

58. a story book 【解析】细节题。根据指南的第三点 Examples are simple stories meant for enjoyment... 可知,如果想要娱乐,读者要读故事书之类的书。

59. important step 【解析】细节题。根据指南的第二点最后一句 You must read such things slowly to remember each important step and understand each important idea. 可知,仔细阅读的目的是了解重要步骤以及信息。

60. important ideas 【解析】细节题。指南的最后一句 You need to read certain pages rapidly and then slow down and do more careful readings when you come to important ideas which must be remembered. 可知,当读者遇到需要记忆的重要信息时应该放慢速度。

Part Ⅳ Translation — English into Chinese

61. C—B—D—A 【解析】译文 A 完全误解了原文的意思,属于错译;译文 B 基本译出了原文的意思,但用词不够准确;译文 C 在准确地理解原文的基础上,用通顺、流畅的中文表达了原文;译文 D 中"很高兴地"为误译。

62. B—A—C—D 【解析】译文 A 基本译出了原文的意思,但用词不够准确;译文 B 在准确地理解原文的基础上,用通顺、流畅的中文表达了原意;译文 C 中"广泛地"和"习惯的"为误译;译文 D 完全误解了原文的意思,属于错译。

63. A—D—C—B 【解析】译文 A 在准确地理解原文的基础上,用通顺、流畅的中文表达了原意;译文 B 完全误解了原文的意思,属于错译;译文 C 中 senior 在此处应意为"老年人",所以"高级的"和"上层社会"为误译;译文 D 基本译出了原文的意思,但"观点"用词不够准确。

64. B—D—A—C 【解析】译文 A 中"面对"在原文中没有提到;译文 B 在准确地理解原

文的基础上,用通顺、流畅的中文表达了原意;译文 C 完全误解了全文的意思,为错译;译文 D 中"基础"属于误译。

65.【参考译文】2008 年,这一年内国际油价就经历了过去五年内的最高潮和最低潮。中石化业绩在这剧烈的波动中也是高潮迭起,险象环生。其中暴露出了很多中国石油化工类企业在面对国际油价波动时的不成熟事实。油价对国民经济影响具有特殊的传导机制。

Part V Writing

解题步骤:

第一步:审题

1. 题型:提纲作文;

2. 文体:应用文。

第二步:框架分析

1. 简历格式;

2. 点出每个要点。

第三步:列出写作思路

1. 说明简历的主要内容;

2. 注意简历的格式。

第四步:列出关键词和词组

  can fully display my specialty in management, opportunities based on performance, manager assistant, etc.

第五步:落笔成文

Resume

Personal Data:

  Name: Sany

  Date of Birth: July 20th, 1981

  Sex: Female

  Health: Good

  Family Status: Single

  Address: 38 Xueyuan road, Haidian district, Beijing

  Telephone No: 010-67×××92

Job Objective: Position in which I can fully display my specialty in management with advancement opportunities based on performance.

Education:

  1996 — 1998 101 middle school in Beijing

  1998 — 2001 Beijing University

Work Experience:

  2001 — 2002 Manager assistant, Southern Computer Company

  2003 — 2008 Manager assistant of Beijing Import & Export Company

Specialty: English

模拟试题(三)

Part Ⅰ Listening Comprehension

Section A

1. A 【解析】录音中女士说 11 月 30 号会有足球比赛,男士说那是在后天。那么今天很显然就是 11 月 28 号。

2. C 【解析】根据 I have to go home. I have to help my mother to do the housework. 可知,他要回家帮妈妈做家务。

3. A 【解析】录音中提到现在是 4:45,而飞机会在半小时后起飞。所以飞机起飞的时间是 5:15。

4. D 【解析】录音中两个人是在讨论张老师的课,根据 I never miss his class... 可知,男士非常喜欢张老师的课。

5. B 【解析】根据 I'll be working part time in a shop. 可知,他会在商店做兼职。

Section B

Conversation 1

6. D 【解析】根据 I need a part time job, both for money and experience. 可知,女士为了收入和经历才来做的兼职。

7. B 【解析】根据 Are you computer trained? 可知,他对所招人员的计算机技能感兴趣。

Conversation 2

8. B 【解析】根据 We'll arrive the day after tomorrow. That is November 10th. 可知,他们到达的日期是 11 月 10 日,即后天,那么计算可得今天是 11 月 8 号。

9. C 【解析】根据 200 yuan a night, including breakfast. That will be fine. 可知,男士想订 200 元一晚上的房间,故选 C。

10. C 【解析】根据 One double room. 可知,他订的是一个双人间。

Section C

11. hero 【解析】根据第一句 The cowboy is the hero of many movies. 可知,牛仔在电影中是英雄的形象。

12. courage and adventure 【解析】根据 The cowboy is the hero of many movies... a symbol of courage and adventure. 可知,牛仔是勇气和冒险的象征。

13. take care of cows and other cattle 【解析】根据 Cowboys were men who took care of cows and other cattle. 可知,牛仔的工作就是照看牲口。

14. several months 【解析】根据 A cattle drive usually took several months. 可知,一次要持续几个月。

15. sixteen hours 【解析】根据 Cowboys rode for sixteen hours a day. 可知,牛仔一天能骑马 16 个小时。

附：听力原文

Section A

1. **W:** The football match will be held on Monday, Nov. 30th.

 M: You're right. That's the day after tomorrow.

 Q: What date is it today?

2. **W:** John, would you like swimming with me?

 M: I'd love to, but I have to go home. I have to help my mother to do the housework.

 Q: What will John do?

3. **W:** The plane is leaving in half an hour.

 M: Yes, now it's a quarter to five.

 Q: When will the plane leave?

4. **W:** Do you like Mr. Zhang's classes?

 M: I never miss his class, you know.

 Q: What do you learn from the conversation?

5. **W:** I'm planning a trip to Beijing this summer vocation. Do you want to join me?

 M: I'd love to, but I'll be working part time in a shop.

 Q: What will the man do during the summer vocation?

Section B

Conversation 1

 M: Good morning, Miss Zhao. Please sit down.

 W: Thank you. It's nice to meet you, Mr. Zhang.

 M: I have your application here. You are a university student?

 W: Yes, I'm a business major.

 M: So you are interested in working for our company.

 W: Yes, I need a part time job, both for money and experience.

 M: We'll have an opening for an office clerk this summer.

 W: That would be wonderful.

 M: Are you computer trained?

 W: Yes, I can handle Windows, Power Point, and Excel. Here is my certificate.

 M: Ah, that's very good. You'll need some training in our methods, though. Every office is different, you know.

 W: Thank you. That will be very helpful for my future. When do I start exactly?

 M: We'll let you know as soon as possible. Goodbye.

 W: Goodbye.

 Q6. Why does the woman want to do a part time job?

 Q7. What kind of skill is the employer interested in?

Conversation 2

 W: Tussion Hotel. Can I help you?

 M: Yes. I'd like to book a room for three nights.

 W: When will be arriving?

M: We'll arrive the day after tomorrow. That is November 10th.

W: Yes, sir. Single or double?

M: One double room.

W: All right. One double room until 13th.

M: How much will that be?

W: 200 yuan a night, including breakfast.

M: That will be fine.

W: May I have your name, please?

M: Lining, Mr. Li.

W: Thank you, Mr. Li. Goodbye.

M: Bye.

Q8. What is the date today according to the conversation?

Q9. What is the rate of the room he'd like to book?

Q10. What kind of room does the man want to book?

Section C

The cowboy is the hero of many movies. He is, even today, a symbol of courage and adventure. But what was the life of the cowboy really like?

The cowboy's job is clear from the word "cowboy". Cowboys were men who took care of cows and other cattle. They should send cattle from one city to another. The trips were called cattle drives. A cattle drive usually took several months. Cowboys rode for sixteen hours a day. Because they rode so much, each cowboy brought along about eight horses. A cowboy changed horses several times each day.

Q11. What is the image of "cowboy" in the movie?

Q12. What can "cowboy" symbolize?

Q13. What is cowboy's job?

Q14. How many days will a cattle drive last?

Q15. How many hours can cowboys ride a day?

Part Ⅱ Structure

Section A

16. D 【解析】本题考查日常用语。句意为:——对不起让你久等了。——没关系,林。根据语境,对方表示歉意时,我们应该表示"没关系"。A、C 项用来回答"谢谢";B 项不合题意;D 项既可以回答"谢谢",也可以回答对方表示歉意,故选 D。

17. B 【解析】本题考查冠词的用法。句意为:《小公主》这部小说中,小公主是一个勇敢的女孩。根据句意,本句中所提到的 novel 应表特指,应用 the,排除 A、D 项。在第二个空中,指小说中的某个人物,应用不定冠词,故选 B。

18. C 【解析】本题考查动词的时态和语态。句意为:我淋雨了,我的衣服被糟蹋了。此题是由两个并列句组成,第一个句子用一般过去时说明过去发生的事情,第二个句子强调过去发生的事情对现在造成的影响,用现在完成时;又因此处 my clothes 与 ruin 之间存在着被动关系,故用现在完成时的被动形式。

19. C　【解析】本题考查情态动词的用法。句意为:在危险的地方,你必须照看好你的孩子。根据句意此处应为"必须"之意,故选 must。

20. A　【解析】本题考查介词。句意为:虽然王教授反对我的观点,但并没有提出自己的观点。A 项意为"反对";C 项意为"支持,拥护(in support of sth./sb.)";D 项意为"依我看"。A 项符合句意,故选 A。

21. B　【解析】本题考查的是非谓语动词。句意为:虽然我说过她的工作做得不好,但是我认为我并不比她更有本事。A 项和 C 项,用不定式,应是表目的,不符合句意。根据句中的 did 可知这种话已经说过,应用完成时,故选 B。

22. A　【解析】本题考查非限制性定语从句的用法。句意为:他放学后写作业。在非限制定语从句中关系代词不能用 that, 因此排除 B、D 两项;C 项干扰性最强,which 这里并非指代地点——school,因此 C 项错;which 是指"放学"这件事,故选 A。

23. A　【解析】本题考查动词辨析的能力。句意为:谁解决问题不重要,重要的是怎样解决问题。count 作动词,意为"值得考虑,有价值";apply 意为"应用,申请";stress 为及物动词,意为"着重,强调";function 意为"运转,起作用"。count 符合句意,故选 A。

24. D　【解析】本题考查引导状语从句的关联词的用法。句意为:虽然我不怎么懂因特网,但我发现它很有用。while=although(虽然,尽管),用于句首。A 项意为"当……时,随着,因为,照……方式";B 项意为"自从……,既然";C 项意为"如果"。因为两个分句在语意上含有转折的意思,故选 D。

25. C　【解析】本题考查现在完成时的基本用法——动作发生在过去,但对现在有影响。A 项强调现在习惯性的或经常发生的动作,与过去无关;B 项表示现在正在进行或近段时期内正在进行的动作, 不与 for long 时间状语连用;C 项强调发生在过去的动作对现在造成的影响;D 项表示过去经常发生的动作,与现在无关。故选 C。

Section B

26. heavily　【解析】本题考查词性转换。这里需要一个副词来修饰 rain 这个动词,故应将形容词(heavy)变成其副词形式(heavily)。

27. unlucky　【解析】本题考查词性转换。这里需要一个形容词来修饰名词 day,又根据句意,这里应该用"不幸运的",所以应将 luck 变成 unlucky。

28. wears　【解析】本题考查第三人称单数的用法。这里的主语是单数 the girl,因此谓语动词应该用其第三人称单数的形式 wears。

29. Traveling　【解析】本题考查非谓语动词。动名词可作主语,故 travel 应变成 traveling。

30. leave　【解析】本题考查时态。一般现在时表示经常性习惯性的动作或行为。助动词 do 用了三单的形式,因此这里要用原形 leave。

31. wonderfully　【解析】本题考查词性转换。这里需要一个副词作状语修饰动词 draw。

32. twins'　【解析】本题考查复数名词所有格的表示方法。根据句意,这应是这对双胞胎的房间,故应用 twins,但又因以"s"结尾的复数名词的所有格应加"'",所以应用 twins'。

33. meet　【解析】本题考查 shall 的用法。shall 作为助动词一般用于第一人称 I 和 we,表示一个将来的动作,其后动词应用动词原形。

34. finishes　【解析】本题考查一般现在时表经常性习惯性的动作或行为。以 sh 结尾的动词的第三人称单数加 es。

35. listening 【解析】本题考查固定搭配。enjoy doing something 意为"喜欢做某事"。

Part Ⅲ Reading Comprehension

Task 1

【文章概述】 本文讲述了成为聪明儿童要具备的几个条件。天生聪慧是不够的,要加上后天的锻炼。在后天的锻炼中,父母起到了至关重要的作用。父母不仅要经常陪孩子玩耍,给孩子足够的思考空间,并且要经常给予孩子表扬而不是批评。

36. C 【解析】词汇猜测题。第一段提到 What makes one person more intelligent than another? What makes one person a genius, like the brilliant Albert Einstein... 在这几句话中我们看到有"天才""爱因斯坦"等词,根据上下文的意思我们不难推断出 intelligent 意为"聪明的",故选 C。

37. C 【解析】细节题。根据第二段第四句 Mental (done with the mind) exercise is particularly important for young children.可知,后天思维的锻炼是很重要的,故选 C。

38. D 【解析】总结归纳题。根据第二段第五六句可知经常由父母陪伴并勤于思考的孩子长大后会比较聪明,故选 D。

39. A 【解析】推理题。根据最后一段最后一句 So it is probably better for parents to say very positive (helpful) things to their children,可知,父母应该多给予孩子赞扬和鼓励(positive things),故选 A。

40. C 【解析】总结归纳题。通读全文,A、B、D 选项的内容我们都能在原文中找到。但 C 选项与第一段最后一句... or is intelligence the result of where and how you live? These are very old questions and the answers to them are still not clear.不符,故选 C。

Task 2

【文章概述】 本文以美国人为例介绍了中西文化的差异。在美国人看来,友好和友谊不是一回事。美国人对人都很友好,但这并不意味着他想和你做好朋友。美国人相信友谊是要慢慢培养的。因此,作者得出结论,人际关系需要在不同情况下采取不同的处理方法。

41. B 【解析】细节题。根据第一段第二句 Silence makes most Americans uncomfortable.可知,沉默会使美国人感到不舒服,故选 B。

42. C 【解析】细节题。根据第二段第六句 Americans are open and they trust relationships that develop slowly.可知,美国人都很开放,他们认为友谊是需要慢慢培养的,故选 C。

43. D 【解析】推理题。根据第二段后半部分可知,他们很容易也经常微笑,这只是表示美国人很友好,但这并不意味着他和你就是朋友关系或者被你所吸引,更不一定是想和你有更亲密的关系,因此可以排除 A、B、C 项,故选 D。

44. C 【解析】总结归纳题。通读全文可知,本文重在讲美国人对待友谊的看法,他们认为友谊是需要时间来慢慢培养的,故选 C。

45. D 【解析】细节题。根据第二段第一句 However, don't mistake friendliness for friend-

ship.可知,美国人认为友谊和友好不是一回事,故选 D。

Task 3

【文章概述】　本文是一则邀请信。信中邀请来北京参加国际会议的 Professor Mike Whitney 为研究生们做一个关于美国文学的讲座。

46. Professor Mike Whitney　【解析】细节题。根据信头可知答案为 Professor Mike Whitney。

47. American literature　【解析】细节题。根据邀请信的第一二段关键句 We are inviting you to deliver a lecture on American literature... We have long been noticed that you have done a lot of substantial and creative work in this field.可知,他对美国文学这一领域很有研究。

48. textbooks　【解析】细节题。根据邀请信第二段第二句 Two of your books have become textbooks for our students...可知,他的两本书已经成为学生的教科书。

49. international conference　【解析】细节题。根据邀请信第一段第一句 We are very glad to hear that you are attending an international conference in Beijing.可知,他正在北京参加一个国际会议。

50. postgraduate students　【解析】细节题。根据第一段最后一句... for our postgraduate students on the evening of March 15.可知,是为研究生讲课。

Task 4

【说明】　本文是一系列电脑专业用语。

51. J, D　52. K, M　53. B, E　54. C, N　55. L, G

各项的译文:

A —— 因特网密钥交换协议	B —— 虚拟局域网
C —— 单用户账号	D —— 需求发送
E —— 局域网	F —— 个人隐私安全平台
G —— 网际协议	H —— 文件传输协议
I —— 数据终端设备	J —— 流控制
K —— 清除发送	L —— 拨号控制管理
M —— 只读光盘	N —— 激光唱盘
O —— 只读存储器	P —— 随机存取文件

Task 5

【文章概述】　本文主要介绍了关于商品交易会的情况。城市为了经济发展举办商品交易会的。商品交易会的目的就是为各公司提供展示自己的产品、服务、学习交流其他重要信息的机会和场所,交易会分为"面向公众开放"和"只交易"两种。

56. demonstrate / show　【解析】细节题。根据第一段第一句 A trade fair is an exhibition organized so that companies in a specific industry can showcase and demonstrate their latest products...可知,商品交易会的目的就是为各公司提供场所展示自己的产品以及其他重要信息。

57. **Public** 【解析】细节题。根据第一段第二句... trade shows are classified as either "Public" or "Trade Only".可知,商品交易会分为两种。

58. **members of the press** 【解析】细节题。根据第一段第二句提到 Some trade fairs are open to the public, while others can only be attended by company representatives (members of the trade) and members of the press...可知,只有公司代表和媒体工作者才能参加。

59. **economic development** 【解析】细节题。根据第一段最后一句... cities often promote trade shows as a means of economic development.可知,城市是为了经济发展才举办商品交易会的。

60. **relatively low cost** 【解析】细节题。根据第二段最后一句 They are increasing in popularity due to their relatively low cost and because there is no need to travel whether you are attending or exhibiting.可知,相对低的花费以及旅行时间的节省使交易会很流行。

Part Ⅳ Translation — English into Chinese

61. **C—D—B—A** 【解析】译文 A 完全误解了全文的意思,为错译;译文 B 中的"承担责任"为误译,assume 在此处应意为"假定";译文 C 在准确地理解原文的基础上,用通顺、流畅的中文表达了原意;译文 D 基本译出了原文的意思,但"很可能不会"用词不太准确。

62. **B—C—D—A** 【解析】译文 A 中"不是……而是"为误译,not only ... but also 意为"不仅……而且";译文 B 在准确地理解原文的基础上,用通顺、流畅的中文表达了原意;译文 C 基本表达了原文的意思,但是个别词汇不准确,"短暂"为误译;译文 D 中"兴趣"为误译,interest 在此处应意为"利益"。

63. **D—B—C—A** 【解析】译文 A 完全误解了原文的意思,为错译;译文 B 基本表达了原文的意思,但是用词不是很准确;译文 C 漏译了原文中的 in sale 以及 by his boss;译文 D 在准确地理解原文的基础上,用通顺、流畅的中文表达了原文。

64. **C—B—A—D** 【解析】译文 A 中"证明"为误译;译文 B 中"应聘者"为误译;译文 C 在准确地理解原文的基础上,用通顺、流畅的中文表达了原意;译文 D 完全误解了原文的意思,属于错译。

65. 【参考译文】射击最初只是生存的手段,直到 19 世纪才成为一项体育运动。1896 年射击第一次成为奥运项目。在 1904 至 1928 年中断,直到 1932 年重回奥运会。1968 年第一次允许妇女参加奥运射击比赛,在 1896 年的奥运会只有三项射击项目,现今已有 17 项。

Part Ⅴ Writing

解题步骤:

第一步:审题

1. 题型:提纲作文;

2. 文体:应用文。

第二步:框架分析

1. 演讲格式;

2. 点出每个要点。

第三步:列出写作思路

1. 说明演讲的主要内容;

2. 注意演讲的格式。

第四步:列出关键词和词组

have a completely new life, keep in mind, arrange your time properly, make a timetable, take advantage of, deal with, help from others will make things easy, get along well with, speak ill of, bear in mind, take an active part in, etc.

第五步:落笔成文

Good morning, everybody. Welcome to Sichuan University!

As a freshman, you are going to have a completely new life. So here is something you should keep in mind.

First, arrange your time properly. You'd better make a timetable so that you will know what to do and how to do it and take advantage of every minute. It will make your work more efficient. Living in the university, sometimes you will face some problems that you can't deal with all alone. Then help from others will make things easy for you. So get along well with all the people around you. Always be open-minded and warm-hearted. Don't speak ill of others at will. You should always bear in mind that we are in a big family. At last, take an active part in societies. Societies at school are your second teachers. It will not only provide you more chances to make friends and challenge yourself, but make your school life rich and colorful as well.

Enjoy your university life!

模拟试题(四)

Part I Listening Comprehension

Section A

1. A 【解析】根据... now it's 1 dollar for two.可知,现在只要 1 美元就可以买到两支钢笔。

2. A 【解析】根据 I did. But your line was always busy.可知,男士打过电话了,可是总是占线,故选 A。

3. C 【解析】女士说:现在 10:45 了,我要错过 11 点的飞机了。男士回答说:不用担心,这个表快半小时。由此可知,现在的时间是 10:15,故选 C。

4. B 【解析】根据... he was having his breakfast at the dining room when I saw him.可知,当时布莱克先生在餐厅,故选 B。

5. D 【解析】根据... he is 3 years younger. He is 18.可知,他今年 21 岁,故选 D。

Section B

Conversation 1

6. A 【解析】根据 I went back to visit my grandma in the countryside.可知,他周末回乡下看望祖母了,故选 A。

7. D 【解析】根据 I have got a cold. I could do nothing but lie in bed.可知,她是因为生病才躺在床上的,故选 D。

Conversation 2

8. C 【解析】通篇全文可知,两人正在讨论在校刊上登广告的事,故选 C。

9. A 【解析】根据... it was 10 yuan for the first 30 words and 50 fen for each word added. 可知,前 30 字收费 10 元,以后每加一字 50 分,故选 A。

10. B 【解析】根据... you can call Berne Li. He is the head...可知,如果女士想登广告她应该给 Mr. Berne Li 打电话,故选 B。

Section C

11. China and France 【解析】根据 Among the leading countries in apple production are China, France and the United States.可知,除了美国另外两个产苹果大国是中国和法国。

12. size and taste 【解析】根据 Apples are different in color, size, and taste.可知,苹果在颜色、大小以及味道上有所不同。

13. green or yellow 【解析】根据 The color of the skin may be red, green, or yellow.可知,苹果除了有红色外还有绿色和黄色。

14. twelve meters 【解析】根据 Apple trees may grow as tall as twelve meters.可知,苹果树能长到 12 米高。

15. cold period 【解析】根据 Although no fruit is yielded during the winter, the cold period is good for the tree.可知,一段时间的寒冷对于果树生长有利。

附:听力原文

Section A

1. **W:** How much are these pens?

   M: They used to be 60 cents each but now it's 1 dollar for two.

   Q: How much will the man pay if he buys two pens?

2. **W:** Why didn't you call me last night, Peter?

   M: I did. But your line was always busy.

   Q: What does the man mean?

3. **W:** It's 10:45 already and I'll miss my 11 o'clock plane.

   M: Don't worry. The clock is half an hour fast.

   Q: When does the conversation take place?

4. **W:** Did you see Mr. Black this morning?

   M: Yes, he was having his breakfast at the dining room when I saw him.

   Q: Where was Mr. Black when the man saw him?

5. **W:** Is your brother older than you?

   M: No, he is 3 years younger. He is 18.

   Q: How old is the man?

Section B

Conversation 1

W: Hi, Mike. How did your weekend go?

M: Fine. I went back to visit my grandma in the countryside.

W: Lucky you. What did you do there?

M: I went for a walk in the hills with some of my friends.

W: Was it good?

M: Yes, the scenery was amazing. The whole hillside was very red.

W: How wonderful! Do anything else?

M: We went on a picnic on Sunday.

W: Did you like it?

M: Very enjoyable. By the way, Lisa, what about your weekend?

W: Don't ask me, Mike.

M: What happened?

W: I have got a cold. I could do nothing but lie in bed.

M: Oh, dear.

Q6. What did Mike do last week?

Q7. Why did Lisa lie in bed and do nothing at weekend?

Conversation 2

W: David, have you ever placed an ad in the *Campus Daily*?

M: Yes, I once did that to sell my bike I no longer needed.

W: When was that?

M: Last May, I think. Why do you ask?

W: I'm thinking of selling my old book since I am going to graduate.

M: Are they in good condition?

W: Pretty good.

M: Well, you can call Berne Li. He is the head of the advertising department of the paper.

W: Do you know what rates they charge?

M: Last May it was 10 yuan for the first 30 words and 50 fen for each word added.

W: 10 yuan for the first 30 words. That is not too bad.

M: Yeah, it's reasonable.

W: Do they charge extra for pictures?

M: No, that's free. But they do charge you more if you want to put in a bow or something.

W: I see. Thanks. That's very helpful.

M: It's a pleasure.

Q8. What are the speakers talking about?

Q9. What rates do they charge?

Q10. Who can the woman call if she wants to place an ad in the *Campus Daily*?

Section C

For thousands of years, man has enjoyed the taste of apples. Apples, which are about 85 percent of water, grow almost everywhere in the world but the hottest and coldest areas. Among the leading countries in apple production are China, France and the United States.

Apples are different in color, size, and taste. The color of the skin maybe red, green, or yellow. Apple trees may grow as tall as twelve meters. They do best in areas that have very cold winters. Although no fruit is yielded during the winter, the cold period is good for the tree.

Q11. Which two countries are the leading ones in apple production besides the United States?

Q12. In which three aspects are apples different from each other?

Q13. What are the colors of apples?

Q14. How tall can apple trees grow?

Q15. Why do apple trees grow best in areas that have cold winters?

Part Ⅱ Structure

Section A

16. D 【解析】本题考查副词比较级、最高级的用法。句意为:汉娜是一位勇敢的骑士,但是她是我的同事中骑马最不勇敢的了。应该用最高级,故选 D。

17. C 【解析】本题考查代词的用法。句意为:网上的信息比报纸上的信息传播得快得多。根据句意,前后比较的内容都是 information,但指代不同的内容,A 项 it 指代同类同物,B、C、D 三个选项所指代的是同类不同物, 但 information 是不可数名词, 排除 B、D,故选 C。

18. D 【解析】本题考查动词词组。句意为:我努力想通过考试,但是结果并不如愿。find out 意为"发现";give out 意为"用尽";hand out 意为"分发";work out 意为"结果"。根据句意,work out 为正确选项。

19. B 【解析】本题考查的是交际英语的运用。句意为:——你能戴上耳机吗?——对不起,打扰你了吧?take it easy 意为"别紧张",用于安抚情绪、精神;I'm sorry 意为"对不起";not a bit 意为"一点也不……",与对话情景矛盾;it depends 意为"视情况而定"。依上下文情景,因打扰别人而表示歉意,故选 B。

20. C 【解析】本题考查语态。首先考虑主句主语与分词之间的关系为逻辑上的主动关系,排除 A、B 两项;分析句意,face 并不在 take an optimistic attitude 之前,排除 D 项,故选 C。

21. C 【解析】本题考查动词时态。本题是个一般陈述句,用以说明一个客观情况,应该用一般现在时的第三人称单数形式,故选 C。

22. A 【解析】本题考查固定搭配的用法。句意为:孩子不应该被迫去学习,兴趣才是最好的老师。be made to 后面接动词原形表示被迫去做某事,故选 A。

23. C 【解析】本题考查强调句的用法。句意为:是约翰这么快就改变了她的想法。it is / was... that 是强调句的基本句型结构,故选 C。

24. B　【解析】本题考查词语辨析。句意为:没有人能知道她是谁。yet 常用于现在完成时的否定句中,意为"尚,还",符合句意,故选 B。

25. A　【解析】本题考查词语辨析。call for 意为"要求";call forth 意为"使起作用";call off 意为"放弃";call up"召唤"。根据句意应选 A。

Section B

26. container　【解析】本题考查词性转换。这里需要一个名词,所以应该将动词(contain)转换成名词(container)。airtight container 意为"密封容器"。

27. goes　【解析】本题考查时态。句意为:露西一个月去一次电影院。这种行为是经常性的、习惯性的,故应该用一般现在时。

28. to watch　【解析】本题考查固定用法。continue to do something 意为"做完一件事,继续做另一件事情"。

29. studies　【解析】本题考查时态。根据后一句可知这里表示一个一般性的客观事实,应该用一般现在时。注意 study 变成第三人称单数时应该将 y 变成 i 加 es。

30. to help　【解析】本题考查固定用法。ask sb. to do sth.意为"让谁去做某事"。

31. has　【解析】本题考查时态。本句表示一个客观事实,在这里 have 作实义动词表拥有,故应该用第三人称单数的形式。

32. is feeding　【解析】本题考查时态。根据 look 一词可知,鸟妈妈喂小鸟的动作正在进行中,所以动词应该用现在进行时的形式。

33. is ringing　【解析】本题考查时态。根据后一句"请快点接电话。"可知,电话正在响,所以应该用现在进行时表示正在进行或发生的动作或行为。

34. shopping　【解析】本题考查固定用法。do some shopping 为固定搭配,意为"购物"。

35. reads　【解析】本题考查时态。根据 always 一词可知,这是一个习惯性的动作,所以应该用一般现在时的形式,来表示经常性习惯性的动作或行为。

Part Ⅲ　Reading Comprehension

Task 1

　　【文章概述】　本文介绍了安全避雷电的常识,其中包括雷电的强度,雷电给人们造成的伤害以及雷电到来时人们应该选择什么样的避雷电方式等。

36. B　【解析】判断正误题。B 选项明显与文中首段第一句 People who are hit by lightning and survive often have long-term effects.不符,故选 B。

37. C　【解析】词义题。第四段第一、二两句说的是一个意思。第一句提到... should stay away from anything with wires or pipes that lead to the outside.其中 stay away 意为"远离",与 disconnect 同义,cut off 意为"迅速远离,切断",故选 C。

38. D　【解析】判断正误。根据第三段第三句 And do not stand near a tree or any tall subject.可知,雷电来时不能站在树下,故选 D。

39. D　【解析】细节题。在文章的第四段我们可以找到 A、B、C 三个选项的内容。根据第五段第一句 Some people think a person struck by lightning carries an electrical charge afterward. Experts say this is not true.可知,被雷电触击后的人是不带电的,故选 D。

40. B　【解析】总结归纳题。通读全文可知,本文主要介绍的是安全避雷电的常识,故选 B。

Task 2

【文章概述】 本文主要讲述了候鸟等动物是怎么迁移的。作者通过科学家的实验证明了候鸟有精确的时间感和方向感。

41. C 【解析】细节题。第二段介绍了科学家的实验过程，根据 This proved that they could see the stars and respond to them.可知，候鸟可以看到星星，并能根据星星来辨别方向，并对根据位置的改变来变换方向，故选 C。

42. D 【解析】细节题。根据第三段第一句 Many animals, especially birds, have a very precise sense of time, which is called their "internal clock".可知，很多动物，尤其是候鸟有一种很精确的时间感和方向感，故选 D。

43. B 【解析】细节题。根据第三段第三句... they are able to steer by following the magnetic field of the earth. 可知，当多云的天气持续很长时间后，候鸟能根据地球磁场来辨别方向，故选 B。

44. A 【解析】细节题。根据最后一段第一句 Most migrating animals travel in groups, sometimes in very large numbers.可知，很多迁徙动物是以群体的形式迁徙的，故选 A。

45. B 【解析】总结归纳题。通读全文，我们可以得知整篇文章都在讲动物是怎么迁移的，故选 B。

Task 3

【文章概述】 本文讲述了世界著名的服装设计师——Vera Wang 的一些经历。

46. skating 【解析】细节题。根据第二段第一句 Vera Wang herself is a very good skater and she had Olympic dreams too.可知，她的爱好是滑冰。

47. liberal arts 【解析】细节题。根据第一段第三句 After earning a degree in liberal arts, Vera worked as an editor at Vogue...可知，她有文科学位。

48. editor 【解析】细节题。根据 Vera worked as an editor at Vogue for 17 years...可知她的第一份工作是做编辑。

49. design director 【解析】细节题。根据第一段... as a design director of Ralph Lauren for two years.可知，她曾在拉夫·劳伦公司作过两年的设计总监。

50. stylish costumes 【解析】细节题。根据第一段最后一句 She became a household name in 1994 when she designed stylish costumes for figure skater Nancy Kerrigan to wear in the Winter Olympics.可知，她曾设计过时尚束装。

Task 4

【说明】 本文是一系列法律用语。

51. A, M 52. J, D 53. G, F 54. N, C 55. P, B
各项的译文：
A —— 非法禁锢　　　　　B —— 会见当事人
C —— 案件受理费　　　　D —— 案由
E —— 本地律师　　　　　F —— 辩护律师
G —— 辩护要点　　　　　H —— 财产租赁

I —— 出庭	J —— 当事人陈述
K —— 吊销执业证	L —— 调查笔录
M—— 法律意见书	N —— 法院公告
O —— 鉴定结论	P —— 待决案件

Task 5

【文章概述】 本文是一封关于不能参加 Cindy 的毕业典礼的道歉信。

56. apology 【解析】总结归纳题。信件的大意是发信人因为不能参加收信人的毕业典礼而道歉,所以这是一封道歉信。

57. seriously ill 【解析】细节题。根据第二段第二句 But the person who was originally appointed to it is now seriously ill in hospital.可知,原来指派的人得了很重的病住院了。

58. make a speech 【解析】细节题。根据第二段第三句 And I have been asked to take his place to attend the meeting and make a speech on behalf of my company.可知,Jocy 是代替原来的同事去参加会议并代表公司发言。

59. display and enhance 【解析】细节题。根据第二段第五句... I do regard it as an opportunity to both display and enhance my abilities.可知,Jocy 认为这是一次展示和提高自己能力的机会。

60. sincere congratulations 【解析】细节题。根据第三段第一句... I really regret that I cannot give you my sincere congratulations on the spot...可知,她是因为不能当面送上诚挚的祝贺而感到遗憾。

Part Ⅳ Translation —— English into Chinese

61. A—D—C—B 【解析】译文 A 在准确理解原文的基础上,用通顺、流畅的中文表达了原意;译文 B 完全误解了原文的意思,为错译;译文 C 中"措施就越基本"为误译;译文 D 漏译了"越……越……"。

62. C—D—A—B 【解析】译文 A 中 certain 不应意为"一定的",另外还漏译了 such as;译文 B 完全误解了原文的意思,属于错译;译文 C 翻译正确,用词准确;译文 D 漏译了 such as。

63. B—A—C—D 【解析】译文 A 基本表达了原文的意思,但用词不够准确;译文 B 准确理解了原文,用通顺、流畅的中文表达了原意;译文 C 漏译了 near;译文 D,完全误解了原文的意思,属于错译。

64. C—A—B—D 【解析】译文 A 中"姓"为误译;译文 B 中"起外号"为误译;译文 C 为正确译文;译文 D 中"领导"为误译。

65.【参考译文】首先,眼睛工作一两个小时之后要注意休息。然后每天要坚持做两次眼保健操。不时向远处望几次对眼睛是有好处的。不要卧床看书,不要在行驶的车上或光线较暗的地方或太阳底下看书。如果有东西掉进眼睛里,不要揉,应用凉开水冲洗。如果不行,应去找医生。如果你需要眯着眼睛才能看清东西的话,那就需配戴眼镜。

Part V Writing

解题步骤:

第一步:审题

1. 题型:提纲作文;

2. 文体:应用文。

第二步:框架分析

1. 招聘启事格式;

2. 点出每个要点。

第三步:列出写作思路

1. 说明职位的要求;

2. 注意招聘启事的格式。

第四步:列出关键词和词组

looking for a secretary for the general manager, arrange the general manager's schedule, be responsible to, meet the following requirements, communication ability, have a basic writing skill, get in touch with, etc.

第五步:落笔成文

Secretary Wanted

Our company is looking for a secretary for the general manager. The job mainly includes two parts: One is to arrange the general manager's schedule. The other is to be responsible to daily reception job.

We hope that he/she could meet the following requirements: First, he/she has communication ability. Second, it's necessary for him/her to have a basic writing skill. Those who are interested in the job, please get in touch with the Personnel Department this week.

Personnel Department

模拟试题(五)

Part I Listening Comprehension

Section A

1. B 【解析】根据 My mother cooked it for me.可知,是男士的母亲做的汤,故选 B。

2. A 【解析】根据 doctor 和 tablets 可知,对话发生在医院,故选 A。

3. D 【解析】根据 I've only been here one week myself.可知,他刚来这个城市一周,对这个城市并不熟悉,故选 D。

4. C 【解析】根据 ... but I have promised my sister to see a movie with her tonight.可知,男士今晚要陪他妹妹去看电影,故选 C。

5. B 【解析】根据"你和我一起健身吧。我可以给你一张贵宾卡。以后吧。但是我真是懒于做那些。"可知,男士不喜欢健身,故选 B。

Section B

Conversation 1

6. B　【解析】根据女士的话 I love it. It's so convenient. But, as a working woman, I think New York has all the conveniences, including the best tomatoes. 可知，她喜欢生活在城市,故选 B。

7. C　【解析】根据 But I'm afraid that she cannot adapt herself to the new environment. 可知,男士怕自己的女儿不能适应新环境,故选 C。

Conversation 2

8. D　【解析】录音的第二句和第八句提到了 A、B、C 三项,男士在银行中并没有取钱,故选 D。

9. B　【解析】录音的第四句提到了 A、C、D 三项,只有 B 没有提到,故选 B。

10. C　【解析】根据 If you could just complete this form, we'll be happy to arrange that for you. 可知,开账户之前男士需要填一张表。

Section C

11. Spring Festival　【解析】根据第一句 Spring Festival is the most important festival in China. 可知,春节是中国最重要的节日。

12. get together　【解析】根据 In the evening before the Spring Festival, families get together and have a big meal. 可知,在除夕之夜,各个家庭都会聚在一起吃年夜饭。

13. Dumplings　【解析】根据 Dumplings are the most traditional food. 可知,饺子是春节的传统食物。

14. delicious food　【解析】根据 Children like the festival very much, because they can have delicious food and wear new clothes. 可知,孩子们喜欢过春节是因为他们可以吃到美味的食物,穿上新衣服。

15. 15 days　【解析】根据最后一句 The Spring Festival lasts about 15 days long. 可知,春节会持续 15 天。

附:听力原文

Section A

1. **W:** Did you cook the soup yourself, Mike? It's delicious.

   M: No. My mother cooked it for me.

   Q: Who cooked the soup?

2. **W:** How do I take the medicine, doctor?

   M: Three times a day and two tablets each time.

   Q: Where does the conversation most likely take place?

3. **W:** Excuse me, can you tell me the way to the central station?

   M: I'm afraid I can't. I've only been here one week myself.

   Q: Why can't the man help the woman?

4. **W:** Michael, would you like to eat out tonight?

M: Oh, I'd really like to, but I have promised my sister to see a movie with her tonight.

Q: What will the man do this evening?

5. W: Why don't you join me at the gym sometime? I can get you a guest pass.

M: Well, maybe someday, but I'm pretty lazy about things like that.

Q: What do you know about the man?

Section B

Conversation 1

M: You like living in New York, don't you?

W: Oh, I love it. It's so convenient. I can take the bus to work or the subway or a taxi. And there's so much to do.

M: I know what you mean. I'd like to live in the city, but living in the suburbs is better for Michelle. Trees, grass. There are a lot of good things about suburban living.

W: I grew up in suburbs, remember? So I know. But, as a working woman, I think New York has all the conveniences, including the best tomatoes.

M: The truth is, Michelle has lived in suburbs for more than ten years. It is very hard for her to leave her friends.

W: I don't think so. Michelle is at the right age. There are lots of things for her here.

M: But I'm afraid that she cannot adapt herself to the new environment.

W: Don't worry. It is never too late to learn or change.

M: OK, I will think about it.

Q6. What is the woman's choice?

Q7. What do you know about the man?

Conversation 2

W: Good afternoon. May I help you?

M: Can you change some money for me, please?

W: Certainly. What currency do you want to change?

M: Here it is: some Hong Kong dollars, American dollars and Japanese yen. How much will they be in English pounds?

W: Just a moment. Let me find out all the exchange rates.

M: Thanks.

W: Here we are. That'll be 456 pounds altogether. How would you like the money?

M: I'd like to open an account. I want to deposit the money in it.

W: If you could just complete this form, we'll be happy to arrange that for you.

Q8. What of the following things did not the man do in the bank?

Q9. Which of the following currency is not mentioned in the conversation?

Q10. What should the man do before the woman open an account for him?

Section C

Spring Festival is the most important festival in China. It's to celebrate the lunar calendar's new year. In the evening before the Spring Festival, families get together and have a big meal. In many places people like to set off firecrackers. Dumplings are the most traditional food. Children like the festival very much, because they can have delicious food and wear new clothes. They can also get some money from their parents. This money is given to children for good luck. People put New Year scrolls on the wall for good fortune. The Spring Festival lasts about 15 days long.

Q11. What festival is the most important one in China?

Q12. What do families do in the evening before this festival?

Q13. What is the most traditional food on this festival?

Q14. Why do children like this festival?

Q15. How long will this festival last?

Part Ⅱ Struture

Section A

16. D 【解析】本题考查短语辨析。look out 意为"照料,留神";make out 意为"辨认出,了解";get across 意为"(使)被理解";take after 意为"像"。句意为:凯特是个漂亮的女孩,她长得更像她的妈妈。故选 D。

17. D 【解析】本题考查词义辨析。Eventually 和 finally 都意为"最终";yet 意为"然而";accordingly (=for that reason, therefore)意为"因此, 所以"。根据句意可知这里有因果关系,故选 D。

18. A 【解析】本题考查短语辨析。nothing but 意为"只不过";anything but (=far from being)意为"根本不";above all 意为"最重要的";rather than 意为"而不是"。句意应是明星只是普通人,故选 A。

19. B 【解析】本题考查短语辨析。break off 意为"中断";take off 意为"起飞";write off 意为"报废";pick up 意为"获得,捡起"。句意为:飞机半小时后起飞,故选 B。

20. C 【解析】本题考查短语辨析。even so 意为"即使如此";ever so (=very) 意为"非常",但在与名词搭配时则用 ever such;so far 意为"到目前为止"。句意为:周先生是一位非常出色的教授。故选 C。

21. D 【解析】本题考查固定搭配。take place 意为"发生";take effect 意为"生效";take office 意为"就职"。句意为:新校长下周将就职。故选 D。

22. B 【解析】本题考查近义词辨析。accept 是经过考虑"接受"下来,表示当事人的态度,是主观接受;receive 意为"收到, 接到",指"收,接"这一动作,客观收到。句意为:我昨天收到了妹妹的信。这是一种客观的行为,故选 B。

23. A 【解析】本题考查短语辨析。in relation to 意为"关系到";in excess of 意为"超过";in contrast to 意为"与……相对照";in favor of 意为"赞成"。句意为:我们定计划的时候要考虑到将来。故选 A。

24. A 【解析】本题考查连词。However 意为"然而",表示转折关系;therefore 意为"因此",表示因果关系;so 意为"因此",表示因果关系;although 意为"虽然",表示让步。句意为:这个秘书很勤奋,然而却得不到老板的认可。这里是转折关系,故选 A。

25. A 【解析】本题考查词义辨析。get over 意为"恢复";get off 意为"动身";hold back 意

为"阻止";hold up 意为"支撑"。根据句意应是"恢复",故选 A。

Section B

26. product 【解析】本题考查词性转换。观察句子可知这里需要一个名词,而且根据句意也应是"产品",故应该把动词变成名词。

27. advertisement 【解析】本题考查词性转换。观察句子结构可知这里需要一个名词作宾语,所以要把动词变成名词。

28. amusement 【解析】本题考查词性转换。根据句意和句子结构可知这里应指 "游乐园",所以应把动词变成名词。

29. spreading 【解析】本题考查时态。观察句子可知这个动作是正在进行的动作,应该用现在进行时,又因 and 一词可知这里的词应该与 flying 一样的形式,故这里应用 spreading。

30. skiing 【解析】本题考查词的用法。enjoy doing sth.意为"喜欢做某事",所以要用 skiing。

31. harmful 【解析】本题考查固定搭配。be harmful to 意为"对……有害",harm 一般构成 do harm to 短语。

32. tell 【解析】本题考查词的用法。why not 后接动词原形,意为"为什么不",表示建议,所以应用 tell。

33. washes 【解析】本题考查时态。根据句意可知这是一般现在时,一般现在时表示经常性习惯性的动作或行为,而且主语是第三人称单数,所以要用 washes。

34. breathe 【解析】本题考查情态动词的用法。情态动词后接动词原形, 所以要用 breathe。

35. fossils 【解析】本题考查名词复数。fossil 是可数名词,所以在 a lot of 后应该用其复数形式。

Part Ⅲ　Reading Comprehension

Task 1

　　【文章概述】　本文介绍了情人节的起源。根据民间传说,情人节的名字来源于一个罗马的基督教徒——瓦伦丁。在当时,罗马教皇不允许教徒结婚,而瓦伦丁却秘密地帮助教徒结婚,这一行为触怒了教皇,最终于公元 270 年 2 月 14 日惨遭教皇杀害。为了纪念瓦伦丁,人们定 2 月 14 号为情人节。

36. C 【解析】推断题。文章的第一段介绍了情人节的庆祝方式以及表达的意思。其中 lovers 出现了三次,因此,可以推断出情人节礼物是为了表达彼此的爱的,故选C。

37. B 【解析】细节题。根据第二段第一句... it gets its name from a Christian named Valentine who lived in Rome...可知,这个节日的名字来源于一个基督教徒的名字,故选 B。

38. D 解析】细节题。根据第二段第三句... the Emperor of Rome didn't allow Christian marriages. So they had to be performed in secret.可知,基督教徒要秘密举行婚礼是因为罗马皇帝不允许,故选 D。

39. A 【解析】细节题。根据第二段... Emperor offered to release Valentine if he would stop performing Christian marriage.可知,罗马皇帝提出如果瓦伦丁停止帮助教徒结婚就可以释放他,故选 A。

40. D 【解析】总结归纳题。通读全文,可以得知作者是在探讨情人节的来源问题,故选D。

Task 2

【文章概述】 本文主要讲述了一种由美国和加拿大科学家发明的新型植物。这种植物能够解决人类的吃饭问题。利用这种新型技术,科学家可以在更多的土地上种植,并希望能增产,以解决人类的吃饭问题。

41. A 【解析】推断题。短文第二段第一句是第二段的主旨句,也就是论点。下面的内容都是解释说明并论证第一句的。第二段整段都是在讲这项新技术的重要性。所以可以推断 significance 的意思应该是选项 A。

42. D 【解析】细节题。根据第二段第二句 The new technology can help mankind solve the problem of feeding its ever-expanding population.可知新技术可以帮助人类解决一直膨胀的人口的吃饭问题,故选 D。

43. B 【解析】计算题。根据 It is estimated that by 2025 the world population will amount to more than 9 billion, an increase of 3 billion over 2000.可以计算出 2000 年的人口为 60 亿,故选 B。

44. C 【解析】细节题。根据第二段最后一句 Salts destroy most plants' ability to draw up water through their roots.可知,盐可以破坏很多植物通过根系吸收水分的能力,故选C。

45. B 【解析】细节题。根据最后一段第一句... the new variety of tomato... can store salts in its leaves so that the fruit doesn't taste salty. 可知, 新型的土豆可以将盐储存在叶子中,因此不感到咸,故选 B。

Task 3

【文章概述】 这是一篇新闻报道。文章介绍了 2008 年四川地震的情况。

46. earthquake 【解析】细节题。根据第一句 On the afternoon 14:28 of May 12, 2008, an earthquake measuring...可知,是地震爆发了。

47. Sichuan Province 【解析】细节题。根据第一句... an earthquake measuring 8.0 on the Richter scale hit Sichuan Province, a mountainous region in Western China.可知,事发地点是四川省。

48. 69,000 【解析】细节题。根据... the death toll stood at 69,000... 可知, 死亡人数为 69,000。

49. 18,000 【解析】细节题。根据... with another 18,000 still missing.可知,失踪人数为 18,000。

50. Over 15 million 【解析】细节题。根据 Over 15 million people live in the affected area...可知,还有 15,000,000 人生活在受地震影响的地区。

Task 4

【说明】 本文是一系列关于职业的名称。

51. H, M   52. O, N   53. E, B   54. A, G   55. J, K

各项的译文:

A —— 行政人员	B —— 证券交易员
C —— 计算机工程师	D —— 外销部经理
E —— 总经理	F —— 保险公司理赔员
G —— 公关部经理	H —— 销售主管
I —— 办公室助理	J —— 应用工程师
K —— 业务主任	L —— 电气工程师
M —— 财务主任	N —— 进口联络员
O —— 法律顾问	P —— 市场分析员

Task 5

【文章概述】 这是一份天气报道。文章介绍了长春的天气情况。

56. around 8:00 p.m. 【解析】细节题。根据第一段第二句 The storm lasted about three minutes from around 8:00 p.m.... 可知,暴风雨在下午 8 点左右发生。

57. power failure 【解析】细节题。根据第一段最后一句... causing serious damage and a widespread power failure.可知,在这场暴风雨中除了四人死亡外还有大规模的损失情况,其中包括电力中断。

58. Fine and pleasant 【解析】细节题。根据第二段... a fine day is in store nearly everywhere, with the best of the sunshine in southern and central areas of China.可知,当天天气很好。

59. 22 degrees 【解析】细节题。根据 These will be light with a maximum temperature of 22 degrees Celsius.可知,今天的最高气温为 22 摄氏度。

60. heavy showers 【解析】细节题。根据最后一句 Looking at the outlook for the next few days, it will become mostly cloudy with heavy showers moving in from the west.可知,未来几天多云并且伴有阵雨。

Part Ⅳ Translation — English into Chinese

61. B—A—C—D 【解析】译文 A 基本表达了原文的意思,但用词不准确;译文 B 为正确译法;译文 C 中"文化程度"为误译;译文 D 中"衣、食、住、行是必要的"为误译。

62. D—B—A—C 【解析】译文 A 用词不准确;译文 B 中"击败"为误译;译文 C 完全误解了原文的意思,为错译;译文 D 准确译出了原文的意思。

63. A—C—D—B 【解析】译文 A 准确译出了原文的意思;译文 B 中 so as to 不应译为"……的目的";译文 C 基本表达了原句的意思,但用词不够准确;译文 D 中"翻译"为误译。

64. D—A—B—C 【解析】本题的考查重点是 by far,它修饰比较级和最高级表示"最……"。译文 A 中"较为"为误译;译文 B 中"远远不是"为误译;译文 C 中"离……最远"为误译;译文 D 准确翻译出了原文的意思,为正确答案。

65.【参考译文】

校规:

1. 在学校里要戴校徽、穿校服。

2. 上午 7:30 上课,下午 4:30 放学,不许迟到、早退。

3. 放学后扫地,保持学校清洁。

4. 如果要骑单车上学,需办理自行车许可证。

Part V　Writing

解题步骤:

第一步:审题

1. 题型:提纲作文;

2. 文体:应用文。

第二步:框架分析

1. 通知格式;

2. 点出每个要点。

第三步:列出写作思路

1. 说明的通知主要内容;

2. 注意通知的格式。

第四步:列出关键词和词组

　　is going to be held, issues to be talked about at the meeting, are required to be present, take notebooks, arrive on time, take notes carefully, etc.

第五步:落笔成文

Notice

　　A meeting is going to be held in Room 401 of Building 4 at 7:00 on the evening of March 7. Issues to be talked about at the meeting include the conclusion of the last term and the plan for the following term and so on. All the students are required to be present. They should take notebooks with them and arrive on time. They should take notes carefully.

Class 1 of Grade 2

March 2nd, 2010

专家预测试题(一)

Part Ⅰ　Listening Comprehension

Section A

1. C　【解析】根据 I had pork yesterday. I think I'll have the beef.可知,他昨天刚吃了猪肉,因此想吃点牛肉,也就是变换一下,故选 C。

2. A　【解析】本题问的是女士为什么道歉。男士提到 I asked for filet mignon.女士回答 I'm sorry. I'll see that it's changed. 由此可知,女士端错了菜,故选 A。

3. A　【解析】根据回答"在我十岁的时候妈妈给我买的,现在我都 20 岁了。"可计算得知选 A。

4. B　【解析】男士说"安迪,请你把这份文件送到怀特先生的办公室。"根据安迪的回答"好的,我马上去。"可知选 B。

5. C 【解析】根据回答"我喜欢黑色中号的衬衫。"可知选 C。

Section B

Conversation 1

6. A 【解析】根据 First class is 24 dollars more.可知,男士如果买头等票就要多花 24 美元,故选 A。

7. B 【解析】根据 Then give me one second class ticket on the express, please. 可知,男士最后买了直达的二等舱的票,故选 B。

Conversation 2

8. C 【解析】根据 I'm terribly sorry. I'm late. 可知,男士是因为迟到而道歉,故选 C。

9. D 【解析】根据 But I didn't know the number of the restaurant. 可知,他们打算在饭店见面,故选 D。

10. A 【解析】根据 I've only been waiting for over an hour, that's all. 可知,女士等了一个多小时,故选 A。

Section C

11. in the morning 【解析】根据 But air is never as fresh as early in the morning. 可知,一天中早晨的空气最新鲜。

12. easier to remember 【解析】根据 We learn more quickly in the morning,and find it easier to remember what we learn in the morning. 可知,早起学习能使我们记得更快并且不容易忘记。

13. a good plan 【解析】根据 We cannot work well without a good plan. 可知,好的计划是做好工作的前提。

14. faces and hands 【解析】根据 ... such as to wash our faces and hands and eat our breakfast properly.可知,准备工作包括洗脸和手,还有吃早餐。

15. helpful 【解析】根据 Early rising is helpful in more than one way. 这一论点以及后面的四点论据可知,段落的大意是:早起对人的益处很多。

附:听力原文

Section A

1. **W:** Well, what are you going to eat? The pork is very good here.

   M: Umm... I had pork yesterday. I think I'll have the beef.

   Q: Why doesn't the man want to eat pork?

2. **M:** Pardon me. I asked for filet mignon.

   W: I'm sorry. I'll see that it's changed.

   Q: Why did the woman apologize?

3. **W:** Your bike looks quite new. When did you buy it?

   M: My mother bought it for me when I was ten years old. Now, I'm already 20 years old.

   Q: How long has the man used his bike?

4. **M:** Andy, could you send this document to Mr. White's office?

W: Sure, I'll do it right away.

Q: What will the woman do?

5. **W:** What kind of T-shirt would you like?

　　M: I'd like black T-shirt in medium size.

　　Q: What color does the man like for his T-shirt?

Section B

Conversation 1

M: We want to take a train to New York.

W: Regular or express train?

M: How much time would I save if we took the express?

W: About one hour. The next express train arrives in New York at 3:15.

M: And how much more do I have to pay for the express?

W: First class is 24 dollars more, and second class is 15 dollars more.

M: As long as we can arrive one hour earlier, I don't mind paying a little extra. Then give me one second class ticket on the express, please.

W: OK, one second class ticket. Here you are.

M: Thank you.

Q6. How much more does the man have to pay for the first class express?

Q7. What kind of ticket has the man bought?

Conversation 2

M: I'm terribly sorry. I'm late.

W: I've only been waiting for over an hour, that's all.

M: Yes, I know, I... I tried to get here in time, but just after I left home, the car broke down.

W: The car broke down?

M: Yes, and... well... luckily... there was a garage near me, and... and it took them a while to repair it.

W: Why didn't you at least phone?

M: I would have! But I didn't know the number of the restaurant.

W: You could have looked it up in the telephone book!

M: Yes, but... You'll never believe this... I couldn't remember the name of the restaurant. I knew where it was, but forgot the name.

W: I see, well, it was lucky you find a garage to repair your car.

Q8. Why did the man apologize?

Q9. Where did they plan to meet?

Q10. How long has the woman been waiting for?

Section C

Early rising is helpful in more than one way. First, it helps to keep us fit. We all need fresh air. But air is never as fresh as early in the morning. Besides, we can do good to our health from doing morning exercise. Secondly, early rising helps us in our studies. We learn more quickly in the morning, and find it easier to remember what we learn in the morning. Thirdly, early rising enables us to plan the work of the day. We cannot work well without a good plan. Just as the plan for the year should be made in the spring, so the plan for the day should be made in the morning. Fourthly, early rising gives us enough time to get ready for our work, such as to wash our faces and hands and eat our breakfast properly.

Q11. At what time is the air the freshest in the day?

Q12. Why do early rising help us in our study?

Q13. How can we work well according to the author?

Q14. What should we prepare before our work?

Q15. What is the main idea of this passage?

Part II Struture

Section A

16. C 【解析】本题考查固定搭配。have a narrow escape 意为"幸免于难,侥幸逃脱"。句意为:在过马路的时候,这个年长的妇人在一辆车前侥幸逃脱,幸免于难,故选 C。

17. A 【解析】本题考查固定搭配。take charge of 意为"负责,掌管,看管"。句意为:李华是班长,所以他应该对这件事负责,故选 A。

18. D 【解析】本题考查词义辨析。sure 经常用于"I am sure that +从句"结构中。但在 it 作形式主语, that 引导主语从句时,主句中表语只能用 certain,不能用 sure,故选 D。

19. B 【解析】本题考查动词短语辨析。 put down 意为"放下,拒绝";shut out 意为"把……关在外面,排除,不让入内";cut short (=interrupt)意为"打断, 中断";take off 意为"起飞"。根据句意,应是不让尘土飞进窗户里,故选 B。

20. D 【解析】本题考查语法。awake 为形容词,意为"醒着的(作表语)";woke 和 waken 是动词 wake 的过去式和过去分词,不能作表语。而且根据句意,应该是孩子们自己醒来,不是被叫醒,故选 D。

21. B 【解析】本题考查短语辨析。but for 意为"若非,要不是";in spite of 意为"尽管";because of 意为"由于";as for 意为"至于"。根据句意应是要不是你的帮助,我们就不会及时完工,故选 B。

22. C 【解析】本题考查词的用法。entitle sb. to sth.意为"给予……权利",句意:军官们有权乘头等车旅行。故选 C。

23. A 【解析】本题考查固定搭配。lie in 意为"在于"。句意为:问题在于他们缺乏资金。故选 A。

24. B 【解析】本题考查交际用语。by the way 意为"顺便问一句"。根据上下文的逻辑关系,故选 B。

25. D 【解析】本题考查代词的区别。代词 one 可以用来替代前面提到过的名词,以避免重复。如果它替代的名词是复数,则用 ones。本题中它代替 apples,又因特指,应用 the ones,故选 D。

Section B

26. bad 【解析】本题考查同级比较。as +形容词+as 意为"像什么一样",表示同级比较,要用原形。

27. **is** 【解析】本题考查语法。不可数名词作主语,谓语动词应用单数形式,there be 句型中 be 的形式要依据临近原则。

28. **fun** 【解析】本题考查词性转换。观察句子结构可知这里需要一个名词作介词的宾语,所以要把形容词变成名词。

29. **does** 【解析】本题考查时态。根据时间状语 every weekend 可知这里是一般现在时,而且主语是单数第三人称,所以要用 does。

30. **diligent** 【解析】本题考查词性转换。观察句子结构可知这里需要一个形容词作表语,所以应该把名词变成形容词。

31. **lost** 【解析】本题考查词性转换。根据句子结构可知这里需要一个形容词作定语修饰名词 watch,所以应该把动词变成形容词。

32. **making** 【解析】本题考查语法。介词后接动词的现在分词形式,所以要用 making。

33. **electricity** 【解析】本题考查词性转换。观察句子结构可知这里需要一个名词作宾语,所以应把形容词变成名词。

34. **watching** 【解析】本题考查固定搭配。have fun doing sth.意为"做某事有趣",所以要用 watching。

35. **been attacked** 【解析】本题考查被动语态。根据句意应该是"电脑被攻击",而且是现在完成时,所以要用 been attacked。

Part Ⅲ Reading Comprehension

Task 1

【文章概述】 本文主要讲述了电子游戏给人们生活带来的种种影响。无论是儿童还是成年人都有人沉迷于电子游戏,各国政府对于电子游戏也有自己不同的政策,但多数正在努力采取措施限制其发展。

36. **A** 【解析】细节题。根据第二段第一句 In Singapore, the battle of man against the machines takes place in licensed amusement centers. 可知,人们对抗机器的斗争发生在有营业执照的娱乐场所,故选 A。

37. **C** 【解析】细节题。根据第二段倒数第二句 Many of them are schoolchildren who have changed out of their uniforms.可知,他们是脱掉校服后进入娱乐中心的,故选 C。

38. **C** 【解析】细节题。根据第一段第一句 In some countries video games are fast becoming a social problem. 可知,由于在很多国家电子游戏已经逐渐变为一个社会问题,所以各国不得不采取措施,故选 C。

39. **A** 【解析】推断题。根据短文第二段作者对于新加坡采取的措施的叙述可以得知,即使政府规定穿校服的学生不允许进入娱乐中心,但是后来发现他们完全可以脱掉校服再进去娱乐。所以这一措施基本上是无效的,故选 A。

40. **B** 【解析】态度题。通读全文可以发现作者用了大部分篇幅来介绍电子游戏的负面影响。短文的结尾作者又用一个反问句表明了自己的态度,因此可推断出作者对电子游戏持消极的态度,故选 B。

Task 2

【文章概述】　本文主要介绍了蚊子的习性。其中介绍了什么样的蚊子吸血及其原因,以及会吸什么样的人的血,吸完血后又做些什么等问题。

41. B　【解析】细节题。根据第二段第六句 Only the female mosquito bites because she needs blood to lay eggs. 可知,母蚊子吸血是为了排卵,故选 B。

42. C　【解析】判断正误题。根据第二段 If she likes what she finds, she bites. But if she doesn't like your blood, she will turn to someone else... 可推断出蚊子会有选择性地吸血,因此 C 不符合这一点,故选 C。

43. B　【解析】细节题。根据第二段 If she likes what she finds, she bites. 可知,如果蚊子找到了它们喜欢的猎物,它们就会发动攻击,故选 B。

44. C　【解析】细节题。根据第三段第三句 After she bites, you will have an itch(痒)on your body... 可知,C 是正确答案,其他选项与文章内容不符,故选 C。

45. D　【解析】细节题。根据第四段 ... after her delicious dinner, the mosquito feels tired... she begins to lay eggs. 可知,蚊子吸完血后开始产卵,故选 D。

Task 3

【文章概述】　本文是一则简历。文章介绍了 Lidia 的一些情况。

46. regional sales representative　【解析】细节题。根据 Objective 这一项中提到的 To work as a regional sales representative who is responsible for sales activity and coordination 可知,她申请的是区域销售经理。

47. finance　【解析】细节题。根据 Education 这一项中提到的 2002—Present Studying at Peking University Bachelor of Arts in finance 可知,她的专业为金融。

48. Student Teacher　【解析】细节题。根据 Work Experience 这一项中提到的 Student Teacher, Yucai High School. 可知,她曾做过教师。

49. Swim Team　【解析】细节题。根据 Work Experience 一项中的 Assistant Coach, New Star Swim Team. 可知,她曾在新星游泳队做助理教练。

50. dancing　【解析】细节题。根据 Hobbies 这一项的 swimming, tennis, Internet surfing, dancing 可知,她的爱好是游泳、网球、上网和跳舞。

Task 4

【说明】　本文是一系列新闻用语。

51. A, K　52. B, L　53. H, N　54. G, J　55. I, P

各项的译文:

A —— 编辑部	B —— 自由撰稿人
C —— 不宜公开报道	D —— 小道消息
E —— 文字编辑	F —— 醒目位置
G —— 调查性报道	H —— 民意测验
I —— 新闻发布会	J —— 传真照片
K —— 深度报道	L —— 特派记者

M —— 特约编辑   N —— 隐性采访

O —— 侵犯隐私权   P —— 年度新闻人物

Task 5

【文章概述】 本文介绍了两种互相矛盾的教育体系:第一种是以考试为目的的;第二种是新的以素质教育为目的的。

56. traditional exam-oriented 【解析】细节题。根据第一段第一句 At present there exists side by side two contradictory educational systems: the traditional exam-oriented system and the new quality-oriented one... 可知,现在有传统的以考试为目的和新的以素质为目的的两种互相矛盾的教育体系。

57. practical ability 【解析】细节题。根据第二段最后一句... they always bury themselves in multiple choices and never attach importance to practical ability and originality. 可知,传统教育的缺点是不注重学生的实践技能以及创造性。

58. all-round development 【解析】细节题。根据第三段第一句... the quality-oriented educational pattern stresses the creativity of students and their all-round development. 可知,素质教育注重学生的独创性以及全面发展。

59. competitive 【解析】细节题。根据第四段... the new quality-oriented pattern aims to train and bring up are not merely learners successful in studies, but responsible citizens fit in health, rich in knowledge and competent in their work" 可知,素质教育要培养有责任感、有知识、有竞争力的学生。

60. new quality-oriented 【解析】主旨题。根据作者的结论... it's high time we reformed our existing exam assessment system and adopted the new one. 可知,作者倾向素质教育。

Part Ⅳ Translation — English into Chinese

61. B—A—D—C 【解析】本题的重点在于 so... that,意为"以便,以致"。译文 A 虽然译出了基本意思,但"了"为误译;译文 C 完全误解了原文的意思;译文 D 中"我挑了这么多书"为误译。

62. B—D—C—A 【解析】本题的重点是 the least,意为"最少"。译文 A 中"和……一样没有雄心"为误译;译文 B 为正确译法;译文 C 中"干有雄心的事最少的"为误译;译文 D 中"是……之一"为误译。

63. A—B—D—C 【解析】本题的重点是 based on,意为"以……为基础"。译文 A 准确地翻译出了原文的意思,为正确译法;译文 B 没有翻译出"在……的基础上"的意思;译文 C 中"以他的精彩报告为基础,做了实验"为误译;译文 D 中"以最近的国际会议为基础"为误译。

64. D—B—A—C 【解析】本题的考查重点是 whether... or not,意为"无论,是否"。译文 A 中"是否喜欢这个世界"为误译;译文 B 中"我们的生活发生了变化"为误译;译文 C 中"我们的生活方式令世界改变"为误译;译文 D 准确表达了原文的意思。

65.【参考译文】我们从信中得知,贵公司已经生产并出口各种纺织机械给我们。根据来函所述,似乎有可能在发货时有些疏忽,我们正在安排驻巴黎代表于下周内前往你公司,检查材料。

Part Ⅴ Writing

解题步骤:

第一步:审题

1. 题型:提纲作文;

2. 文体:应用文。

第二步:框架分析

1. 便条格式;

2. 点出每个要点。

第三步:列出写作思路

1. 说明便条的主要内容;

2. 注意便条的格式。

第四步:列出关键词和词组

check on the car, remind the car driver of this, be sure of, show up, sorry to trouble you, be useful to, etc.

第五步:落笔成文

Miss Li,

Could you please check on the car to take me to the airport? Please remind the car driver of this. I want to be sure of this car, because it will be too early in the morning to call a taxi if the company car doesn't show up. I am sorry to trouble you again. Here I thank you again for all that you have done for me during my stay in your company. I really enjoy working here, and will never forget the day I spent with my colleagues. Probably I will come back some day. I leave some material to you. I hope they will be useful to the company.

Yours

专家预测试题(二)

Part Ⅰ Listening Comprehension

Section A

1. B 【解析】根据 Take the second turn on the right and there you are. 可知,她要转两个弯,故选 B。

2. C 【解析】根据对话"珍妮,请把明天会议的报告准备好。好的,我马上做。"可判断两人是上下级的关系,故选 C。

3. A 【解析】根据对话"我想买双鞋。请去三楼。"可推断出他们应该在商店,故选 A。

4. B 【解析】根据回答"我喜欢流行乐和摇滚乐,但是最喜欢摇滚乐。"可知,她最喜欢摇滚乐,故选 B。

5. D 【解析】根据 I think it's a bit too bright for me. 可知,她认为红色太艳丽,故选 D。

Section B

Conversation 1

6. C 【解析】根据 I have an important exam at that time. 可知,凯西不能参加杰纳森的生

日宴会的原因是那天她将有一个重要的考试,故选 C。

7. B 【解析】根据 I think we can hold the party ahead of time. 可知,他可以提前举行宴会,故选 B。

Conversation 2

8. D 【解析】根据 I am going to the cinema. 可知,他要去电影院,故选 D。

9. C 【解析】根据 It tells a story about a fight between cats and dogs. 可知,电影是关于猫鼠之战的,故选 C。

10. A 【解析】根据 In fact, it is wonderful. 可知,她认为电影很好,故选 A。

Section C

11. rich tobacco planter 【解析】根据... the son of a rich tobacco planter. 可知,他的父亲是一名富裕的烟草种植者。

12. April 1775 【解析】根据 When the war broke out between America colonies and England in April 1775, 可知,战争爆发于 1775 年 4 月。

13. in 1789 【解析】根据... in 1789 Washington became the first president of the U.S.A. 可知,华盛顿是在 1789 年成为美国第一任总统的。

14. strong character 【解析】根据 But Washington's wisdom and strong character won him great respect. 可知,是他的智慧和坚毅的性格为他赢得了尊重。

15. in honor of 【解析】根据 The new capital of the U.S.A. was named Washington D.C. in honor of him. 可知,人们是为了纪念这位伟人才将首都以他的名字命名的。

附:听力原文

Section A

1. **W:** Excuse me. Can you tell me the way to Central Square?

   M: Take the second turn on the right and there you are.

   Q: How will the woman go to Central Square?

2. **M:** Jenny, could you prepare the report for tomorrow's meeting?

   W: OK. I'll do it right away.

   Q: What's the possible relationship between the two speakers?

3. **M:** I'd like to buy a pair of shoes.

   W: Please go up on the third floor.

   Q: Where does the conversation most likely take place?

4. **M:** What kind of music do you like?

   W: I like pop music and rock music. But, rock music is my favorite.

   Q: What kind of music does the woman like best?

5. **M:** How about this red dress, Ann? It's very fashionable.

   W: I don't know. I'm not crazy about red. I think it's a bit too bright for me.

   Q: Why doesn't the woman buy the red dress?

Section B

Conversation 1

M: Hello, this is Jonason speaking.

W: Hello, Jonason, I am Kasy. I am sorry to tell you that I may not attend your birthday party this weekend.

M: Oh, what's up?

W: Nothing much... but...

M: What's happened then?

W: I have an important exam at that time.

M: If so, I think we can hold the party ahead of time. What do you think about it?

W: Yeah, It is a good idea. I can't agree more.

M: Great and I wish you success.

W: Thank you, happy birthday to you.

Q6. Why can't Kasy attend Jonason's birthday party?

Q7. What will Jonason do to solve this problem?

Conversation 2

W: Hi, Ben! Where are you going now?

M: I am going to the cinema.

W: What is on today?

M: *Cats and Dogs.*

W: I saw it yesterday. It tells a story about a fight between cats and dogs.

M: Sounds interesting.

W: Yes. In fact, it is wonderful. All the actors in the film are real dogs and cats, not cartoons. By the way, what time is it?

M: It is 3:15.

W: I have got to leave now because I have got to visit my aunt in the hospital.

M: See you later.

W: See you.

Q8. Where is Ben going?

Q9. What does the film tell about?

Q10. How dose the woman feel about the film?

Section C

Gorge Washington(1732—1799) was born in Virginia, the son of a rich tobacco planter. His grandfather emigrated to America from England. Washington was brought up like an English gentleman and, as a young man, served in the British army.

When the war broke out between America colonies and England in April 1775, he was elected leader of colonists' army. Under his strong leadership and with French help the colonists defeated the British, and in 1789 Washington became the first president of the U.S.A.

It was not an easy task to govern a new country. But Washington's wisdom and strong character won him great respect. The new capital of the U.S.A. was named Washington D.C. in honor of him.

　　Q11. Who is Washington's father?

　　Q12. When did the war break out between America colonies and England?

　　Q13. When did Washington become the first president of the U.S.A.?

　　Q14. What won Washington great respect?

　　Q15. Why was the new capital of the U.S.A. named Washington D.C.?

Part Ⅱ Struture

Section A

16. C 【解析】本题考查短语辨析。above all 意为"最重要的"；in all 意为"总计"；at all 意为"全然,真的(常用于肯定句中)"；after all 意为"毕竟,终究"。句意为:你若真做,就得做好。故选 C。

17. D 【解析】本题考查词义辨析。almost 意为"几乎,差不多"；even 意为"甚至"；nearly 意为"几乎"；hardly 意为"几乎没有"。句意为:时间有限,我几乎不能按时完成工作。故选 D。

18. B 【解析】本题考查词义辨析。somehow 意为"不知怎么地"；anyhow (= any rate; in any case)意为"无论如何,不管怎样"；somewhat 意为"在某种程度上,有点"；anywhere 意为"任何地方"。句意为:无论如何,我都不会放弃梦想。故选 B。

19. D 【解析】本题考查词义辨析。equal 意为"等于"；agree 意为"同意"；help 意为"帮助"；match 意为"匹配;相配"。根据句意应是在物理知识方面你无法与他相比,故选 D。

20. A 【解析】本题考查固定搭配。all too 意为"实在太……",all too soon 意为"太快了",带有惋惜的意味。句意为:汤姆觉得暑假结束得太快了。故选 A。

21. D 【解析】本题考查词义辨析。 hit 意为"击,击中"；beat sb. 意为"打败某人"；win 意为"赢得",常用于赢得比赛或赢得奖项等。根据句意应是他在比赛中获得了第一名,故选 D。

22. A 【解析】本题考查固定搭配。give away 意为"暴露,泄露"；give in 意为"让步,屈服"；give out 意为"分发,释放"；give up 意为"放弃"。根据句意应是我已经答应琳达不泄漏秘密,故选 A。

23. B 【解析】本题考查短语辨析。in general 意为"总的来说"；above all 意为"最重要的"；after all 意为"毕竟"；in all 意为"总共"。根据句意应是汤姆斯善良、幽默、聪明,但最重要的是他勤奋,故选 B。

24. C 【解析】本题是考查 little, few, a little, a few 的用法。little 表示否定意义,a little 表示肯定意义,都用来修饰不可数名词；few 表示否定意义,a few 表示肯定意义,都用来修饰可数名词。某一语言不可数,而且根据题干的意思应为肯定,故选 C。

25. B 【解析】本题考查代词的用法。the others 特指某一范围内的"其余的人(物)"；others 泛指"其余的人(物)",它常和 some 对比使用,即"some... others..."；the other 特指"(两个中的)另一个"；other 泛指"另一个",故选 B。

Section B

26. will be 【解析】本题考查语法。这是一个复合句,根据句意"快点,要不就迟到了。"

可以确定主句是一般将来时,故应用 will be。

27. stores 【解析】本题考查名词。根据 many 可知,后边应该用名词的复数形式,故应用 stores。

28. cheaper 【解析】本题考查比较级。根据 than 可知应该用比较级,而且 and 连接并列结构,所以应用 cheaper。

29. walk 【解析】本题考查固定搭配。have to do sth. 为固定搭配,意为"不得不做某事",所以要用动词原形。

30. to do 【解析】本题考查固定搭配。use sth. to do sth. 为固定搭配,意为"用什么去做什么"。

31. cut 【解析】本题考查词的用法。have sth. done 为固定搭配,意为"让别人做某事"。这里要注意 cut 的现在分词形式为原形。

32. were planted 【解析】本题考查被动语态。根据句意应该是"树被种",而且其中含有表示过去时间的时间状语 last summer,所以应该用一般过去时的被动语态。

33. countries 【解析】本题考查名词。different 后边应该用名词的复数形式,所以应该用 countries。

34. cleaning 【解析】本题考查词性转换。观察句子结构可知这里需要一个名词作宾语,所以应该把动词变成名词。

35. was reading 【解析】本题考查时态。句意为:电话铃响时他正在读书。又根据 rang 可知从句用的是一般过去时态,所以主句应该用过去进行时。

Part Ⅲ Reading Comprehension

Task 1

【文章概述】 地球上生物种类繁多,科学家每天都有新的发现。

36. D 【解析】总结归纳题。通读全文,可以发现世界上生物种类繁多,每天都有新的发现,所以生物种类不是固定的,而是不断变化的,故选 D。

37. B 【解析】细节题。根据第一段 Most people agree on an estimate of somewhere near 10 million...可知,大部分科学家认为地球上有大约一千万种物种,故选 B。

38. C 【解析】细节题。根据第二段可知 A、B、D 三项生物是新发现的物种,但文中并没有提及 C 选项,故选 C。

39. A 【解析】推理题。根据短文最后一段的介绍以及最后一句 How many species these communities contain is still anyone's guess. 可以推断, 很多地方还没有被完全开发,故选 A。

40. C 【解析】主旨大意题。通读全文可以发现,作者一直在介绍地球物种的局限性。因此 C 选项最符合题意,故选 C。

Task 2

【文章概述】 泰勒先生的珠宝店开张了,一大早他就带着伙计把宝石饰品摆在了摆台上。可还没来得及细细品味,就遭遇到一伙抢劫犯的袭击。他们只用了几分钟时间就把店里价值数千英镑的钻石抢走了。

41. C 【解析】细节题。根据第一段第三句 Mr. Taylor, the owner of a jewellery shop...可知，他是一家珠宝店的老板,故选 C。

42. B 【解析】推理题。根据第一段 Two of his assistants had been working busily since 8 o'clock and had only just finished.可排除 A, D 两项。又根据第一段最后一句 After gazing at the display for several minutes, Mr. Taylor went back into his shop. 可排除 C 选项。通过推理可得知泰勒先生刚进门就发生了抢劫,那么在他欣赏时那些劫匪也就正在抢劫的准备中,故选 B。

43. B 【解析】细节题。根据 One man stayed at the wheel two others with black stockings over their faces jumped out...可知,劫匪共三人,故选 B。

44. D 【解析】细节题。根据第二段 While this was going on, Mr. Taylor was upstairs. He and his staff began throwing furniture out of the window.可知,当抢劫发生时泰勒先生正在楼上。他们在向窗外扔家具,故选 D。

45. A 【解析】细节题。根据 The raid was all over in three minutes...可知,A 项内容与文章内容不符,故选 A。

Task 3

【文章概述】 本文是一则关于学生会要举行中文演讲比较的通知。

46. National Day 【解析】细节题。根据第一段第一句 The Student Union has decided to hold a Chinese speech contest to celebrate the coming National Day.可知,中文演讲比赛的目的是为了庆祝国庆节的来临。

47. seven experts 【解析】细节题。根据第一段第三句 We will invite seven experts to serve as judges.可知,比赛要邀请 7 位专家作评委。

48. reaction of audience 【解析】细节题。根据第一段第四句 Every speaker will be judged from three aspects: script(文字材料), eloquence(口才), and the reaction of the audience.可知,可以从文字材料、口才以及观众的反应三方面来评判。

49. September 18 【解析】细节题。根据第二段第二句 The preliminary contest（初赛）falls on September 18...可知,初赛时间为 9 月 18 号。

50. the cinema 【解析】细节题。根据最后一句 The final contest will be held on September 30 in the cinema of our university. 可知,决赛会在大学的影院举行。

Task 4

【说明】 这是一些金融用语。

51. G, C 52. I, P 53. L, O 54. J, A 55. N, F

各项的译文:

A —— 单位信托	B —— 未上市证券
C —— 上调风险	D —— 风险值
E —— 创业资金	F —— 短期持股
G —— 提款计划	H —— 预扣税
I —— 周转资金	J —— 产业基金
K —— 种子资金融通	L —— 卖空

M —— 优先债务   N —— 独立上市

O —— 股东价值   P —— 空壳公司

Task 5

　【文章概述】　本文是一封应聘经理助理一职的求职信。

56. in newspaper　【解析】细节题。根据第一段第一句 I am writing to apply for the position... that you recently advertised in newspaper. 可知,应征者是在报纸上发现广告的。

57. the general assistant　【解析】细节题。根据第一段第一句 I am writing to apply for the position as the general assistant... 可知,此人应聘的是经理助理一职。

58. Public Relations　【解析】细节题。根据第二段第一句... I pursued my graduate study in the direction of Public Relations... 可知,他的专业为公共关系。

59. Shanghai　【解析】细节题。根据第二段最后一句 As Shanghai is my hometown... 可知,求职者的故乡是上海。

60. telephone　【解析】细节题。根据最后一句 Please contact me at 13977652398. 可知,可以和求职者电话联系。

Part Ⅳ Translation — English into Chinese

61. C—B—D—A　【解析】本题考查的重点是 put the clock back to an earlier age, 意为"将时钟拨回到早先的时代"。因此我们可以排除与此意思不符的选项 A、D;C 选项为正确翻译;译文 B 漏译了 even if one wanted to。

62. A—B—C—D　【解析】本题的重点是 in attempts to, 译文 A 准确地译出了原文的意思,为正确译法;译文 B 中"行为"为误译;译文 C"试图欺骗来证明有智能"为误译;译文 D 完全误解了原文的意思,为错译。

63. B—D—C—A　【解析】本题的重点是 no one can fail to... 的用法,意为"没有谁不会……"由此,D、C、A 三个选项的翻译都为误译。

64. D—A—C—B　【解析】本题的重点是 as 的用法。译文 A 没有翻译出"像……一样";译文 B 中"我和你在非洲的经历"为误译;译文 C 中"像我一样"为误译;译文 D 准确表达了原文的意思,为正确译法。

65.【参考译文】能源短缺是世界上一个非常严重的问题。许多人担心如果我们无节制地使用,能源将被使用殆尽,这将导致严重的后果,甚至危及人类的生存。这个问题可以用某种方法解决。其中之一是保护和拯救我们的能源。另一种方式是开发新的能源。

Part Ⅴ Writing

解题步骤:

第一步:审题

1. 题型:提纲作文;

2. 文体:应用文。

第二步:框架分析

1. 简介格式;

2. 点出每个要点。

第三步:列出写作思路

1. 说明简介的主要内容;

2. 注意简介的格式。

第四步:列出关键词和词组

　　the biggest university in the district, altogether 40 professors and more than 200 teachers, two semesters for each year, spend two thirds of the time studying in the classroom and one third practicing on our training site, rich and colorful, various kinds of competitions, have a good time, etc.

第五步:落笔成文

Introduction

　　Good morning, honorable guests. I am glad to make you warm welcome. Ours is the biggest university in the district, with 10 colleges, a library and two campuses. There are altogether 40 professors and more than 200 teachers in our university, 30% of whom have studied abroad. There are 15,000 students in our university. We study 4 years here, two semesters for each year. During our studies, we spend two thirds of the time studying in the classroom and one third practicing on our training site. Our school life is rich and colorful. We often have various kinds of competitions. That's all for my introduction. I hope you will have a good time in our university.

2009 年 6 月真题

Part Ⅰ　Listening Comprehension

(略)

Part Ⅱ　Structure

Section A

16. D　【解析】本题考查将来完成时的用法。将来完成时主要表示一个动作在将来某时之前,将要完成,还可表示可能性和猜测。句中 by 和时间连用也是该时态的常见用法,故选 D。

17. B　【解析】本题考查固定搭配。sth.+be+worth+doing 意为"(某事)值得……",用主动表被动。worth 后用及物动词的现在分词形式,或不及物动词加介词构成短语,故选 B。

18. A　【解析】本题考查连词用法。until 表示"在……以前";because 表示"因为";if 表示"如果"或"是否";since 可表示"自从"或"因为"。原句中前半句和后半句不存在因果和假设关系,而运用 not... until...结构,表示"直到……才",故选 A。

19. C　【解析】本题考查代词 it 的用法。此题中,it 为形式主语,真正的主语为 that 引导的主语从句。故选 C。

20. B　【解析】本题考查动词过去分词的用法。过去分词在意义上表示被动和完成。在本句中主语 manager 与动词 shock 之间是被动关系;主句使用一般过去时,表明动作已经发生。所以 B 项为正确答案。A 项是不定式, 表示目的; C 项为动词被动结构, 不用在从句中; D 项表主动, 故排除。

21. A 【解析】本题考查名词性从句。除了 D 项中的代词 whom "谁" 以外, whether, what, where 都可引导表语从句, 并且它们分别有 "是否"、"什么" 和 "哪里" 的意思, 根据句意应是 "明天我们是否去那那么早", 只有选择 whether, 句子才符合逻辑, 故选 A。

22. D 【解析】本题考查连词用法。A 项表示 "如果不、除非"; B 项表示 "当……时候"; C 项表示 "但是"; D 项表示 "否则"。本句前半句为对过去事实的叙述, 后半句为与过去事实相反的虚拟语气, 对过去事实的假设, 从句意可判断 D 项为正确答案。

23. A 【解析】本题考查时态。enclosed 是动词的过去分词形式, 表示 "被随函附寄的", 修饰句中的 application form。读者还未看到所提及的申请表 application form, 应该使用一般将来时, 故选 A。

24. C 【解析】本题考查动词不定式。A 项为动词原形; B 项为动词的过去式或过去分词形式; D 项为动词的第三人称单数形式。这三种形式都可以作为句子的谓语动词出现。而本句为一般现在时, 谓语动词为 spends, 需要的是动词不定式作目的状语, 故选 C。

25. D 【解析】本题考查定语从句。在定语从句中, A 项 whose 表示所属关系, 应与名词连用, 在本句中, whose 后未有其他名词, 故排除; B 项 which 指物, 而本句中的先行词为人; C 项 whom 为宾格形式; D 项中的关系代词 who 可作从句中的主语, 指先行词 designer, 故选 D。

Section B

26. lucky 【解析】本题考查词性转换。enough 一词常用在 be+*adj.*+enough to do sth. 结构中。luck 是名词, 意思是 "幸运, 运气", 对应的形容词是 lucky "幸运的"。本句中 is 后需加形容词作表语, 所以应使用 luck 的形容词形式。所以, 空格处填 lucky。

27. introduction 【解析】本题考查词性转换。空格前为不定冠词 an, 显然空格处需要使用名词。introduce 是动词, 意思是 "介绍", 对应名词是 introduction "介绍"。所以, 空格处填 introduction。

28. informed 【解析】本题考查过去分词。短语 inform sb. of sth. 意为 "告知某人某事", keep sb./sth. doing/done 结构中, 当 sb./sth. 与动词间是主动关系时, 用动词的现在分词形式, 意为 "使某人或某物一直做……"; 当 sb./sth. 与动词间是被动关系时, 用动词的过去分词形式, 意为 "使某人或某物 (被)……"。本题为 inform the manager of the advertising campaign, manager 与 inform 之间是被动关系, 所以, 空格处填 informed。

29. (should) make 【解析】本题考查虚拟语气。表示建议、要求或命令等动词后接的宾语从句要用虚拟语气, 谓语动词为 "should +动词原形", should 可以省略, 能这样用的动词有 suggest, request, demand, decide, propose, order, insist, recommend, advise, desire, ask, require, command 等。所以, 空格处填 (should) make。

30. rebuilt 【解析】本题考查被动语态。本句主句使用一般现在时, rebuild 意为 "重建", 主语 city 与 rebuild 是被动关系, 需要使用 rebuild 的过去分词 rebuilt。所以, 空格处填 rebuilt。

31. had been living/had lived 【解析】本题考查时态。本句首选答案使用了过去完成进行时, 表示动作完成于另一过去动作或时间以前, 并在所述时间段内持续进行, 结构为 had been *v*-ing。本句中从句的动作 live(居住)完成于主句动作 described(描述)之前, 从句时间状语 for years 为一段时间, 强调动作 live 持续进行。而主句使用一般过去时, 从句应使用过去完成进行时。所以, 空格处填 had been living。本句亦可使用过去完成时, 表示动作完成于另一过去动作或时间之前, 如果强调动作的结果, 亦可用过去完成时。所以, 空格处还可填 had lived。

32. winning 【解析】本题考查现在分词。本句使用了一般现在时, 短语 be confident of 意为"对……有信心"。介词 of 后要加动词的现在分词形式, win 的现在分词为 winning。所以, 空格处填 winning。

33. more 【解析】本题考查比较级。本句出现一个比较级的标志词 than, 表明两者之间进行比较, 使用 adj./adv.的比较级。much 在这里作副词, 修饰谓语动词, 它的比较级是 more。所以, 空格处填 more。

34. heavily 【解析】本题考查词性转换。本题是一个简单句, 根据句意可知需要一个副词来修饰谓语, 故应填入形容词 heavy 的副词形式 heavily。所以, 空格处填 heavily。

35. left 【解析】本题考查 with 的独立结构。这是分词独立主格结构, 即分词有其自己的主语, 独立于主句的主语。一般作伴随状语。在这个结构里, 分词也要和它的主语保持逻辑上的一致, 本句中 time 和分词是被动关系, 所以, 空格处填过去分词 left。

Part Ⅲ Reading Comprehension

Task 1

【文章概述】 这是一篇说明文。文章介绍了如何用阅读器阅读电子书, 以及电子书的用途。电子书是印刷图书的数字版, 可以下载阅读。但是, 若要看电子书, 必须有电子书阅读器。电子书是普通图书奇异的替代品, 可以下载到任何一台计算机上, 创建自己的图书馆, 存入成百上千册书。如果把电子书都存入笔记本电脑, 就可以在旅行时带上。有的电子书还能互动。最大的好处是, 买电子书不用等, 没有运输费。下载电子书的时间取决于链接的速度和电子书的大小。

36. D 【解析】细节题。根据第二句 But if you want to read an ebook, you must have an E-book Reader, which is a kind of free software used by your computer.可知, 当阅读器这个软件安装后才能看电子书, 故选 D。

37. A 【解析】推理题。根据文章的上下文对阅读器的定义可知 an Ebook Reader 是 software, 而第四句的主语为 the software 指的就是 Reader。根据 The software allows you to turn the words on the screen into the size you like. It also helps you turn pages and change your viewing options.可知, 电子书阅读器是用来阅读已下载的图书的, 故选 A。B 项曲解了文章的意思; C、D 选项文中未提到。

38. A 【解析】细节题。根据第八句 If you load them onto your portable computer, you can take them with you when you travel.可知, 旅行时可以看笔记本电脑上的电子书, 故选 A。B、C、D 选项在文章中没有提到。

39. C 【解析】判断题。A 项意为"电子书以印刷图书同样的方式订购。"B 项意为"电子书中的单词大小不能改变。"C 项意为"下载时间由电子书的大小决定。"D 项意为"看电子书不如看印刷图书有趣。"A项和D项文中未提及；B项与37题的答题依据相悖(见37题解析)；根据最后一句The amount of time it takes to download your ebook depends on the speed of your connection and the size of your ebook.可知，下载电子书的时间取决于链接的速度和电子书的大小，故选C。

40. B 【解析】主旨题。首句就提出ebook(电子书)。接下来各句都是对如何阅读电子书及其特点的介绍。A、C项文中未提及；D项片面，故选B。

Task 2

【文章概述】 这是一份航空公司的乘机说明。首先是入检要求。乘客及行李要求提前入检，所有乘客提供政府颁发的附有照片的身份证。跨境旅游的乘客要备有所有必需的旅游文件。如果旅游文件不齐全，就会被拒绝登机。乘客必须在起飞前20分钟到达登机口，准备登机。Frontier航空有限公司允许每位持票乘客免费携带两个包，超重行李收费。

41. D 【解析】细节题。根据第一个小标题下第一句Passengers and their baggage must be checked in at least 45 minutes before departure for domestic flights and 60 minutes for international flights.可知，国际航线的乘客应该至少提前60分钟入检。A、B项文中未提及；C项指国内航线乘客，故选D。

42. C 【解析】细节题。根据文章第一个小标题下第二句Government-issued photo identification is required for all passengers.可知，要求所有乘客入检时提供政府颁发附有照片的身份证。A项是邀请函；B项是公司的工作邀请；C项是官方照片证件；D项是官方移民许可。A、B、D项均未提及，故选C。

43. B 【解析】细节题。根据第二个小标题的内容Frontier Airlines, Inc. will accept, per ticketed passenger, two free checked bags...可知，每位持票乘客免费托运两个包。A、C、D项文中均未提及，故选B。

44. A 【解析】推理判断题。根据最后一句An excess charge will be made for each piece of baggage over the free allowance and for each piece of over-sized or over-weight baggage.可知，每件超过免费限额的行李以及超出标准尺寸或超重的托运行李都会额外收费，故选A。B、C、D项文中均未提及。

45. B 【解析】推理题。全文多次多处提到passengers(乘客)和flight(航班)，并说明入检要求、行李限额、注意事项等，可推断出答案为B项(给航班旅客的注意事项)。A项为一则航线的广告；C项为国际航班时间安排；D项为航空公司介绍。本文并无宣传或介绍公司字样，故可排除A项和D项；C项只讲了国际航班，比较局限，很容易排除。

Task 3

【文章概述】 这是一份广告。介绍了樱花奖学金。它给学生们提供到东京学习为期三个月的日语课的机会。奖学金涵盖免费的住宿、餐饮和学费。而且提供学生从自己国家的居住地到大阪之间的往返机票，以及1,000美元零用钱。此外还介绍了奖学金的申请方式、截止日期和地址。

46. tuition 【解析】细节题。根据第一段第二句The scholarship covers free accommoda-

tion, meals and tuition.可知,奖学金包括食宿费和学费。

47. **return** 【解析】细节题。根据第一段第三句前半句 Return air fares between their country... 可知,是往返机票,因此答案为 return。

48. **pocket money** 【解析】细节题。根据第一段第三句后半句 ... and $1, 000 pocket money is also provided. 可知,是 1, 000 美元的零用钱,因此答案为 pocket money。

49. **educational career** 【解析】细节题。根据第二段前半句 To apply for one of these Scholarships, you should write a letter of about 300 words, describing your own educational career so far...可知,要求在信件中说明申请者到目前为止的学习经历,因此答案为 educational career。

50. **February 1, 2009** 【解析】细节题。根据第三段第一句 The closing date for application is February 1, 2009.可知,申请的截止日期是 2009 年 2 月 1 日,因此答案为 February 1, 2009。

Task 4

【说明】　本文是一些医疗用语。

51. D, Q　52. L, J　53. A, E　54. N, P　55. G, I

各项的译文:

A —— 装配线		B —— 包装工	
C —— 铲车		D —— 易爆材料	
E —— 灭火器		F —— 装载码头	
G —— 机器操作员		H —— 触电危险	
I —— 输送带		J —— 安全靴	
K —— 运务员		L —— 工时卡	
M —— 仓库		N —— 安全帽	
O —— 耳塞		P —— 手推车	
Q —— 安全耳罩			

Task 5

【文章概述】　这是一封求职信。信件介绍了求职者的实习经历,自己的技能,以及将给公司带来的改变,并希望得到面试的机会。

56. **Fourteen weeks** 【解析】细节题。根据第二段第二句 My fourteen weeks with your company... 可知,他工作了 14 周。

57. **sales support activities** 【解析】细节题。根据第二段第二句... involved me in a whole variety of sales support activities including...可知,他参与到了各种支持销售的活动。

58. **business communication skills** 【解析】细节题。根据第三段第一句 During the past two semesters I have concentrated on developing my electronic publishing and business communication skills.可知,他提高了电子刊印和商务沟通的技能。

59. **an online catalog** 【解析】细节题。根据第三段第三句 This would include designing and maintaining an online catalog...可知,他通过设计和维护网络目录来帮助支持区域市场营销代表们。

60. **an interview** 【解析】细节题。根据最后一段 I am available for an interview at...可知,

劳迪斯·圣地亚哥写这封信是为了得到面试的机会。

Part Ⅳ Translation — English into Chinese

61. D—C—B—A 【解析】本句是带有条件状语从句的复合句。本题重点把握 for your safety "为了安全起见", electrical appliance "电器" 和 operate "运行, 操作"的确切含义。综合来看 D 项最贴切;correctly "正确地"是修饰"安装", 而不是"运行", C 项将此处误译;B 项关键词"为了安全起见""正确地"未译, electrical 误译为"电子", 还添加"持续";A 项的翻译无论从单词还是从语法上都有严重错误, 偏离原意甚远。

62. A—B—C—D 【解析】本句是一个由 not only... but also...连接的并列句。本题重点把握 asking questions at a meeting "会上提问", involve sb. in..."使某人参与到……中", demonstrate "展示" 和 it 的指代含义。综合来看 A 项最贴切;B 项未译出 involve sb. in..., 将"展示"误译为"利用";C 项将"会上提问会使你(involve you)参与到……中", 误译为"使会议讨论……", 对句子结构理解不清楚;D 项没有理解 not only... but also... 连接的是两个句子, 而将"会上提问"和"参与讨论"理解为并列, 将"展示"误译为"提高", 与原句相去甚远。

63. B—D—C—A 【解析】本句是含有一个宾语从句的主从复合句。本题重点把握 interdependence "相互依存", statesmen "政治家" 和 reality "现实, 实在"的确切含义;以及对 so long talked about by statesmen 过去分词短语作定语的翻译。综合来看 B 项最贴切;D 项将 so long talked about "长期谈论"误译为"以前认为";C 项将"相互依存"误译为"独立", 未译出"政治家"之意;A 项中上述关键词都误译, 句子本身也不通顺。

64. D—C—B—A 【解析】本句是一个简单句。本题重点把握 purchaser "买主" 和 not be responsible for "不负责"的确切含义。综合来看, D 项最为贴切;C 项把"不负责"误译为"不予过问", 并未译出"成本";B 项颠倒了买卖双方的关系, 将"买主"误译为"卖主";A 项不但颠倒了买卖双方的关系, 并对 not be responsible for 理解不清, 译为"卖方不是没有责任解决……问题", 与原文相去甚远。

65. 【参考译文】市政府认识到市民们有某些新的需求。为了更好地满足大家的需求, 我们在 2009 年已经给社区设施带来了一些变化。三个服务郊区的火车站也已纳入西部火车服务体系。宽带电缆现在通达全市。市图书馆购进 5,000 本新书。市医院一些新的设备已安装完毕。明年, 我们会尽最大的努力, 使大家生活得更好。【解析】这是一段市政府官员的讲话。在翻译时应该注意措辞清楚、亲切。如 your 就不要翻译成"你们的", 为表亲切, 拉近官员和市民的距离, 应翻译为"大家的"。最后表决心和希望时采用了一般将来时。

Part Ⅴ Writing

解题步骤:

第一步:审题
1. 题型:提纲作文;
2. 文体:应用文。

第二步:框架分析

1. 书信格式格式；

2. 点出每个要点。

第三步：列出写作思路

1. 说明图画含义；

2. 加以引申；

3. 总结自己的看法。

第四步：列出关键词和词组

consult some traveling information, arrange a holiday trip, give me some advice about the route, be available, get back to work, send me some relevant materials about it, your early reply will be well appreciated, etc.

第五步：落笔成文

20 June, 2009

Dear Sirs,

I am writing to consult some traveling information. Our department intends to arrange a holiday trip for 20 clerks. Would you please give me some advice about the route? What would be the price and the discount(if there is)? The clerks will be available from July 1st to July 3rd. They need to get back to work on July 4th. Could you please send me some relevant materials about it, especially the traveling schedule?

My phone number is 024-23×××80. My e-mail address is *smilingdaisy@yahoo.com.*

Your early reply will be well appreciated.

Yours sincerely,

Wang Lin

Personnel Department

2009 年 12 月真题

Part Ⅰ　Listening Comprehension

（略）

Part Ⅱ　Struture

Section A

16. A　【解析】本题考查词义辨析。without 意为"没有"；with 意为"和"；despite 意为"尽管"；for 意为"为了"。句意为：我们必须找到一种既调低价格又不会过多降低利润的办法。应该是不发生后边的情况，故选 A。

17. D　【解析】本题考查疑问词辨析。which 意为"哪一个"；what 意为"什么"；why 意为"为什么"；how 意为"怎样"。根据句意应该是她不知道如何在公众面前用英语清楚地表达自己的意思，故选 D。

18. D　【解析】本题考查语意。as, since 意为"由于"，表示原因；while 意为"当……时候"，引导时间状语从句;unless 意为"除非,如果不",等于 if... not。根据句意应该是如果天气不好转,旅游业将会遭受巨大损失,故选D。【知识拓展】unless 是从属连词,引导条件状语从句,含有否定意义,相当于 if 条件状语从句的否定形式。所以 unless = if not。注意:unless 引导的条件状语从句和 if 条件状语从句,与其他时间状语从句一样,用一般现在时代替将来时。

19. A 【解析】本题考查语法。这是一个含有同位语从句的复合句,说明消息的内容。that, which, what, whether 都可以引导名词性从句,但是 that 只起连接主句和从句的作用,在从句中不担当任何成分,本身也没有词义,而 which, what, whether 引导从句时都在句子中充当成分,而且一般保留本意。观察句子可知从句中不缺少成分,故选A。

20. C 【解析】本题考查虚拟语气。important 后边的从句一般用虚拟语气,其构成是(should)+动词原形,故选C。【知识拓展】表情绪、观点的形容词或名词要用虚拟语气, 常见的有:necessary, impossible, natural, strange, surprising, funny, right, wrong, better, a pity 等。句型:It is... that 结构后从句的谓语动词都要用 should+原型或只用动词原型。

21. B 【解析】本题考查定语从句。根据句意可知后边是一个关系词引导的定语从句,故 D 不正确,从句中不缺少主语或宾语,故 A、C 不正确,cover 和 book 之间是所属关系,故选B。【知识拓展】which 和 that 在定语从句中可作主语或宾语,而且 that 既可以指人,也可以指物,whose 在定语从句中只能作定语,表示所属关系。

22. A 【解析】本题考查非谓语动词。根据句意可知马克变得精通商业谈判是在公司工作了三年之后,所以前边的"工作"这个动作发生在后边的动作之前,所以应该用分词的完成式,应选 A。【知识拓展】非谓语动词包括动名词、分词和不定式。其中分词包括现在分词和过去分词,现在分词表主动,时间一般指现在;过去分词一般表被动,时间一般指过去。动词不定式一般表示将来。

23. B 【解析】本题考查倒装句。not until 用于句首时,后边的主句要用倒装语序,而且是一般过去时态,故选B。【知识拓展】常见的需要用倒装的情况有:only +状语或状语从句置于句首,句子用部分倒装。hardly, in no way, little, scarcely, seldom, never, no more, no longer, not, not only, no sooner, not only... (but also), not until... 等具有否定意义的词或词组位于句首,句子用部分倒装。so / such... that 结构中的 so 或 such 位于句首可以构成部分倒装句,表示强调 so / such 和 that 之间的部分。

24. C 【解析】本题考查连词。because 意为"因为",引导原因状语从句;though 意为"虽然",引导让步状语从句;so 意为"所以",表示结果;while 意为"当……时候",引导时间状语从句。这里表示因为约翰之前从没出过国,所以觉得这次出差很令人兴奋。后边是结果,故选 C。

25. B 【解析】本题考查连词。since 和 because 都表示原因;if 意为"如果",表示假设;while 意为"尽管",引导让步状语从句。根据句意尽管一些学生毕业后可以就业,但另外的学生却不得不回学校继续学习,故选B。

Section B

26. to make 【解析】本题考查词的用法。"允许某人做某事"用 allow sb. to do sth.。

27. puttin 【解析】本题考查介词的用法。介词后边应该用动名词形式, 所以应该用

putting。

28. **easier**　【解析】本题考查比较级。根据语意和后边的 more difficult 这里应该用比较级,所以应该用 easier。

29. **will be discussed**　【解析】本题考查时态和语态。根据时间状语可知这里是一般将来时,而且应该是建议被讨论,所以应该用一般将来时的被动语态。

30. **occasionally**　【解析】本题考查词性转换。观察句子可知这里需要一个副词修饰谓语动词,所以应该把形容词变成副词。

31. **advanced**　【解析】本题考查语法。观察句子可知这里需要一个形容词修饰后边的名词,所以应该把动词变成形容词。

32. **correcting**　【解析】本题考查介词的用法。介词后边应该用动词的动名词形式,所以应该用 correcting。

33. **complaint**　【解析】本题考查词义辨析。根据句子结构可知这里需要一个名词作宾语。所以要把动词 complain 变成名词 complaint。

34. **were interviewed**　【解析】本题考查时态和语态。句中有表示过去时间的状语 yesterday,所以应用一般过去时,而且根据句意应该是被采访的学生,是被动语态,故要用 were interviewed。

35. **brought**　【解析】本题考查语法。观察句子可知后边需要一个分词作定语,而且是被动关系,所以应该用过去分词 brought。

Part Ⅲ Reading Comprehension

Task 1

【文章概述】　谷歌是一家网络搜索引擎公司,公司声明将投入 2,500 万美元来帮助贫穷的人们。他们说将利用信息和技术的力量来提高人们的生活。之后文章分别列举了谷歌是从哪几方面来投资的。

36. **A**　【解析】细节题。根据第一段第一句可知,谷歌投资的目的是为了帮助穷人,故选A。

37. **B**　【解析】细节题。根据第二段第二句可知,第一项工程的目的是帮助识别传染性疾病是在哪发展的,故选 B。

38. **D**　【解析】细节题。根据第三段第一句可知,第二项工程是帮助中小型企业发展的,因为受益的应该是中小型企业,故选 D。

39. **D**　【解析】细节题。根据第四段第一句可知,谷歌今年早些时候还声明要投入资金到协助气候变化的规划中,故选 D。

40. **A**　【解析】总结归纳题。根据最后一段可知,谷歌投入的这些资金百分之一来自公司的利润还有百分之一来自股票市值,故选 A。

Task 2

【文章概述】　本文讲的是老板掌握着你未来事业的发展。并且员工和老板之间的关系情况是一个员工升职与否的主要因素,文中还讲了与老板保持好的关系最重要的就是交流与沟通。

41. C 【解析】总结归纳题。文章第一段第一句 Your boss holds your future prospects in his hands.就是第一段的主题句,由此可知,你的老板掌握着你未来事业的发展,故选C。

42. C 【解析】词义猜测题。rise up the career ladder 意为"在职业生涯这个梯子上的攀升",这里把职业发展的线比喻成为"不断向上攀的梯子",与 C 项(在职位上的提升)相符合,故选 C。

43. A 【解析】细节题。根据第三段第一句 Your boss also needs you to perform at your best in order to accomplish his objectives.可知,为了达成自己的目标,他需要你更好地工作,故选 A。

44. D 【解析】细节题。根据第四段第一句 The key is communication. 和第三段最后一句的提问可知,与老板保持好的工作关系最重要的因素是沟通,与 D 项(有效的沟通)相符合,故选 D。

45. B 【解析】主旨题。纵观全文,作者都在写如何与老析建立良好工作关系的事,故选B。

Task 3

【文章概述】 这是一份东航的乘机指南。为了旅途的安全,应在"系好安全灯带"指示灯亮时一直系着安全带,只有在飞机未起飞时可以使用手机,航行中不准播放 CD 或 DVD。飞机上提供音乐和录像,并且提供免费的食物和饮料。

46. fastened 【解析】根据第二段第三句可知,应在"系好安全灯带"指示灯亮着时一直系着安全带。

47. on the ground 【解析】根据第二段倒数第二句可知,只有在飞机未起飞时可以使用手机。

48. not allowed 【解析】根据第二段最后一句可知,航行中不准播放 CD 或 DVD。

49. video programs 【解析】根据第三段第二句可知,飞机上提供音乐和录像。

50. Nothern China 【解析】根据第四段最后一句可知,所有 9 点前起飞和到中国北方的航班都提供快餐。

Task 4

【说明】 这是一些与安全有关的用语。

51. A, J   52. I, B   53. E, P   54. D, O   55. F, Q

各项的译文:

A —— 空中交通管制系统   B —— 武装警察
C —— 预防犯罪   D —— 入境要求
E —— 国际刑警组织   F —— 安全保障级别
G —— 警戒线   H —— 警察局
I —— 巡逻车   J —— 安全预防措施
K —— 安全控制装置   L —— 保安指挥中心
M —— 保安服务   N —— 安全控制中心
O —— 安保人员   P —— 有效证件
Q —— 安全监控

Task 5

【文章概述】 这是一封商业信函。这家公司决定聘用史密斯先生做售后经理,因此给他寄了合约,让史密斯先生考虑上边的条款,但如果不能在规定日期之前寄回合约,将被视为自动放弃工作。

56. the after-sales manager　【解析】根据第一段第一句可知,提供给他的工作职位是售后经理。

57. a lawyer　【解析】根据第二段第一句可知,可以跟家人、工会、律师或是其他信任的人商量。

58. Employment Service Office　【解析】根据第二段最后一句可知,可以跟用工服务部联系或是访问他们的网站。

59. June 1, 2009　【解析】根据第四段第一句可知,应在 2009 年 6 月 1 日前交回副本。

60. automatically withdrawn　【解析】根据第四段最后一句可知,如果不能在规定日期前交回签好的副本,这次机会将自动作废。

Part Ⅳ Translation — English to Chinese

61. D—B—C—A　【解析】翻译这句话的关键在于认清几个重点词汇的意思。renew the contract 意为"续签合同",submit a written notice to 意为"书面通知",prior to 意为"提前",the expiration of the contract 意为"合同期满"。所以最佳答案应是 D。

62. C—B—A—D　【解析】翻译这句话的关键在于认清句子结构和几个重点词汇的意思。这是一个复合句,although 引导让步状语从句, 主句中含有一个同位语从句。there is no sign that 意为"没有……的迹象",in sight 意为"看得见,出现",a certain degree of recovery 意为"一定程度的经济复苏"。所以最佳答案应是 C。

63. B—A—C—D　【解析】翻译这句话的关键在于认清句子结构和几个重点词汇的意思。现在分词短语 concerning personnel management 作后置定语修饰主语,所以应先翻译定语。personnel management 意为"人事管理",secondary importance 意为"次要",remain to be disscussed 意为"有待讨论"。所以最佳答案应该是 B。

64. B—A—C—D　【解析】翻译这句话的关键在于认清句子结构和几个重点词汇的意思。这是一个倒装句。improve their competiveness 意为 "提高竞争力",avoid doing 意为 "避免……",entry into the WTO 意为"加入世贸组织"。所以最佳答案应是 B。

65.【参考译文】非常感谢,布莱克先生。被任命为海外销售经理使我深感荣幸。说实话,这次升职令我非常吃惊。我认为这是整个团队的贡献。我要感谢公司里所有努力工作并给予我支持的同事们。由于他们的努力,我们成功地开展了一些海外项目。展望未来,即使我将在管理层工作,我仍愿与大家共同合作。【解析】这些句子基本都是简单句,只有最后一句是复合句,含有一个让步状语从句。it's a great honor to 意为"深感荣幸",to be honest 意为"实话实说",thank sb. for sth.意为"由于……感谢某人",due to 意为"由于",look to the future 意为"展望未来",maintain contact with 意为"保持合作",at the management level 意为"在管理层"。

Part Ⅴ Writing

解题步骤:

第一步:审题

1. 题型:提纲作文;

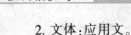
2. 文体:应用文。

第二步:框架分析

1. 书信格式;

2. 点出每个要点。

第三步:列出写作思路

1. 说明如何得知这款手机;

2. 询问详细情况;

3. 希望和对方建立长远的合作关系。

第四步:列出关键词和词组

get to know, new-style cellphone, ask about detailed information, have a good prospect for sales, establish long-term cooperations with, etc.

第五步:落笔成文

Dec. 22nd, 2009

Dear Mr. Smith,

I got to know Mr. Smith at the recent Guangzhou Trade Fair, and I'm very interested in your new-style cellphone displayed at the fair. Now I'm writing to ask about detailed information about it, such as specifications, price, function and etc. I'm sure this new-style cellphone will have a good prospect for sales, so I want to establish long-term business cooperations with you.

Look forward to your reply.

Best wishes!

Faithfully yours,

Mark Zhang